Dancing
to the
End of Love

Adrian White

BLACK & WHITE PUBLISHING

First published 2016
by Black & White Publishing Ltd
29 Ocean Drive, Edinburgh EH6 6JL

1 3 5 7 9 10 8 6 4 2   16 17 18 19

ISBN: 978 1 78530 012 7

ALBA | CHRUTHACHAIL

A CIP catalogue record for this book is available from the British Library.

Typeset by Iolaire Typesetting, Newtonmore
Printed and bound by Nørhaven, Denmark

For all the lost sons and daughters.

PRELUDE

I live in Pisa with Maria. She's the reason that I'm here. Maria Gabriela Carbone – an Italian Scot, or a Scottish Italian, depending on her moods, which are many and extreme. Carrier of a gene that will kill her sooner rather than later, so I forgive the mood swings. I forgive her because she is what she is – everything to me and everything that I'm not. No doubt she'd tell me that she's not mine to forgive and I'd agree; but I'd forgive her anyway.

So I'm back in Pisa, staring again at the Leaning Tower. It leans. It's not wasted on me that I've returned here, but I gave up long ago being amazed at where my life might take me. It doesn't really matter to me where I live and I try not to draw any conclusions or comparisons or circles. I'm here because Maria is here, and she won't be here forever and neither will I.

Of all the Italian cities Maria might have chosen in which to study, Pisa wouldn't have been the first on *my* list. Bologna, I think, I like the feel of above all others. Before I lived in Pisa, Bologna was my idea of an Italian university town, perhaps because the tourism isn't so blindingly in your face. Bologna's appeal reveals itself to you gradually and it gets to feel more personal. You can believe you're part of a select few who appreciate its beauty. Pisa, on the other hand, is a city of instant gratification when it comes to tourism – it does exactly

1

what it says on the postcard – but it also has one of the best hospitals in the world and so, for now, this is where I live.

Don't get me wrong; I like a lot of things about Pisa and the longer I live here the better it gets. It's the opposite of Bologna: Pisa reveals its mundane reality over a period of time. People live here and work here, study here and die here. The white marble of its public buildings is a temporary distraction, conveniently packaged together in the Campo dei Miracoli so Pisa can point and say, '*si*, all that is over there, that's where you want to be'. And, if truth be told, it's where I go just about every day. I love the grass around the Duomo; I particularly like the contrast of the grass and the marble. And the blue sky, of course, I'm forgetting about the cornflower blue of the sky. The green, the white and the blue – what a combination. I can be at peace here, sitting alone in the shadow of the Baptistry, and it never fails to blow me away.

If I'm not in her room when Maria finishes her lectures for the day, she knows to come and find me here. It's quite a walk from where we live and more often than not she'll get on with her studies first – we share a desk and she has essays and a thesis to write. Early evening, or late afternoon, is Maria's desk time. She also has a job in a local bar and this means she has to grab what opportunity she can to get her coursework completed. It's a little intense for my liking and occasionally a little tense too, but this is Maria; she's never going to change and I wouldn't want her any other way.

We do okay. I thought at first we'd be too much on top of each other but it hasn't been like that at all. I do most of my writing early in the day while Maria's at college and I can go over my work again in the evening. Also, she has the use of the university library and this leaves me free to work or to not work; whatever I feel like doing. She worried about me for the first week – would I manage on my own in a strange city, or would I get lonely? I think she forgets sometimes who I am, or else she blanks out how I lived my life for most of the past three or four years before we met; whether she does so subconsciously or deliberately, I don't know. Perhaps she just has a natural concern, or a determination to be normal in abnormal circumstances? I let it go and smile; it's nice to have someone care for you, even if the cause for their worry doesn't actually exist. Lonely – how can I be lonely? Look at all these people, thousands of them, every day, holding up their arms to support the Leaning Tower for their photographs. Families, lovers, strangers, tourists. Some argue over nothing, made irritable through tiredness and the heat, while others flop down on the grass beside me and just enjoy. I love it here and I'm happy.

I used to leave Maria a note in the room – *gone for a walk, gone to buy groceries* – but the notes soon became redundant. We live along the river and my walks usually take a circular route along Via Santa Maria to the Campo and then back through the side streets to the Piazza del Cavalieri, stopping off at the market to shop for tonight's dinner. My rests at the Campo have become longer and longer, partly in recognition of Maria's need for space – work space and personal space – but also through sheer contentment. After everything – this. I know how to count my blessings and I count them every day.

Maria came looking for me one day, early into my routine, and neither of us was surprised when she found me on the grass between the Duomo and the Baptistry.

'You're such an English tourist,' she said.

And I am. I don't ever want to lose my wonder at this place, this beautiful island of green, white and blue.

So sometimes now when Maria comes to join me in the Campo, she walks in the opposite direction, through the market, glancing in the shops she knows I like to frequent. I am that predictable, but I also like to wait to see her arrive in the Campo, among the crowds of people, and watch for the moment when she switches from her thoughts of whatever to her thoughts of finding me. It's good to see her from a distance, but only because I get to see her up close too. That girl there – she's looking for me, and when she sees me, her walk changes from an unconscious swing of happiness to a very deliberate come-on. She knows what she can do to me, and even though I know she knows it, I fall for it every time. I play my part; I sit back, resting on my outstretched arms, and I stare. I'm lucky and I know it. She's smart and she's sexy, and she's with me – or rather, I'm with her.

'Am I in heaven?' I ask.

She deliberately stands where I can see up her dress, so I shake my head and smile.

'What?' she asks, all innocence.

'You're shameless.'

'You're the one doing the looking.'

'I'd be crazy not to.'

'I'm starving. I'm at college all day and I have to come looking for you if I want something to eat?'

'You could always try shopping and cooking for yourself.'

'Yeah, right – that's not the deal.'

'We have a deal?'

'You know we do – you feed me, you get to have sex with me.'

'Which would you like to do first?'

'Very funny,' she says. 'You know the rules – you don't do one, you don't get to do the other.'

4

I miss Maria on the days she doesn't come to the Campo, but once it gets to a certain time and she still hasn't arrived, I know she must have some college work to finish before heading out later to her job at El Greco's. I also know she's avoiding me. She's been avoiding me for days, which is no easy thing when you share a single study bedroom. She has a secret she's keeping from me – which isn't that much of a secret, all things considered – and the consequences of it are worrying her. I understand why she's nervous about telling me but I hope she's not scared; fear like that can sit in your belly like a cannonball.

Tonight, perhaps, I'll talk to her about the baby.

The sun dips behind the Duomo and I stand to brush the grass from my clothes. Maria might joke about the cooking and the eating but she has to cram that food inside her, so I head off to shop for tonight's dinner.

LAURA

2004

As soon as I see her, I know what I want to do to her. And I know it's not a very nice thing to do.

I have my Brad Pitt look about me. I'm not saying I look like Brad Pitt – I'm a long way from that – but there's a look: a scruffy but clean look, a *happy and content with who I am* look, a *seen a lot of the sun but taking care of my skin* look.

Thelma and Louise without the cowboy hat . . . *A River Runs Through It* . . . any of the outdoor, sunshine movies. Happy to be alone, but open to conversation. Enviably self-possessed – you get the picture?

I'm travelling alone. I always travel alone these days. I live alone; I am alone. It's so much easier when you're on your own. There are no worries about finding a seat with the kids. I often wait until last before boarding a plane and enjoy the lack of hassle and responsibility. This flight today is only half-full – or half-empty, you choose – and still the parents are panicking and pushing, watching out for any sneaky queue-jumping, resenting the older passengers who block the way and take an age to hobble down the stairs and across to the plane. When I walk out from the departure lounge, all the passengers are lined up at the first set of steps, baking in the hot afternoon sun, babies bawling in the heat, toddlers trying their parents' patience. I walk to the rear steps; I'm comfortable and settled into my aisle seat before she's even entered the cabin.

I'm not looking for her – I hadn't noticed her in the terminal – but something happens as she looks down the cabin, searching for the best seats for her family. There's a second as she sees me – a moment of indignation at my having jumped the queue – before she looks up and notices the other passengers who have followed me to take the rear steps of the plane. There's a smile at not being sharp enough to have thought to do the same, a shake of the head at the futility of all the pushing and shoving when the flight is so empty, and she catches my eye and smiles. I sympathise – or, rather, I convey my sympathy by returning her smile, acknowledging the joys of parenting with a slight shake of my head – but I know right away that this isn't how she sees me. I am the antithesis of parenthood. I'm freedom; I am lack of responsibility – all this in one look and in the space of a second.

Still, now, she could disappear beneath my radar. In that one shared moment, I've seen something in her – something nice and good, something I know I would like – but it doesn't have to come to anything. It could be one of a thousand thoughts I have today – well, maybe not a thousand, but you know what I mean – of the different women, of the many different lives we all could have, if only we choose to pursue them. What she chooses to do, though, is to walk on down the cabin and take the seats opposite me.

I wonder why. I mean, it's obvious who and what she is: a mother with her family – these five words define her. She can't allow the likes of me into her world. From now on, she refuses to acknowledge my existence and my role is to similarly deny that anything so much as a smile has passed between us. These are the games we play. I'm not stupid: I know that brief acknowledgement we shared is just that and nothing more, but I like that she's allowed herself this little lapse of sitting close by. I like that I might be the briefest of glimpses into another life for her, one that she's chosen not to take and is happy not to have taken, and I smile because it makes me feel good.

Englishness is all around me. You have to be away for a while before you can feel this, how quaintly odd and typically English they are when they're together like this. Or is it just that when you see them abroad, they're so much more obviously English, and stand out from their different surroundings? And I don't mean the football shirts – the shirts are more for the English airports, before the holiday flights to foreign countries. Have shirt, will travel – always the England shirt and not the club team you happen to support. You might not know much about where you're going, but you want the friendly recognition from another shirt-wearing Englishman once you get there ... and not the rivalry of a City or a United. The shirt gives you the confidence to fly off to the strange places, to the darker faces that, funnily enough, might not think so much of you for what you're wearing.

I'm on a Ryanair plane in Italy – in Pisa – and yet the whole tone of the cabin is one of Englishness and the English. There must be a few Italians on the plane, and I suspect there are a few Irish people planning to fly on from Stansted once we arrive, but the English dominate the cabin and make it their own. With their over-politeness that makes them sound a little slow and stupid, with their worried faces as they check for seats and their loud, southern English accents that will always

9

be alien to me – I'm happy not to count myself amongst their number.

It's funny, the reasoning that allows me to think of the English as though I'm not English myself. It's as if, because I've not lived there for so long, I'm somehow different to all these passengers. Or have I always thought of myself as different, first by choosing to live in Ireland and then by travelling for so long that I've effectively made myself stateless? Yet it's still a British passport I carry in my pocket; I'm not that much of a vagrant. I know it's my Britishness I would cling to if I ever found myself in a tight spot, if ever I had to find my way home in a hurry.

This is the difference: these English passengers are going home. I have nowhere to call home and haven't had for almost three years.

My 'friend' across the aisle is travelling with her husband and young children, two little girls.

'If you sit in there with Jenny,' she says to her husband, 'we can maybe keep the seats for Bob and Laura.'

Her husband sits in the row in front with the elder of the two girls. I deliberately don't look across, and close my eyes to concentrate on my breathing. Nobody asks to sit in the seats next to me. It wouldn't bother me, but there's no need for anybody to ask, as there are plenty of free seats. Hearing all these English voices suddenly makes me conscious of the fact that I'm on my way back into the world. I've spent the best part of three years hearing many different languages spoken, most of which I don't understand well enough to follow, and one – Greek – that I've given up on even trying. I know enough to be polite and to get what I need, whether it's accommodation, food or directions, but it's a long time since I've been in an environment where I understand every word I hear spoken. I guess this is why I'm picking up on all these holidaymakers' petty concerns: because I can understand them.

Bob and Laura arrive; already I call them by their names in my head. This makes six of them travelling together and I can see why it makes sense to save the seats – two rows of three to keep them all together. Her husband moves back to sit with her; she has the window seat and he the aisle, with their baby daughter safely between them. I'm surprised the baby's old enough to require a seat of her own as she doesn't look much more than one, or maybe a very young two-year-old. I used to be pretty good at guessing ages, but perhaps I'm not as good as I once was. The elder daughter, Jenny, sits on her own between Laura and Bob – three, is she, or maybe four?

I used to have a daughter of my own – Ciara – but I lost her. She'll be almost four now, a little older perhaps. It's almost time for her to start school. This September, I guess – just a few short weeks away.

I can see that Laura is the sister and that Bob is Laura's boyfriend. That was a pretty good idea for them all to go away together – more variety for the kids and the chance of a break for the parents. One night out together, alone, while Bob and Laura mind the kids. It makes sense.

All this and they haven't even closed the cabin doors yet. I deliberately look away before they pick up on my listening in.

It's easy to figure out the family dynamic though, even without watching closely. Her husband reads his *Daily Mail* while she settles their younger daughter with a picture book. The elder daughter refers back constantly to her mother – never her father – for sweets and a drink for the flight, or to show a page from the book she's reading. Bob sits in front of

11

the husband and reads the in-flight magazine, turning around occasionally to point out the interesting bits from an article on Amsterdam. Her husband says he'll read it later and returns to his *Mail*. Laura seems very close to her sister and I can see she enjoys her role as the children's aunty. She's young – in her early twenties, I think – but you can see she wants a family like this for herself. The talk between the four females is easy and natural; the men are content, if quiet. No one here has fallen out over the past week or so, and the holiday has been a success.

But I don't think either man appreciates just what he has. Bob must be secure, almost smug, in the knowledge that he's Laura's boyfriend. He has reason to be – if anything, she's the more obviously attractive of the two sisters. Bob's the one with the least responsibility here: all he has to do is get along with the kids and doing so puts him in a stronger position with Laura. She has the feeling he'd make a good dad; all he has to do is bide his time and he's there. But I don't think he knows just how easily she could be taken from him.

Pay her more attention, I want to tell him.

And the husband: does he think it's enough that he just turned up on this holiday? Sure, he works hard all year and yes, he deserves a holiday, but this is supposed to be quality time with the family, and he seems oblivious to the three of them. There's a lot to lose here: two daughters and a wife. It's not enough just to read your paper. She prompts any conversation they have and any help he gives her is asked for rather than offered. I gave more for my one daughter than he gives for two and still I lost her.

Horses for courses, I think. Different strokes for different folks. They all seem happy enough. The kids don't suffer with

12

their ears as the plane takes off. She chats away to her sister in between listening to her daughters. What more do you need from your partner than to carry the bags and to be there for a cuddle in bed at night?

As I said, I pick up on all this without even trying. I catch her eye every now and again when she leans forward to speak to Laura but there's nothing there for me. She changes at one point from her contact lenses to her glasses and it adds a few years. She looks even more like the mammy, even more content with her lot in life, but I recognise something when I see it and I see a quality in her that she can't hide, no matter how hard she might try.

The flight is uneventful. This is the first time in a long time that I've been up in the air. I've been travelling by trains, buses and ferries, with the occasional hitched ride in a car. I've been clinging to the surface of the earth. When we land, they announce we can leave the plane by either the front or the rear steps, but I resist the temptation to catch her eye. I notice the husband carries the younger daughter as she sleeps, that's all.

The weather gives me an immediate reality check and the difference in temperature has me wishing I had a jacket or a coat. I run across to the bus carrying us to the terminal, no longer harbouring any fancy notions about Brad Pitt.

It might be this lack of a coat or it might be something else that alerts the attention of immigration control. They take me to one side, away from the passport queue.

'Can I ask you where you're travelling from, sir?'

'Pisa.'

'And your destination in the UK?'

'I'm travelling on to Ireland, to Dublin,' I say.

'Do you mind if I just check through your bag?'

I pull the small rucksack off my shoulder and hand it to him. He scans it first with some sort of long stick and then opens the buckles. What are you going to do? These people: their authority derives from your fear that if you kick up a fuss they can probe your anus with a camera. So I wait for him to go through my things. It takes only a few seconds.

'You live in Ireland, do you?'

'Yes,' I say for simplicity.

'Do you mind if I make a note of your address there?'

Well, yes, I do mind but there's nothing I can do about it, so I give him Siobhan's address – our home, as was.

'And you've been on holiday in Italy, yes?'

Jesus – what is this?

'I've been travelling around Europe for a year or so,' I say.

'Very nice – and what do you do that allows you that kind of luxury?'

I shrug and reach for my bag but he doesn't let me take it.

'Seriously, sir, what do you do for a living? I just need you to tell me that and then I can let you go.'

Should I tell him? That I live off the money given to me when I agreed never to see Siobhan and Ciara again?

'I'm a writer,' I say, dreading the conversation, but he releases the grip on my bag.

'That's fine, sir, thank you. Have a safe onward journey to Ireland.'

It's routine, I know, but it throws me and I have to remind myself of the reason for coming back when there's nothing here for me to come back for.

I was based for a while in North Africa – Morocco, mainly, and then Tunisia for last winter – before returning in the spring to the Greek Islands. As the temperatures rose, I had the idea of travelling up from the bottom of Italy, inching further north each time it became too hot or the mosquitoes moved in. And that's what I did, catching the ferry first to Brindisi and then hitching, or walking when rides were hard to come by. Having shipped my things to Pisa, I was happy in the knowledge that if necessary I could always just jump on a train. I diverted for a week or so to Rome to meet up with Danny – or Brother Daniel as he is now called. He's studying at the Irish College, preparing for the priesthood. We argued, about money mostly – his money and my money, how he'd given his away and how he suggested I do the same. I stayed with Danny for a couple of days in the accommodation the college provides for tourists on a pilgrimage to Rome, but I couldn't suffer the piety for long and had to put some distance between us again. I swapped the noise of the city for the open countryside along the spine of Italy. Some part of trekking across those barren mountains must have stirred a desire for the colour and the rain of Ireland, and I decided to fly home for the month of August. When I arrived in Pisa, I collected my few belongings from the station and booked a flight for the following week to Dublin.

But I hadn't reckoned on the cold, and I still haven't really thought where I will go once I get to Dublin. I thought I had my shit sufficiently together but now I'm not so sure. I'm already having my doubts and this is only England. What will I do once I get to Dublin? It's one thing to wander through a foreign country in the sunshine, quite another to wander through Ireland in weather that's changeable at best. Being pulled aside by Immigration is enough to shake me out of the smug contentment I've been used to – just as those English voices had on the flight – and it brings the real world sharply

15

back into focus. This is a world where you worry about the stamps from foreign countries on your passport, especially if those foreign countries are in North Africa.

This is England.

At baggage reclaim the monitor says belt number one, but when I walk across, our flight number isn't there; this is obviously going to take a while. I recognise a few faces from the flight. Some passengers decide to stay by the belt, while others return to the monitor. I notice a teenage girl looking at me and how she quickly turns away. She looks good – tanned and well dressed, waiting for a jacket from her baggage, just like me. Her sister joins her and she's just as good-looking – a little older but still in her teens. They chat and both look my way. Now it's my turn to look away but it feels good. They're joined by their father and the three of them consult with each other. The girls walk by me on their way back to check the monitor – how come I didn't notice them on the plane?

I stroll over to their father and catch his eye. He smiles – typical, his face says to me. I walk the circular length of the baggage carousel and he's still alone when I return.

'No sign of the bags, so?' I ask.

'No, nothing yet,' he says. 'My girls are over by the monitor; they'll let us know if there's any change.'

He's very affable, very easy-going. I could be his friend, in another world.

'Have you far to go, if they ever decide to give us our bags back?' I ask.

'Not too far. Cambridge.'

'That's a nice part of the country.'

'You know it well, do you?'

'I'm often there through my work,' I say, lying. 'Are you in one of the colleges?'

He laughs.

'Is it that obvious? Yes, just been away for a few days with the girls – try to instil some culture in them.' The belt starts up. 'Ah, maybe now,' he says.

'Best of luck,' I say, and move over to a space by the belt. His daughters are making their way back over and I don't want to be too obvious – caught talking to their father.

Yes, we could be friends. I could meet him one day in Cambridge, in town or in his college – invent some business or other. Fancy a pint some time? Is he alone – separated? Sees the girls occasionally; I could be there by chance one time and get to know them. Not move too soon, build up the trust. Our parents don't understand us, they'd tell me. I'm a little younger than their dad so it might make all the difference. See both sides – he loves you, you know, don't give him a hard time. Find a shared interest with the girls – the movies, perhaps? Ask his permission. Pleased to have them taken off his hands – safer off with me than out with some of those young bucks. Where's the mother – some frosty academic bitch? Too busy doing research to take time off for the family holiday? Might be something there for me too? I could fuck up his life big time. If I can't have his happiness, at least I can take his happiness away.

This is the ease with which my world might change. Who knows what may happen? I take one last look at the girls – yes, I'm right, there's something there for me – but then turn my back on them and watch out for my bag.

The family of six from the plane approach the belt now that our luggage is about to appear. They have two trolleys

– Bob wheels one, Laura the other. Her husband carries their sleeping baby while she holds the hand of the elder child, Jenny. No culture trip to Tuscany for these guys, I think – they've been in Viareggio for the week, maybe caught a glimpse of the Leaning Tower but almost certainly didn't make it as far as Florence.

They stand close by. It's one of those days when what I hope might happen does happen. If I'd been coming on too strong, I'm sure she might have avoided standing close by. I get the feeling she's happy to be seen with her family – look at what I have here, she's telling me. Bob stands beside me with the trolley behind him; he's the luggage man. I consider using the same conversation I had with the Cambridge professor – try to discover where they're heading – but again, I don't want to be too much, too obvious. It's enough that I can listen in on their happy family group.

The bags go by on the belt. I see my own as it appears down at the far end and I decide not to take it on the first run past.

Bob muscles in to pick up a huge suitcase. There's an identical one immediately behind and I can picture how it is – Bob and Laura have one case, while her family of four share the other.

'Is this one yours too?' I ask Bob. I can see him struggling with the weight of the first, trying to lodge it on to Laura's trolley.

'Cheers mate,' he says, twisting around to look at the bag.

I drag it off and on to Bob's trolley. I catch a glimpse of the label – Springfield, I think it says, and Brighton, although that's a long way from Stansted. I know she's watched me lift the bag and I walk away, further along the belt.

Cheers mate – fucking English, commonly used by blokes

who wish to get along. Or occasionally used in an aggressive way, but not here, not by Bob. Brighton – Jesus, that's a long way. Surely there are flights out to Italy from Gatwick? Yet I can picture them all, piling into the husband's SUV – yes, makes sense in a way. Last-minute booking, cheap flight – come on, let's fuck off to Italy for a week. Cheers mate!

I see the Cambridge professor walking away with his daughters and the younger one throws me one last look. Yes, I could do that. Be the first, spoil her for everybody else. Make it so that only I will do and then move on to her sister. Sibling rivalry – could I manage them both? Be worth trying at least – be fun trying.

My bag comes around again – a small sports holdall that's seen me through the past three years – and I grab it off the belt. I don't need a trolley. It's easy to travel light when there's only one of you. Once I'd sold the laptop and given up on the whole writing thing, there wasn't much luggage left to carry. I have a few T-shirts – faded by the sun and soon to be replaced – a change of trousers and some underwear. I wear my walking boots when I'm travelling because they're easier to carry on my feet than in a bag.

It's a pain having to check in for Dublin all over again but there's only a small queue so I tag on to the end. I'm on autopilot here, taking out my passport and reservation number and, once I've checked my bag, I revert to that independent-traveller state of mind. I'm hungry and I decide to eat on this side of passport control. There are almost two hours before my flight. I walk the entire way back along the concourse to the Irish pub at the far end. The pint tastes good and when my food arrives I order a second. It's good, everything is good, and I relax into the ambience of the bar.

19

Is it the Guinness that gets me thinking or is it the spare time I have before my flight? Where will I go once I reach Dublin? I'm so used to arriving in new places, finding accommodation and exploring my new surroundings, that to be somewhere I know so well is going to be strange. Where will I go for a cheap room? In Italy and Greece, cheap means humble and basic; in Dublin it means seedy and unsafe. Maybe I should splash the cash for a few days, find a nice room while I figure out where I should go? I haven't really thought this through. I can't just contact friends again after three years and expect them to put me up for a while. Besides, I've alienated just about everybody I ever knew and cut myself off so completely that I doubt I have any real friends left.

Am I going back to Dublin for good – is that it? And where, exactly, do I anticipate living? There are certain no-go areas and this restricts my options. Plus, it's easier to forget, easier to find oblivion, while you're away – am I going to have to face a flood of memories in Ireland? Am I ready to go through that again? Am I that strong?

I pay for my meal but I don't move. I can't go back to Ireland – what was I thinking? A couple of months ago, I was as far away from Ireland as I could be in western Europe; what dragged me all the way up from Greece, through Italy and on to that plane? What was calling me home? And where did I think that home might be – Ireland? England?

My bag is checked in to fly to Dublin; I either fly with it or I stay in Britain. If I stay, should I tell them I'm not flying? Do I want to go through all that hassle? There's nothing in my bag that I'd miss. Walk away, disappear – last seen checking his bag in to fly to Dublin? There's something appealing in simply disappearing, though the first time I use my credit card they'd know exactly where to find me. But who are 'they'? Who would care?

I could catch a train up to Cambridge. Try to meet up with the professor and his daughters – there are worse places to be. Or I could check the departures board and choose a destination beyond Europe and further even than North Africa. Really travel, see some different cultures – India, maybe, South East Asia or South America? But nowhere will ever be home until I settle down, learn a language, find some work, be a part of a new country. And is there really anywhere that's far enough away?

I won't be getting on that plane to Dublin. I like the idea that they'll have to go searching for my bag; they can get that immigration officer to do it. I'm so sorry – I changed my mind.

Brighton sounds okay to me – it's as good a place as any.

I buy a ticket for the Stansted Express to London and have plenty of time to reflect on my decision as I sit on the train. The effect of the two pints of Guinness starts to wear off and I hit a mid-afternoon slump. I rarely drink these days and this is one of the reasons why, but I enjoyed the pints so what the hell. I'm also tired from the flight, which may sound silly given the distances I've covered in the past three years – but there's always a catch-up time after your body has been in motion. Plus, of course, it's been a while since I've travelled by plane. Now I'm on the move again, it's like my body has to crank itself back up into travelling mode.

It's hard to switch off though. I'm used to being able to go brain-dead as I travel but I can't stop tuning in to all that English language. There's a little girl playing peek-a-boo with two male students in the seat across from me. The girl is beautiful and has an infectious laugh that has everybody falling in love with her. I have to change carriages, I feel so sick.

I'm still considering my options when the train pulls into Liverpool Street. Brighton was a whim and it seems such whimsy doesn't make as much sense here as it did on the Continent. While I was in Italy, a diversion to Assisi had worked out just fine, so why should this be any different? Nobody knew I was in Assisi and nobody knows I'm here. If it's anonymity I'm after, perhaps London might be the best idea?

As I step out on to the platform in Liverpool Street, I consciously stop myself from walking at a fast pace. What is it about London that makes you do that? I like London. I may be from the north but I know a good city when I see one, and London has just about everything. If staying lost is what I'm looking for then nobody will find me here. I have as much chance of running into someone I know in London as I had in Assisi. All the lonely people – it has to be the best place in the world if you want to be on your own. And the worst place in the world if you don't.

I decide I can't stay in London – too many memories of flying into City airport from Dublin to join Siobhan at some gig or other. I can no more be in London than I could have travelled on to Dublin. I check out the Tube map. I guess trains to Brighton still go from Victoria, so I make my way there. Having a destination is what matters. Take me down to Brighton where all I know is mods and rockers fighting it out on the beach. Oh, and the IRA, trying but failing to blow up Margaret Thatcher in the Grand Hotel. Siobhan must have sung in Brighton at some time or other, but I was never there. As the train from Victoria crosses the river heading south, I watch the London we knew together disappear safely into the past.

It's evening by the time I arrive in Brighton and I take a cab from the station to the Grand Hotel. It's too late now to start looking for suitable digs. I choose the Grand in honour of the attempt on Thatcher's life, though there's no guarantee there'll be a room. I guess the middle of August is peak season for Brighton.

'Is that rain,' I ask the driver, 'or spray from the sea?'

'Rain unfortunately, mate. We're forecast a big storm here tonight.'

'I thought Brighton was the sunniest place in England?'

'You're thinking of Bournemouth, mate.'

'Oh,' I say. I'm not that keen on tramping the streets of Brighton, looking for a room in the rain.

'But don't worry,' the driver says, looking in his rear-view mirror. 'Brighton's a close second. This'll blow over and it'll be beautiful again tomorrow.'

I appreciate his optimism but I have my doubts. I tip him well because the fare is lower than I expected. Most likely he thinks if I'm staying at the Grand I can afford the tip. I run up the steps to get out of the rain. I must look a bit of a state, but one of things I love about good hotels is they don't make any presumptions on the way you look. If you can afford to stay, you can dress as you please.

The lobby seems quiet; Sunday evening kind of quiet. I get the feeling the guy on reception is just covering for someone, like he's really the concierge or something.

'Have you a reservation, sir?'

'No – is that a problem?'

'Not necessarily. Is it just for tonight?'

23

'I'm not too sure.'

He cocks his head – if I don't know then who does?

'Tonight, definitely, and let's say tomorrow night too.'

'So, one room for two nights and we'll see how you get along.'

I ask for a room at the front of the hotel, if possible, looking out over the sea. The concierge looks at me like now I'm really taking the piss.

'I don't mind paying extra,' I say.

'It's not a question of money, sir; it's a question of availability.'

This puts me in my place and I'm grateful just to be getting a room. No, I don't have a car and yes, this rucksack is my only luggage. I use an address in Manchester – a false one, because what do they need to know? And I tell him I'd like to pay by cash.

'In that case, sir, can I take payment in advance?'

I hand over the money.

'Enjoy your stay, sir. Can you manage your own bag?'

I look up and see a hint of a smile. I smile too when I see the room he's given me: two floors up and overlooking the sea. I love what money can do for you when all you want is a nice place to be for the night.

The taxi driver was right: by the following morning, the storm has blown itself out. I wake up early and hungry and I sense the brightness of the sun behind the heavy hotel curtains. I walk over to the window and pull the cord to let the sunlight shine directly on my face. As I look out, the sun is over to my left and reflected across the sea. I squint to check the time on the digital display of the TV.

'Seven-fifty,' I say out loud. Not so early then.

I walk through to the bathroom, go to the toilet and splash

24

my face with cold water. Back in the bedroom, I put on my one set of clothes, pick up my glasses from the side of the bed and go downstairs. I take a peek outside the main entrance of the hotel and what I see makes me forget about eating for a moment. The light on the sea draws me across the busy road to the prom. The sound of the waves on the pebbles is different to anything I've come across in Greece or Italy – more physical somehow, more English.

I like this piece of England, I think, and decide I've come to the right place.

I watch a young woman walk across the beach by the shoreline with her dog, a huge Alsatian. The two of them stride out across the pebbles. It must be heavy going walking on such an uneven surface but both owner and dog seem to step lightly across in front of me. The dog is off the lead but the woman is carrying a thick chain in her left hand. That sure is a big dog. I guess she's probably walking it before leaving for work.

Above and behind her, I follow slowly in the same direction. The cry of the gulls cuts through the sound of the early morning traffic. There's already some warmth in the sun on the back of my neck. I stop after a short distance and lean on the railings. I look out at the remains of the broken-down pier, a black silhouette in the brightness of the sea. I remember as a child reading in the newspaper – my parents' *Daily Mail* probably – about the time the pier burnt down. Or had it collapsed in a storm? Whichever, that pier's a hell of a statement out there in the waves.

The woman and her Alsatian reach the derelict pier and turn back along the beach. I turn towards the sun and close my eyes against the light, letting it work its magic on my face and listening to the gulls — but then my stomach reminds me about breakfast and I walk back across the road to the hotel.

I go through to the breakfast room, wait to be seated and give the waitress my room number. I've enjoyed living quite frugally for the past couple of years and learnt to appreciate a simple breakfast of fresh bread and good coffee. I guess I'm paying through the nose here at the Grand for exactly the same thing but I don't care. I'm going to look after myself for a while, whatever it takes and however much it costs. While I wait for my breakfast to be served, I do a quick calculation of how long I could afford to live like this before my money runs out. Maybe two thousand nights, or let's say five or six years. And I'm worried about checking in here for a couple of days? I tell myself to relax and enjoy; it's not as though I do this all the time.

After my breakfast I see the concierge from last night and he doffs his cap. I smile and walk over.

'Where in Brighton would you recommend I try shopping for new clothes?'

He looks at the state of me, leaving me in no doubt that it's about time.

'Are we talking about a gentleman's set of clothes, sir, or a younger, trendier range of wear?'

'We're talking absolute basics of shirts, trousers, shorts – casual wear, shall we say?'

'Ye-es.' He's disappointed but not surprised. 'I think you'll find what you're looking for in the North Street area of shops.'

I love this guy; he reminds me of a white and weedy version of Siobhan's bodyguard Stevie.

'And where would I find North Street?'

He reaches beneath his desk and opens out a small map.

'We're on the seafront here,' he says, pointing with the tip of his pen. 'If you turn left outside the entrance to the hotel and then left again here, you'll find a whole range of shops to choose from.'

I pick up the map and thank him. I want to ask him his name – just as I imagine Danny might have done – but I don't share Danny's congeniality. I'd like him to stop calling me sir, but I daren't ask him to do that either. I just thank him again and walk over to the lifts.

I take a shower and have a shave. I swap my glasses for contact lenses and look out the window of my hotel room, shaking my head again in disbelief at the view. This was the right place to have come and already I'm thinking of how I could settle in Brighton, start a new life and, who knows, maybe even be happy here.

I nod to the concierge as I leave the hotel and see an eyebrow raised in acknowledgement. He's getting his money's worth of amusement out of me.

I'm drawn across the road to the seafront again, but I resist the urge and turn left and then left again, away from the prom. I see what Mr Concierge means about North Street; I have no difficulty finding trousers, shirts, underwear, shoes and socks. Perhaps I should ask him where he recommends a 'gentleman' might shop, just out of interest. I could do with a change: I'm too old for most of the clothes I see in these shops, but still too young (I hope) for where Mr Concierge would send me for a fitting.

He's there at his desk when I return to the Grand and I ask if he knows of a cobbler for my boots.

'They're in need of some tender loving care,' I tell him.

'I could organise that for you, sir.' He waits while I untie the laces and hand over the boots. He picks them up between two fingers.

'Thank you,' I say.

'That's not a problem, sir. I shall have these back to you by this evening.'

I walk across the foyer in my dirty stocking feet and take the lift up to my room.

Back downstairs, I drink a coffee in the lobby and head off for another stroll along the prom. It's still the height of the season and the front is gearing itself up for another day. Picking up my pace, I step out a little and feel as though I could go on walking along the coast forever, beyond Brighton, past the Isle of Wight, through all those seaside towns of southern England, through Dorset and into Devon and finally into Cornwall, down to the very end of England – that would be a fine thing to do – but not today and not in new shoes. I buy fish and chips and a takeaway cup of tea for my lunch and make my way down to the beach. I feel content. Brighton seems right to me, a place I might one day call my home.

I sit on the pebble beach and lay out my fish and chips. So this is where they came to fight in the sixties. Hard work, I think, running and fighting on all this shingle.

The horizon line runs straight and uninterrupted for as far as I can see. The sea seems raised above me, stretching out into infinity. I have a little doze after eating my lunch but wake up with a dry mouth from the salt on the chips. Two teenage girls along the beach are kissing, one with her hand down the back of the other's pants. They break away from each other, laughing, and look right back at me. It's like I'm the one that's been outed and I stand up unsteadily in the sunshine. I drop my rubbish in the bin, buy a bottle of water and stroll along the lower level of the prom towards the pier, taking it easy. I make my way up on to the pier where it's crazy busy, but I'm happy and alone in my own private world. I watch and listen without being a part of it all. This is the closest I feel to the Brighton of yesteryear, the Brighton of *Brighton Rock*, and I see the ghost of Pinkie in every piece of seaside tack. The toffee apples and the candyfloss, the ice cream and seafood – they're all here. The noise is relentless but I don't mind; it's like a soundtrack of the seaside playing in my head.

The swirling green water I see through the gaps in the boardwalk – isn't that how Pinkie's story ends, falling to his death from the pier? The scratched record letting Rose off the hook, her still believing Pinkie was a saint.

I walk past the bars where Pinkie and his gang drank and caused trouble. On to the funfair where Pinkie was such a deadeye shot at the firing range. I listen to the music of the carousel and feel like I'm in the story myself. People push past so I move out the way of the crowds, listening to the sound of a time I thought was gone forever. I rest for a while at the railings with my face to the sun before walking on again.

I make my way back to the Grand along the upper prom, shading my eyes from the sun. There's no sign of Mr Concierge at the hotel, but my boots are waiting for me just inside the bedroom door. I run a bath and soak contentedly for the best part of an hour.

I'm up early again the next morning. I leave the hotel and cross the road to look out to sea and, once again, there's that same woman walking her dog. This must be their daily routine; I wonder how far she walks every morning. I hang around until she passes by a second time in the opposite direction, and then I return to the hotel for my breakfast. I ask at reception if I can stay for the rest of the week, giving my credit card as a guarantee but insist on settling my final bill in cash.

I lace up my boots and set off on another day of discovery. I cover the obvious places by lunchtime – the Pavilion, the Dome and the Lanes. The city has that classic seaside combination of grandeur and decay. I see the attraction of the Lanes area but it's not for me. All those bars and restaurants, antique and jewellery shops – the quaintness is fine but I prefer the seafront any day. I'm surprised by how hilly Brighton is and the high-rise flats that overlook the city are a reminder that real people live here – not just tourists and visitors.

I take a break back in my hotel room and order up some room service for lunch. If I'm serious about staying in Brighton, I have to find somewhere to live. That means tramping further afield, buying the local paper to study the ads in search of an area I like. There's no good reason why I shouldn't try. I think back to the luggage label that brought me to Brighton in the first place – Springfield, was it? I check out my map and find a Springfield Road that's not too far from the hotel. It makes sense to start there.

I cut through the Lanes where the pubs are still busy with the late lunch crowd and continue up towards North Laine. This is immediately to my liking, much more my kind of scene. Granted, cafés and shops dominate the area but I can see from the people who work here that this place is alive. I spread out my map – definitely not cool – and decide to cut down to my right towards London Road. This is different again: busy, normal, lots of traffic, like the high street of a small town. There are banks, shops and pubs and if it wasn't for the cry of the seagulls you'd never guess you were so close to the Brighton seafront.

I come across an open market that is just off the main road and it looks like the ideal spot to shop each day for fresh produce; I like that in a place. Plus, there are supermarkets for when you need them, a post office, charity shops; this micro-town looks like it works.

A huge railway viaduct cuts across the road and I stand and stare at it for a while, admiring the balls it took to build such a thing. In its own way, it's a piece of art – a great big fuck-off piece of art that, come to think of it, speaks of money and power and how the two always go hand in hand. I'm kind of glad to see it defaced by graffiti: 'BUSH IS A CRIMINAL', and 'BRIGHTON IS WITH YOU, OMAR'.

I walk underneath as a train goes by overhead and it all adds up to a very different noise to the sounds I've been hearing down on the seafront. Springfield Road is the next road up to the right. This isn't necessarily where the mammy from the Pisa flight lives but I'm interested all the same. It's much quieter than the main road, more residential and homely. The houses are large and I can well imagine my English Rose feeling right at home here.

(What can I call her? I want to call her Laura but that, of course, was her sister's name.)

When I look closer at the houses, however, I think I might be mistaken. Most are divided into apartments and look decidedly run-down. Many have been taken over by builders and are having work done to them while others are in obvious need of renovation. A few houses remain as family homes but this area isn't her. She looked like money to me, as did her kids. I think if she had a fixer-upper it would already be fixed up. I walk on up the hill; it's nice enough but it's just not her.

There's a pub up the road and I call in for a sit down. I

order a Bloody Mary and take a seat at the bar. I try to picture myself drinking here as a regular, having found an apartment along Springfield Road, and I know it's not going to happen. My idea of Brighton is completely tied in to the sea. I've learnt what I needed about finding a place to live and I pick up a copy of the *Argus* off the bar to flick through the property ads. I imagine anything with access to the sea, or even a view of the sea, is going to cost a fortune – though maybe not quite so much as staying in the Grand Hotel for five years.

After finishing my drink, I thank the barman and leave the bar. I've done enough exploring for one day, so I put in my headphones and Eminem takes me back down towards London Road. By chance, as I wait to cross at the busy intersection, I finally see something of what I've been looking for: what looks like a jewel of a pub, almost hidden from the main road. I have to give it a try. There are a few punters outside, sitting in the late afternoon sunshine. I turn off my music and step inside the pub, order a pint and enquire about food. There are two bar areas and I take my drink through to the back room where a few punters sit drinking in the semi-dark. I take a seat but then change tables when I see a young drunken couple directly in my line of sight.

The pub has a good feel to it, despite having the obligatory fruit machine – what is it about the English and their gaming machines?

I order some food and enjoy my pint. There's a steady flow of punters. Most stay for a quick drink but a few regulars look set for the evening. The drunken couple argue, the girl announcing she's leaving to put on the dinner.

'I'm coming after this pint,' he slurs.

Yeah, right, I think.

'Are you sure you're okay?' she asks.

'Just go, can't you?' he shouts, too loud for the pub. Everybody looks and then looks away. She leaves and he grips his stomach in pain. It's pissing me off to watch him so I pick up a paper from a rack on the wall. Naturally, it's the *Daily Mail*.

'AL-QAEDA'S CHILLING PLOT TO TARGET BRITAIN' is the headline.

A young woman comes in, orders a drink, and sits at the bar talking into her mobile phone.

The drunk opposite is shaking so badly, he has to hold on to his arm like he's having a stroke. He tries to stand and knocks his empty glass flying. He has trouble with the side exit door and I'm tempted to help, if only to get rid of him sooner.

'It's a shame,' one of the regulars at the bar says once the drunk has left.

Sure, I think: a shame we have to see it.

'It's happening so quickly,' someone else says. 'I never thought he'd deteriorate so fast.'

So, maybe not a drunk after all? My food arrives and I forget all about him. I order a second pint to have with my dinner.

There's a poster on the wall for a gig at the pub this coming Saturday – the Andy Williams Experience – that might be something worth going to.

A different couple – some young one and her fella – take the drunk's table. They look like students and I can see they're in love. She's hanging on his every word and they keep giving each other that special look that only they know what it means.

The food's good, the beer's good and the music playing in the bar is good; my only problem is watching happy girl

33

opposite stroking her man's stubbly chin while he kisses her on the neck.

The lounge area starts to fill up, mostly with young ones who seem to know each other. I'm tired from all my walking and sleepy after the beer and the food so I decide to leave. Just as I stand up, though, the woman I saw exercising her dog on the beach walks in from the other bar. She looks at me, smiles and says hello.

'Are you here for the meeting?' she asks.

'Meeting? No, sorry.'

I look around and see a couple of tables being pushed together. I feel a bit awkward and make to leave.

'We're trying to build a response to Blair for the Labour Conference next month,' she says. She hands over a pile of photocopies she's carrying to a young lad who can't be more than fifteen. 'Thanks, Damien,' she says. 'About five minutes, yes? We'll just wait and see if we get any late arrivals. You can stay if you like.'

This last bit is to me. She talks like she walks on the beach: strong and confident, taking everything in her stride.

'I – maybe,' I say. 'I recognised you when you came in.'

'You recognised me?'

'From seeing you walk your dog on the beach.'

'Yes?'

'I enjoy watching your dog,' I say, like an idiot.

'That's Max,' she says and then, 'Oh God! You're the man in the dark glasses up on the prom!'

'I guess so, yeah.' I forget sometimes that my glasses have reactor lenses for the sunshine. This is such a mistake. I'm uncomfortable that she's noticed me watching her.

'I thought you might have been Special Branch,' she says.

34

'You looked so mysterious up there on the prom – like a man without a dog to walk.'

'Special Branch? No, I don't think so.' I laugh but it comes out wrong, more like a yelp. I've got to get the fuck out of here before I make a complete fool of myself.

'You might laugh,' she says, 'but that gentleman over there is Special Branch.' She points to some anonymous bloke sitting alone at the bar. 'Aren't you?' she asks him in a loud voice. The bloke turns away without replying.

'You're telling me Special Branch send an officer along to your meetings?' I ask her quietly.

'Yes – it's pathetic, isn't it?'

I'm sure she's talking deliberately loudly to provoke him. I look around and I don't know which is more pathetic – the bunch of losers at the meeting or the fact that somebody somewhere would give a damn what they have to say.

'Please stay,' she says. 'We really do need to let Blair know what we think of all his lies. I'm Juliette, by the way.'

She holds out her hand and I shake it. She says her name in the French way, with a soft 'J'. She looks to be in her late twenties but I may be as bad at guessing the age of women as I am of children.

'Marshall,' I say.

She looks at me oddly, like she has me rumbled.

'And will you stay?'

I'm caught now.

'Sure, why not?'

She smiles and turns to help set up the meeting. I catch the Special Branch guy staring at me and I look away. I take a seat at what I hope will be the back.

'You met Juliette then?' The young woman from the

bar – also in her late twenties – sits down next to me and introduces herself as Anna.

'Marshall,' I say and we shake hands.

'She's very driven.'

'Juliette?'

'*Juliette*,' she corrects me, giving it the full French. She has on a heavy pair of glasses that I guess are meant to hide her striking looks but only succeed in making me look closer.

The meeting is very intense and very predictable. Juliette tries her best to get commitments out of the few people there, mainly with the aim of encouraging others to come along to the next meeting. Everybody talks about what must be done, what it will take to get Blair to understand and how we must build for a real show of strength at the upcoming Labour Conference. I bite my tongue: if he didn't listen before the war he won't listen now. Blair has a direct line to God and believes what he believes; nobody from this world will ever change that.

Anna takes on the responsibility of contacting other groups to form a united front for the week of the Conference. I sneak away as soon as I sense the meeting is about to wrap up, out through the front bar.

On my way out I notice another *Daily Mail* reader, half-sitting on a bar stool and half-leaning against the wall. I look closer to confirm I have it right: it's Bob, Laura's boyfriend from the Stansted flight. So he's the Springfield Road connection. It figures – his address on the luggage and an apartment in one of the sub-divided houses just crying out for renovation. He sees me staring so I nod.

'Cheers mate,' I say. 'Remember me from the flight the other day?'

He folds up his paper and looks at me, not taking too kindly to having his space invaded, but finally he recognises me.

'Yeah,' he says, 'you helped with the luggage. Fucking hell, it's a small world, ain't it?' He holds out his hand and I shake it. 'You live 'round 'ere?'

'Just doing a bit of work, mate. You got back all right then?'

'Yeah, no problem. You prob'ly did the same as us, did ya – cheap flight, last minute?'

'That's right but I had no idea I was going to be sent down to Brighton for work the next day. This is a great pub. Your local, is it?'

'Yeah, it's all right, ain't it? Except for that crowd of shit-stirrers out the back: I don't wanna be rude but . . .'

I nod vaguely in agreement.

'Sorry, mate – you're not with them, are ya?'

'No, Jesus – no way. I got caught by them, is all.'

'Yeah, they're like that.' I think if he was anywhere else but in his own local, he might spit on the floor in disgust. 'Fancy a pint? Bob's the name.'

'Marshall,' I say. 'Cheers, but I'd best be off.'

'Another time, maybe?'

'Yeah, I'd like that – maybe see you here on Saturday night?'

'Whatever rocks your boat,' he says. 'I'll be 'ere as usual.'

I bet you will, I think.

At the door, Anna from the meeting is also about to leave.

'I wondered where you'd got to,' she says.

I hold the door open for her. I look back, raising an eyebrow at Bob and he lifts his paper to salute his approval.

I walk in the direction of the seafront and Anna falls into step beside me.

'Who's Omar?' I ask, indicating the graffiti on the viaduct wall.

'Oh, he's our prisoner in Guantanamo.' She looks at me. 'You don't live in Brighton, do you?'

'No – just working here for a few days.'

'But you came to the meeting anyway?'

'I think it's important to do something, however small it might seem. Let them know they can't get away with just anything.'

'That's the problem, though, isn't it – they can?' she says.

'I think it's great that people are prepared to fight back. We'd be lost without the likes of you taking a stand.'

I feel the warm glow it gives her to know that she's doing her bit. She's like a political version of those Christian evangelists who'll fuck your brains out if only you talk their talk.

A few metres ahead a car is parked up on the pavement. Somebody's leaning in through the open passenger window with his arse stuck out, blocking our way. He looks up and sees us walking towards the car but doesn't move out of the way. I step up my pace and walk right through him, kneeing him hard on the thigh.

'What the—'

He bangs his head on the side of the car as he corrects his balance. I carry on walking.

'Sorry mate,' I say. 'Didn't see you there.'

He catches my shoulder and spins me around to face him.

'Marshall,' Anna says and pulls on my other arm to get me away. I look back at the guy. There's music thumping in the car and voices from inside asking him what's happening.

'You should watch where you're going, mate,' he says.

I just look at him. He's going to have to hit me or turn away; it doesn't matter which to me. He makes his decision and leans back inside the car window. Anna pulls me away, linking her arm through mine.

'Are you crazy?' she asks once we've walked a good distance away. 'What if he had a gun?'

'Then I guess he might have shot me. Maybe he'll move out of the way next time.'

We walk on and I feel her lean into me.

'Where are you staying?' she asks.

'At the Grand.'

'The Grand Hotel?'

This is the moment. The combination of all that political talk and my staying at the Grand is just too much for her. When we get back to my room, I tell her to take off her clothes but to leave on her glasses.

On Saturday I settle my bill at the Grand but check in for another week. They give me a price reduction, but it's still a lot of money. I've given up tramping around the streets of Brighton in search of an apartment. I read through the *Argus* but my heart isn't in it. I'm waiting to see if meeting up with Bob this evening will actually lead anywhere. It'd be nice to find a place close to where my English Rose lives. I could call around during the day while that prick of a husband is out at work. We could have fun.

Bob's already in his favourite spot by the time I arrive in the pub. It's a smarter crowd tonight and an older one too – no socialist agitators taking up valuable drinking space. This is Saturday night. There's a guy in the corner setting up an amp and keyboard in front of a poster announcing the Andy Williams Experience.

'What'll you 'ave?' asks Bob.

'No,' I say, 'my shout. Lager, is it?'

'Cheers mate.'

Bob's *Mail* is beneath his elbow.

'Good 'ere on a Saturday night,' he says.

I agree and compliment him again on having such a great pub as a local.

'I'd say you're here every night, are you?'

'I'm not that bad; just a pint or two during the week and a few more at the weekend.'

Every night it is then.

'Live close by, do you?' I ask.

'Just up the road; got an apartment, ain't I?' He's so easy to read. 'What about you?'

'I'm staying in a hotel on the seafront.'

'And where you from then – up north?'

Ap noaf!

'Yeah but, to tell you the truth, I travel around so much these days there's nowhere I really call home.'

'So what – you just stay in 'otels like, wherever you 'appen to be working? That's all right, ain't it? What is it you do then?'

I've been over and over my cover story in my head, so much so that by now I've even started to believe it myself.

'I'm in property development.'

'That right? So am I, in a way. I'm a builder like, doing up 'ouses and stuff. Is that what you do? That what brought you 'round 'ere?'

'Don't worry,' I reassure him. 'I'm more in the line of hotels and offices. Looking for potential sites – that kind of thing.'

'And what – they pay you to go sniffing out for places to invest in?'

'Well, that and actually persuading the owners to sell.'

'So you make 'em an offer they can't refuse?'

'Yeah. Only more often than not they do refuse and we have to up the price.'

Andy Williams walks by and Bob nods his head by way of a greeting.

'Gone out to the van now to get into 'is gear,' he says of Andy. 'My girlfriend Laura should be in any moment – 'fact, 'ere she is now.'

Laura walks in through the door, exactly as I remember her.

'Laura,' Bob says, 'this is – Marvin, did you say your name was?'

'Marshall,' I say and shake her hand.

'I'll get some drinks in,' Bob says.

I can't believe that this is what Bob does with his girlfriend on a Saturday night. I tell her how I recognised Bob from the plane and then bumped into him by chance during the week.

'I don't remember seeing you,' she says.

'No, of course not – it was just that I helped Bob with his suitcase, that's all.'

'Small world, ain't it?' Bob says when he comes back with the drinks.

'Look,' I say, 'if you two guys want to be alone, I can just stay for the one drink. I had no idea you'd be here on a night out together.'

'Not at all,' Bob says. 'We don't mind, do we, love? Much better than you spending a Saturday night on your own in a strange city, ain't it?'

'Are you sure?' I ask Laura.

'It's fine, really,' she says and smiles. She looks like she means it too.

Andy walks back through the bar and approaches the mike,

the consummate lounge singer, complete with tinted glasses and cufflinks.

'Good evening,' he says, 'and welcome to the Andy Williams Experience.'

'He has the look,' I say.

'Even better once he starts singing,' Laura replies.

He kicks off with 'It's So Easy' and it gets the place going. I glance across at Bob. He doesn't show any response to the music but I can see he's pleased that Laura's enjoying it. I wonder if this is their one night out together all week. Will she sleep with him tonight or was the holiday something special?

Andy follows up with 'Can't Get Used to Losing You'. It's difficult to have any kind of conversation but in between songs I direct any comments to Bob, standing to one side so I can look at Laura.

'Where did you two meet, then?'

'I work for Laura's brother-in-law.'

'Was that him with you at the airport?'

'Yeah, that was Phil and Paula and the kids.'

Paula – I savour her name to the music and feel myself getting closer. It's so easy – indeed.

After a few more songs, Andy takes a break and I get in another round of drinks.

'Thank you,' Laura says.

'No – thank *you*,' I say. 'It's great to have some company for a change. Mostly I just go see a movie or something.'

'On your own?'

I shrug.

'You get used to it. I saw an interesting-looking cinema on my way up here – the Duke of York's, is it?'

'That's right – one of the oldest cinemas in the country.'

'I saw that. It's a beautiful building.'

'Marshall's in property development,' Bob says. 'I guess you notice things like old buildings and that?'

I tell Laura what my fake job entails and pick up a few more snippets of information from Bob. Phil has his own construction company, whereas it sounds like Bob's just a labourer. I guess Laura's hoping Bob might make a step up sometime soon so she can follow in her sister's footsteps.

'What about you?' I ask Laura. 'What do you do?'

'Oh, it's really boring. I work in a bank.'

'Not just any bank,' Bob says. 'Your dad's one of the top guys there, ain't he?'

'Bob!' she says, but I can tell she's proud of her daddy.

'Actually,' Bob says to me, 'he could prob'ly 'elp you out with a few contacts.'

'Oh, I wouldn't want to impose.'

'He wouldn't mind,' Laura says, 'really. In fact, you might find he's interested in investing in whatever it is you're doing here.'

I hold up my hands.

'You're very good – both of you. I'm lucky to have run into you.'

I raise my glass.

'Here's to good company.'

'Cheers mate,' Bob says.

'Cheers,' Laura says and we clink glasses.

I can't figure out if they live together. Part of me wants to believe she still lives at home with her parents. When Bob goes off to the toilet, I take my chance.

'How was your holiday?' I ask Laura.

'Oh, fantastic but just too short. We went for a week and I'd have loved to have stayed for longer.'

43

'Where were you?'

'Viareggio – do you know it?'

'On the coast, isn't it?'

'Yes, though I'd like to see more of Italy now I've been the once.'

I tell her something of my own trip through the country.

'That sounds wonderful.'

'Perhaps you'll go back again soon?'

'Oh, I hope so.'

'You picked up a great colour,' I tell her.

'Thank you.'

'Nice travelling with your sister, I'd say?'

'Oh yes, I love being with the kids, especially now Jenny's old enough to be such fun. Have you any children?'

'No, unfortunately it's just never happened. I guess I've never really settled down anywhere long enough to get close to anyone.'

'It sounds very glamorous, travelling from place to place.'

'I guess it is in some ways, but I think I'd still rather have a family and a home to come back to each night.'

Bullseye, I think, when I see the reaction on her face.

Bob returns and Andy comes back on for the second half of his set. He sings a couple of the smoochy ones like 'Moon River' and 'Danny Boy' and a few of the older couples get up to dance. He livens things up again with 'House of Bamboo' and Laura's eyes light up.

'Is this an Andy Williams song?' she asks Bob and he shrugs. 'We dance to this in class – it's a cha-cha-cha.'

She does a couple of steps, as though she's trying to remember what she's been taught.

'You're taking dancing lessons?' I ask them.

'Not me,' Bob says. 'Laura goes with 'er dad.'

'He's the only partner I could find,' she explains. She's such a daddy's girl.

'Would you like to dance now?' I ask. 'If that's okay,' I add to Bob. 'Or maybe you want to dance together?'

'Feel free.'

The dancing couples have left the floor, leaving a space that will soon be filled by drinking punters. I can see Andy thinks the song was a mistake – he had them up dancing and now he's lost them.

'Can you really do the cha-cha-cha?' asks Laura.

'Sure,' I say, 'but only if it's fine with Bob.'

Bob raises his glass in a blessing and I step back to allow Laura on to the dance floor. She looks down at her feet and I can see her listening to the beat. The song's almost over by the time she looks up and is confident enough to start but I hear Andy adjust to repeat the first verse. There's a second or two while I feel Laura's young body in my hands and I have to stop myself from closing my eyes at the pleasure this gives me. We part to dance but I get to hold her hand and feel how light she is on her feet. She's very good – better than a beginner – and I wonder how long she's been attending the lessons. She relaxes into the song and comes alive to the music. It's easy for me to guide her; she makes me look good and feel even better but then the song is over and I have to stand well apart without a hint of any closeness between us. A few people clap and Andy makes a comment about how good it is to see a person of Laura's age on the dance floor.

'But can you do the rumba?' he asks into the mike. Laura looks at me and then to Bob for permission. I hold out my hands and Laura steps into position.

'I'm not so good at the rumba,' she says.

'You'll be fine,' I say over Andy's intro. 'You're a beautiful dancer.'

Andy sings 'Here Comes That Rainy Day Feeling Again' and it's such a great song that the dancing comes easy. By now Laura has the attention of the whole pub and people are whistling and cheering and I can see how she loves it. She holds herself perfectly, allowing herself a couple of flourishes with her hands. I hardly need do anything but keep the beat. I'm there for her to step back into and to throw her out on to the dance floor again. She's the perfect dance partner.

I step away at the end of the song and applaud her along with the rest of the pub. I look across to Bob and I can see he's both pleased as punch and taken aback at Laura's panache. She takes the applause and beams a smile around the room. Andy does the sensible thing and starts up 'House of Bamboo' again. Laura looks across at me; this is one happy girl. People make space for us again and we dance the cha-cha-cha properly this time.

I know Laura could carry on dancing for the rest of the set but at the end of the song I applaud and walk over to Bob. I finish my beer as though the dancing was thirsty work but Laura was so good I hardly broke a sweat. I can't think what to say to Bob that isn't an insult – he really has no idea what he has here – so when Laura joins us I go off to the toilet and leave them together. It's time to leave; I can do no more here tonight. Bob offers to buy another drink when I get back to them but I refuse.

'It's time I was going,' I say.

I can feel Laura looking at me and Andy is singing 'Can't Take My Eyes Off You' but I focus on Bob.

'Thanks for a great evening.'

'No problem, mate,' he says, his relief that I'm leaving writ large on his face.

'Oh,' I say, 'before I go – do either of you know where I'd find the nearest Catholic Church? It's Sunday tomorrow and . . .' I let it hang there; it's a shot in the dark but I've noticed she's wearing a cross around her neck and every other hunch I've had so far has been right.

'Laura's your woman for that,' Bob says, indicating Laura with his pint.

'St Mary's is the nearest, at the top of the park.'

I smile like I'm an idiot.

'Preston Park, is that?'

'Yes, just up the road here. Make your way to the top corner of the park and you can't miss it.'

'I don't suppose you know what time the Masses are in the morning, do you?'

'Ten o'clock and twelve o'clock.'

I say my goodbyes and leave. It's so easy.

I'm a little hung-over in the morning but I want to make sure I'm there for the ten o'clock Mass. I couldn't ask outright if Laura was going to be there, so if I pray at all it's that I don't have to sit through two services without getting to see her again. I could have done with a Mr Concierge set of clothes to wear but I make do with what I have. I shower and shave and generally try to look my Sunday best. I enjoy a full breakfast and set off in good time to find the church.

I retrace my steps from yesterday up the London Road and, once I'm past the viaduct, I see how it opens out into Preston Park and how it's different once again to anything I've seen of Brighton so far. The houses facing on to the park are large like the ones on Springfield Road but they're well looked after – there's money here. Now this is where I can imagine Laura – and also Paula – growing up with their ballroom-dancing father.

There are lots of people out with their dogs and I guess Juliette and Max might be walking on the beach right now, but this is the place for me today. I head up to the top of the park and see the church above the trees. I'm about twenty minutes too early but people are already arriving for the ten o'clock Mass, the priest greeting a few old ladies on the forecourt. Any hesitation and I'm lost, so I walk straight into the church. I take a seat close to the back and kneel down; if people think you're praying, they tend not to bother you.

The organist starts warming up and a few more people arrive. It's hardly a full house, though, and I'm just thinking perhaps the twelve o'clock service might have been the one to aim for when in walks Laura, along with a man and a woman who I presume to be her parents. They walk on past and – praise the Lord! – in comes Paula with her two kids and my heart beats with excitement. That I could make this happen, that I could track her down from a Ryanair flight to her place of worship here in Brighton – I love that I've been able to do this. She carries her baby and her daughter runs down the aisle to join her grandparents.

So Phil the husband doesn't come to Mass? He's the canny one here, having done whatever he had to do to marry Paula. Then, as soon as the kids arrived, he was secure enough to do whatever the fuck he liked. Bob has a lot to learn: play the game until you're in a position to win. I wonder if Bob realises he doesn't stand a chance? How long before Laura gives up on him? He's never going to make it drinking on his own in the pub each night. Laura must hope he might one day be another Phil, but how long before her daddy puts her right?

The priest comes on to the altar in full fancy dress and we all stand. I'm amazed how the words have barely changed in all these years and how I still remember the responses as if by heart. I think of Danny in Rome; is this really what he wants to do with his life?

The service goes by quickly; there aren't enough parishioners to justify dragging it out. I'm reminded of the happy few that gathered for the political meeting the other night. The priest gives the obligatory five-minute sermon, urging us to have a more Christian attitude towards strangers coming into the country. He might have convinced his parishioners while they're in church, but I fear he might lose them to the *Mail on Sunday* once they get back to the security of their own homes.

'Go in peace to love and serve the Lord,' he says and we're done. I kneel and keep my head bowed in prayer. I'm not too sure about being seen by Paula; I think it might spook her to see me and mess up my chances now that I'm interested in Laura as well. I sneak a look between my fingers as they go past, a family group blessed with the grace of God. I want to fuck them up so bad it hurts. Laura sees me and gives a little wave before walking on out of the church.

I wait a full five minutes before I leave. I know I'm running the risk of missing Laura but it's an even greater risk to run into Paula – way too obvious. Happily, Laura's waiting for me outside the church.

'I thought you'd never come out,' she says.

'I had a few sins to confess.'

'I'll bet. Come and meet Mummy and Daddy.'

There's no sign of Paula and the kids, thank God, and Laura's parents are talking to the priest. She introduces me as Bob's friend Marshall from the pub last night but it's immediately obvious from their reaction that they already know me as the guy who danced the rumba. Her father shakes my hand.

'David Roberts,' he says, 'and this is my wife Margaret.' He also introduces me to the priest. 'Laura tells me you're a property developer? Anything in particular you're here to look at?'

'No, I have a brief from a couple of clients so I'm on the lookout for a suitable site. I leave the developing to the clients, though.'

'Sensible man.' I can see he's no fool and I'm going to have to be careful. I'm also on the receiving end of a serious look of appraisal rather than approval from his wife.

'I was quite taken by some of those empty office blocks facing on to the park,' I say. 'There's a lot of potential there.'

'There is indeed but I hope your clients have a lot of money to spend; land as good as that doesn't come cheap. Will you be in Brighton for a while?'

'I guess that depends on how I get on. What I've seen so far, I like.'

I glance at Laura and she smiles.

'And where are you staying?' he asks.

'For now, I'm at the Grand.' I watch as this does the trick in his mind. 'But I could do with finding somewhere a little more long term.'

'And a little cheaper, I shouldn't wonder?'

I laugh.

'Yes, certainly.'

'Good man,' he says, 'good man. Well, if there's anything I can do to help. Laura told you I'm in banking, I believe?'

'Thank you, sir. That's very generous of you. Everybody's been very kind since I arrived in Brighton.'

'Well – why not? Just doing our Christian duty, eh?'

We shake hands again and I say goodbye. Laura follows me away from her parents.

'You know you could always ask me out to the cinema,' she says.

Her nerve impresses me, as does the way she looks – like she's still in a state of grace from Mass but itching to get spoiled.

'I'd like that.'

We agree to meet at the Duke of York's Picture House the next evening at eight. I have no idea what's showing but I don't really care.

Come Monday evening, the movie allows us to spend some time together, to normalise the idea of there just being the two of us on our own. I ask her afterwards if she'd like to go for a quick drink but she says no and I'm relieved because we'd be obliged to join Bob the Builder and I'm certainly not interested in repeating that experience.

'Should I call you a cab?' I ask.

'It's hardly worth it; I only live across the park.'

'Do you mind if I walk you home?'

'Not at all; that would be lovely.'

I know I have her down as the younger sister and a bit of a daddy's girl, but there's more to her than that. She seems sharp, like her father, and I need to watch my step. It's pleasant to stroll slowly through the park, though, Laura plying me with questions as we walk along.

'Are you really staying at the Grand?'

This seems to be the thing that impresses people the most – the thing that gives me some semblance of worth. I want to tell her that it's nothing – that it's just money – but I let it go. She turns to face me at the entrance to the driveway of her home.

'You don't live with Bob then?'

'God, no! We're a long way from that.' She blushes as though she's said too much and I let the bare fact hang in the air between us as she recovers her composure. 'I know I turned down the offer of a drink but you're very welcome to come inside for one now.'

The rather formal invite is a coping mechanism, a default to politeness to prevent her true feelings being laid bare. A whiskey from Mr Roberts' decanter might well seal the deal for me but I decide to stick to my plan.

'I don't think so.'

She looks confused.

'I'd like you to,' she says.

'Yes, I know.'

'So?'

'Laura . . .'

'Yes? Oh God, I'm sorry – this has been a terrible chore for you, hasn't it, taking me out? I'm sorry.'

'Don't be sorry, and no – this hasn't been a chore. It's been an absolute pleasure,' I say.

'So come inside.'

'No, I don't think so,' I repeat.

'What is it? Are we not to see each other again?'

'Laura, I know it would be the simplest thing in the world to arrange to see you again but you're with Bob. I can't work like that.'

52

'What are you saying?'

'I'm saying that we can't just be good friends. That you're too . . .'

'Too what?'

'Too close to what I want.'

'So?' she says again.

'So I'm a lot older than you, too old to be fucking about – if you'll pardon the expression. If I were to see you, I'd want everything and I'd want it now. No silly games, no wait and see and certainly no Bob hanging around. But I'm in no position to ask anything of you. I don't even know how long I'll be in Brighton.'

She doesn't speak but I know I have her.

'Thank you again for a wonderful evening. If I'm still here next Sunday, perhaps I'll see you at Mass again, yes?'

I turn and walk away. I know she would come after me if I was to give her the slightest encouragement but I keep going and don't turn around. It's a gamble, but one I'm prepared to take. It's a shame really – I'm kind of getting to like her. I'm almost sorry I have to use her just to get at her sister.

Now I have a good reason to find an apartment, I start searching in earnest. I look at a few properties around North Laine but I can't find the right place and, let's face it: it has to be perfect for me to move out of the Grand.

I decide to talk to Mr Concierge. He stands and listens while I describe what I'm looking for.

'Leave it with me, sir,' he says. 'Let me think about it for a day or two.'

Good as his word, he comes to find me in the bar on Thursday morning while I'm having my coffee. He suggests that what I should be looking for is a long-term stay in a boarding house on the seafront.

'I'm not sure I want to live with other guests.'

'Yes, sir, I thought you might say that, which is why I'm going to suggest a place I know. It is a boarding house, run by a Mrs Sullivan, but on the top floor she has a self-contained apartment that she finds difficult to let because it's too small for a family. I believe that if you committed yourself to a minimum stay of a month, Mrs Sullivan would be prepared to let you have it for a reasonable price.'

'And where is it?'

'About a mile from here – more Hove than Brighton – but nice, I think you'll find. I took the liberty of writing down the address and a telephone number for Mrs Sullivan.'

He hands me a note written on Grand Hotel stationery.

'Thank you,' I say. 'Thank you very much.'

'If you intend calling on her, I could telephone in advance by way of an introduction.'

'Thank you. That's very kind of you. I think I shall call on her today.'

'Then I shall let her know.' He calls Mrs Sullivan and arranges for me to see the apartment at two o'clock.

Mr Concierge was right – the place is perfect for me. It may be a little out of town but it's right on the seafront. It has a shared entrance but I have my own little place away from other guests, upstairs in the attic. Mrs Sullivan is charmed by the fact that I've lived in Ireland, even if it was in Dublin rather than Kerry where her family are from. I arrange to move in on Saturday and walk back to the Grand for a celebratory pint in the bar. Finding a place to stay seems to confirm for me that I could make a go of things in Brighton. I feel good here, content.

After breakfast on Saturday, I go down to reception to settle my bill. As I do, Laura calls my name from across the lobby. It looks like she's been crying.

'Laura,' I say and walk over. I can feel Mr Concierge watching; he doesn't miss a thing.

'They had no record of your staying here,' she says. 'I thought you'd gone for good.'

I stand to shield Laura from the reception desk.

'Probably because I've already checked out,' I say. 'What are you doing here? Come and sit down.' I walk into the bar where it's a lot quieter and we sit down, away from anyone wishing to hear my business.

'You're leaving,' Laura says.

'I'm leaving the Grand,' I say, 'but I'm not leaving Brighton. I've found an apartment to move into. I was going to tell you at Mass tomorrow.'

'Really?'

'Really. I'm on my way there now. But you – what are you doing here?'

'Oh God, I feel like such a fool now.'

'Tell me – I won't think you a fool, whatever it is.'

'I wanted to see you,' she says, 'and not at Mass either. So I came here to ask for you and they had no record of you staying here. And when I realised I didn't even know your surname, I started to think – oh God! I'm such an idiot.'

'Stop it. You're here now and we've found each other and I'm not going anywhere very far. Dry your eyes and tell me what you came to say.'

For all my planning, I've avoided adopting a false surname and this is surely indicative of how ambivalent I am about how far I want to run with this. What brought me to Brighton won't keep me in Brighton. After only a few days, I feel like I could make a new life here – with Laura, if I'm lucky – and fucking up her sister is no way to go about it.

'Lanaghan,' I say to Laura, hoping a show of openness will reassure her. 'My surname is Lanaghan. Here.' I hold out the passport I've just picked up from the reception desk. 'My name is Robert Lanaghan but I prefer to use my middle name Marshall.' She doesn't need to know I only chose the name Marshall because I was listening to Eminem on the day I met Bob.

'Oh Marshall, I didn't mean that – I didn't mean that. I just panicked when I thought you might be gone, that's all.'

'Well, I'm not. I'm very much here and delighted to see you.'

'I've finished with Bob,' she says and waits a second or two to gauge my reaction. 'I've finished with Bob because I want to be with you.'

'Are you sure?' I ask. 'I mean, we've only just met.'

'I'd rather take that chance. I've been thinking about it all week and I told him last night.'

'Was he pissed off?'

'Very,' she says and smiles. 'Yes, he was but I'd made my decision and I told him.'

'Then I'm glad.'

'Really?'

'Yes, really. I told you the other night what I want and, like you, I'd rather everything be out and in the open.'

We look at each other across the table and laugh.

'Come here,' I say. We stand up and hug.

'Oh God, Marshall. I was so scared – of making such a rash decision.'

'Did you tell Bob about us?'

'No but I think he might have guessed.'

'I'm happy you made the choice you did.'

'Me too.'

We order coffees and I ask Laura if she'd like to help me move in. I say my goodbyes to Mr Concierge and the staff at the Grand and we walk the half-hour along the prom to my new home. I have a feeling Laura won't be asking too many questions for a while – not since my display of honesty with the passport – but they're bound to come up at some stage. Quite how I can extricate myself from the other lies, I don't know, but if I'm serious about being with Laura then I'm going to have to find a way.

When we arrive at my digs, I introduce Laura to Mrs Sullivan and let my new landlady make of it what she will.

'I've put fresh bedding and towels in your room,' Mrs Sullivan says. 'Just shout if there's anything else you require over the weekend.'

Laura and I climb the narrow stairs to the attic room and I unlock the door. We make love, sleep for a while and make love again. I'm hungry but I don't seem to care. Hours go by just being with her, lying together on the bed. It's a warm room and I open the dormer window, out of which I can see the sea.

'Come and look at this,' I say to Laura and we stand side-by-side, naked, looking out to sea.

I can't get enough of her young body and she seems to have decided to give it over completely to me. I regret now how we came to meet and this makes me determined not to betray the trust she's placing in me.

'Do you know what I'd like?' I say.

'No, tell me what you'd like, Mr Lanaghan.'

'I'd like to walk back into town, buy some fish and chips, eat them on the beach and then go to the funfair on the Pier.'

'Wow, you sure know how to show a girl a good time.'

'Take it or leave it.'

'Then let it be so,' she says and laughs, but still we don't move for at least another hour, by which time I think I might pass out from hunger.

'Come on,' I say and we do as I suggest. I get to see the Pier at night-time and to go on all the rides – screaming on the Crazy Mouse high above the waves, over the end of the Pier so you feel like you're out at sea. We play all the stalls and I feel like Pinkie with his girl, Rose, and then I'm hungry again so we buy toffee apples and eat them down on the beach in the dark. We sit and listen to the waves against the pebbles.

'What time do you have to be getting back?' I ask.

'Do you mind if I don't stay with you tonight?'

'I'd rather do things properly,' I say. 'Today was great but I know you have to think of your mum and dad.'

She links my arm and hugs me.

'Would you come to the house for lunch tomorrow – after Mass?'

'I'd like that.'

We walk back up to the prom and I flag down a cab for her. We kiss goodnight and I walk back home, daring to hope I might get this one right. I played a blinder today, and soon after going to bed I fall into a deep sleep.

INTERLUDE

When they come for me, I'm too scared to move. It's laughable that they think I'm worth taking, but I'm too scared to laugh. The sound of them breaking through the door is what wakes me, and they're on top of me before I have a chance to react. It's not the easiest of rooms to storm. There wouldn't have been a lot of space to get a good swing at the door because of the turn at the top of the attic stairs. They must have crept up before exploding into my room. Not easy to do with the gear they have on and their boots and their guns but once they're inside they shout and stamp – I must have been deep in my sleep not to have heard their approach. Their noise takes over the room. It's dark and they shine a torch in my face. Why don't they just turn on the light? I shut my eyes but I can't shut my ears.

'Don't move,' some prick shouts, like I have a choice.

I don't move. I can't move because they have me pinned across my arms, legs and chest. The barrels of two guns are pressed into my temples, one on either side of my head. I can smell metal. I try to relax into submission but I'm too scared; my body won't stop resisting into a rigor mortis seizure.

'Clear the room,' he shouts but I don't know what he means. They don't let me go. I keep my eyes shut tight because the light is still in my face. I hear a lot of activity, but I can't guess how many men are in the room; they fill it, like they fill my head with their noise and their light. They're searching the room – that's what they're doing. I know they won't find anything. Maybe then they'll leave? I could get through this. I may be sick or I may soil myself, or both, but if they left now then my body could get through it.

'Up!' he shouts and they take away the guns and the limbs that are pinning me down.

'Up!' he shouts again and I realise he's talking to me. I still can't move; I'm petrified.

'Over!' he shouts and I'm rolled on to my stomach. My arms are pinned behind me and I'm handcuffed. They drag me up by the cuffs and I scream at the pain. I realise they've mistaken my inability to move for a refusal to move. I'm thrown towards the door. The flashlight beams are all over the place. Irrationally, I think of *E.T.* and every other Spielberg movie – he loves his flashlight beams, so he'd love this scene.

My shoulder hits the door frame and I feel the splinters in the wood where they've broken through into the apartment. I'm no longer frozen in terror; I experience it fully now. I'm naked, with my arms pinned behind my back. I'm doubly naked because they have on so much gear and are carrying guns. My body shakes – or rattles – and somebody laughs. I think they must have seen this scene before. An unexpected boot kicks me in the testicles and I fall to the floor in pain. The same boot stamps against my chest and pushes me through the doorway. I can't prevent myself from falling and I can't protect myself on the way down. There's no perfect roll like in the movies because the stairway is so narrow. It takes another push with the boot to get me to the bottom.

They're not going to leave me alone is what I think.

'Up!' shouts the prick again and this time I move. But I can't get to a standing position with my hands behind my back and they use the cuffs to lift me again. My feet leave the ground and my upper body flips forward to the floor. I try to reach out to break my fall but of course I have no arms free. I'm carried and dragged along the landing and down the stairs to the guest house below. My weight is nothing to the person dragging me but the pain from the wrenching of my arms is so bad that I think I black out. My body can't stand it and shuts down.

I smell fresh air and I'm naked all over again. I'm out in the street, my knees and shoulder and the side of my face against the pavement. My arse is in the air. It's not so dark out here. I hear the gulls but I don't see the sea. The day is starting; this is my day, starting.

I get an idea of the scale of the operation. The surrounding area has been blocked off. There are spectators in the street. Mrs Sullivan must have helped out; she must have let the soldiers in, unheard, and led them up to my room.

I'm freezing and I start shaking all over again. There's a change in the momentum, like they're taking a break. I wouldn't be surprised if somebody somewhere is enjoying a cigarette. Or am I on show? In the early morning light, I see guns pointed in my direction. I know I'm a pathetic-looking figure and I hope this fact might make them realise I'm not a threat. They must know they have the wrong person and are taking a second or two to decide to let me go. I'm in such pain with my arms. I want to push myself up into a better position but I daren't make any sudden movements and I'm not sure I can anyway. I dread being yanked up by the arms again. There are tiny stones sticking into my knees and gravel against my face. I fall sideways in an attempt to lie down.

'Okay, we're clear,' shouts a voice behind me – a different voice.

The back doors of a van are opened and they throw in a sack or bin bag. They grab my arms and take off the cuffs.

'Get up!'

I use my hands to push myself to a standing position. I don't know if they're soldiers or policemen, but I'm still hoping they're about to let me go back to my room.

'Let's get him into the van.'

This is when I know they're not going to let me go, when I first think about saying something – anything – to stop this now. But I'm grabbed by the upper arms and dragged to the van. The backs of my calves hit the rear bumper and my legs fold beneath me. I land on my arse on a cold metal floor. They tip up my feet so that I fall inside, rolling over backwards and against the bin bag. They shut the doors and it's dark again. The engine of the van starts up and I feel around for something to hold on to. As soon as the van moves, I lose my balance and I'm thrown back hard against the doors of the van. I crawl on to my stomach and lie flat against the metal floor; it's cold but this is the best position I can find.

I'm sick – either with fear or with the motion of the van. I hear the gears change and the van slows down, but each time there's a sudden turn or a brake I have to get up on my hands and knees to clear my stomach. Bile comes up into my mouth and my whole body feels emptied out. I can taste last night's fish and chips. The practicality of needing the toilet is what worries me most on the journey. I can't lie down because of the mess I've made so I sit with my back against the side of the van and use my hands for support and balance. This is better. Some light comes through the join in the doors; enough to see there's just a bin bag and myself in a travelling metal box.

We slow down. There are lots of turns and then we speed up again, only to slow down and turn another corner. I don't know how long I'm in the van; it could be ten minutes or it could be an hour. There's a period when we travel consistently at speed in the same direction so I can't begin to guess how far we've come. I'm fairly certain we're no longer in Brighton.

The van brakes and we come to a stop. I hear the two front doors open and slam shut and I start shaking again. The back doors open and I hold up my left hand to block out the sunlight. I'm sitting in the mess I've made.

'Oh, Jesus,' one of the two men outside says, presumably referring to the smell. He slams the door shut again and I'm back in the dark. I sob a little and make a little mewling noise. My breath comes in short snatches, fast and irregular. When the doors open again, I jump up and scamper to the back of the van, covering myself as best I can. When I look back, there's nothing to see but an empty courtyard in the sunshine.

'Throw out your things,' someone shouts.

I realise my belongings are in the bin bag.

'Throw it,' shouts the voice.

I swing the bag and throw it out into the courtyard. I see a building that looks like the loading bay of a warehouse. A man appears in the doorway carrying a hose. He's different to the army/police guy in Brighton; he looks like a security guard. The water from the hose throws me down on to the floor of the van, rolling me over until I hit the back wall. I try to stop the force with my feet and hands but it's impossible. I turn to face the back of the van but then the guard starts aiming it at my backside and I hear him laughing. The water is freezing.

I curl up into a ball to protect myself as best I can. I learn my first lesson: that there's nothing to do but wait for this to be over.

'Okay, okay,' the guard says, as the water is turned off. Something is thrown at me and I jump, but it's nothing – a rag or a piece of material. The guard laughs again.

'Put that on,' he says.

I uncurl myself and look at what he's thrown me. I can't figure out what it is – sacking of some sort. I shake it out, but there's nothing to shake out. I was expecting some trousers but it's not clothing.

'On your head, you fool,' the guard says, not so amused now.

I look at this security guard and it doesn't make sense. Why would they hand me over from fully kitted-out troops to a pair of rent-a-cops? It changes my perception of what this is – amateur hour, all of a sudden.

'Put on the hood,' he says, 'or you get the water cannon again.' He's just itching for an excuse.

I peel apart an opening in the sack and put it over my head. It smells and blocks out the light.

'Now lie down,' he says, 'on your stomach.'

I feel my way to the floor.

'Put your hands together behind your back.'

Doing so forces my face into the sacking, pressing my head hard against the metal floor of the van. I breathe the material into my mouth and gag on the smell of the stale vomit of previous prisoners.

'Don't move,' the guard says, and I hear two of them climb into the back of the van. They grab my arms and handcuff me again. My ankles are gripped and this takes me by surprise.

64

'Don't struggle,' a different voice says. 'If you struggle, you'll only make it worse.'

I hear a heavy metal object dropped on to the floor and I panic because I don't know what they're about to do. I'm naked and face down in the back of a van with two guards above and behind me. I shake my head because this is the only thing I can move. Even this isn't easy – I have to raise my chin off the floor of the van to thrash my head about and all that happens is the sacking gets caught in my tongue. I can't speak so I make noises at the back of my throat. I know I'm about to be given a lesson but I don't know what and I don't know what for.

'Jesus!' the first guard says. 'What the fuck is his problem? Lie still,' he says to me.

He kneels in between my shoulder blades and this means I can no longer move my head. His mate still has my ankles pinned to the ground.

'Lie still,' he says again.

I do so and he takes away his knee.

'We need to put some leg irons on you and if you fight it you'll only hurt yourself. That's all we were saying – Jesus!'

I do cry now because this is going to continue and the noises I make turn into a plea. I spit out the sacking as best I can but I can't get it away from my tongue.

'Jesus,' the first guard says again, and I can hear the disgust in his voice. 'This is hardly worth it.'

They put on the leg irons and their power over me is now absolute. They grab me under the arms and drag me across the floor of the van into the open air. I don't have a chance to protect myself and I catch my hip against the door. It could have been a lot worse. They stand me up in the open air and hold me there. My breathing doesn't come any easier but I can at least make out the ground at my feet.

'Are you able to walk?' asks number one.

I don't answer but move my feet forward anyway.

'This way,' he says and they guide me away from the van. There are stones cutting into my feet but then I step onto a metal ramp, up to the loading bay. One of them lets go of my arm. There's nothing for a minute or two and then a door opens. I hear some talk but can't make out what they say. I don't like the lull because it gives me time to think.

'What's happening?' I ask the guard left holding my arm.

He doesn't answer. I try to turn towards him but he holds me firmly in place.

'I haven't done anything,' I say. The words sound muffled, even to me.

'You'll be fine now,' he says. He speaks quietly, while the other conversation carries on in the background.

'I don't know what's happening.'

'Shh, you'll be all right.'

I cry again and he makes another noise to quieten me down.

'Okay,' number one shouts. 'We're done here.' Number two lets go of my arm and bends down to unlock the leg irons – all that fuss and it was just for show, to make a point. I stick my chin into my chest and I see the top of his head. Number one unlocks my hands and they free me at the same time. I feel lighter without the weight of the metal. I've already forgotten about being naked – it's no longer such a terrible thing. I stand there nodding in my hood, not daring to reach up to take it off. The material is wet from the soaking with the hose and it clings to my head. I have no thoughts of running; I just wait to be told what to do next.

66

'This way,' a new voice says and a hand grabs my left arm. I'm led inside, away from the light. I hear the van start up behind me but then a door closes and I hear nothing more. It's concrete under my feet – smooth concrete – but still I tread warily.

'This way,' the voice says again.

They've taken delivery of me. I'm a package, and I've arrived.

I put one foot in front of the other and move into a void. Every step I take I expect to trip or fall or hurt myself in some way. The voice lets go of my arm and I hear his shoes walk away. A door is closed and locked behind me. Even with the sacking covering my face, I can sense I'm in a darkened room. I look down at my feet and see nothing but black space. I wait, not knowing if I'm alone. There's the sensation of falling and I hold out my arms to break my fall. I'm in a permanent state of falling over an edge that doesn't exist. I'm falling, I'm falling, but I don't fall.

Nothing happens. There's no sound – nothing. I wait. I could take off the hood but I don't dare. I shout out.

'Hey!'

Nothing, and yet I sense another presence in the room. My body is still wet. I cross my arms and feel my shoulders, gently touching the grazed skin where I was thrown against the broken-in door. The backs of my hands brush against the sacking of the hood. I pull on the material to take it away from my mouth and the rush of oxygen makes me dizzy all over again.

'Can I take this off?' I ask.

Nothing.

I reach up, pull off the hood and let it fall to the floor.

Whatever happens, it's worth it for the air. It's so good – like the air at the seaside – but black and silent. I'm in a perfectly enclosed room. The darkness is complete – and when I say complete, I mean absolute, like the darkness of an underground cave. I run my hands over my face and head, so I know this is real. My upper arms and the backs of my legs are in pain and I reach down to where the leg irons have taken the skin off my ankles. I crouch down and then kneel on the smooth concrete floor. My body dries quickly in the warm, artificial air. How can they block out the light so completely?

'Please,' I say, but I don't know what I would ask for if somebody answered. Let me go? Let me see? Tell me where I am? Tell me why I'm here?

I rest my forehead on the ground. If I believed in a god, I would pray to that god now. I grope across the floor in the dark, stopping after each shuffle to feel the space in front of me.

I shout out again, if only to catch an echo of sound with which to determine the size of the room. Nothing but an empty silence. I touch a wall – the same concrete material as the floor, flat and smooth to the touch – and push myself up into a crouching position. Using the wall as a guide, I stand up straight and reach as high as I can. I step in closer and run the palms of my hands flat along the wall in a slow, sweeping motion.

Now I have a wall, I've lost the sensation of continuous falling and given up completely on the idea that someone else may be with me in the room. I inch my way left along the wall, until I hit a corner – a square corner – and I stand for a while with my two hands on the two walls and my feet wide apart. I set off again to my left, but I kick a metal bucket with my foot.

The metal makes a scraping noise on the floor and I have a sound to relate to – something other than the thoughts inside my head. I nudge the bucket with my foot and it feels weighty, as if it has something in it. I lean over and smell – nothing. I tip the bucket over and pour the contents on to the ground. It makes a different sound and I listen out again for some reaction but nothing happens. I reach out and touch some material. After a moment's hesitation, I drag it towards me and lift it in both hands. It's material all right; quite heavy, like strong cotton – a pair of jeans, perhaps? I lift it up to my face and smell – definitely an article of clothing of some sort. Overalls maybe? I'm in prison and these are my overalls? What kind of a place is this?

'Hey!' I shout. 'Hey!'

I throw down the overalls and back myself into the corner. My heel hits the bucket. I bend down to pick it up and bang it hard against the wall.

'Hey!' I shout again.

The bucket makes some noise but not enough for my liking. I want a dustbin lid to bang on the ground, loud enough to wake the world. I want everyone who cares to know where I am.

'Hey, out there!' I shout, but my shout disappears into a vacuum; it goes nowhere.

What am I thinking? Nobody I know would care where I am.

After a few minutes – or what I think is a few minutes; I've already lost the ability to judge the passing of time – I push myself back up to a standing position against the wall. The overalls, if they are overalls, are beneath my feet. The bucket is somewhere out on the floor. I have another shaking fit; I'm not particularly cold but I can't stop my body from shaking. I reach down for the material and throw it out in front of me. Using the palms of my hands, I smooth out the folds until I have it flat on the ground. I was right: a pair of overalls. There's a strip of Velcro and I pull it apart. I lean back into my corner and step into the overalls. They're a good fit, as though somebody already knew my size.

I slide down into a crouching position in my corner and give myself a few minutes' break.

I have to find out the extent of this room. I stand up and turn to face the wall on my right. Taking the same sideways steps, I use the sweeping motion of my arms to guide me along. I reach another square corner after four steps and continue along my third wall. Five steps and another square corner; one more corner and I'm on my way home.

Home – you're a long way from home, Robert Lanaghan.

My hand catches on something on the final wall – a joint or a crack. I pull my hand away and stand perfectly still, waiting.

Nothing.

I reach out with my left hand again and find the line in the wall. It's a vertical joint of some sort – a fault line maybe? I'm excited that this may be a clue to the room. I follow the line down to the floor and then along where the floor meets the wall. This is the door – it must be – although it's made from the same concrete material as the wall. I go back to my vertical line and reach up. The line cuts across to my left at about the height of seven feet. Yes, this is a doorway. I follow the crack along the wall and then it cuts back down to the ground. I sweep my arms across what I believe to be the door but there's nothing. There are no hinges or locking mechanism, nothing to suggest how this door might work, and yet this must have been where I came into the room.

Cell, I tell myself. I'm in a cell.

Knowing I can't get lost in my square cell, I get on my knees and sweep my arms across the floor. I find my bucket and also the piece of sacking I wore as a hood. I squat down in a corner and feel as though I've achieved something, only the satisfaction is short-lived – it's still just a bucket and some sacking in an empty cell.

The darkness and the silence take their toll. I'm not stupid. I know what's happened: I've been taken and I'll be held without trial. It's not remarkable or unusual. I've done something that somebody somewhere didn't like. Call me a threat to national security. They can do what they will. I know the world we live in.

I must have fallen asleep because I'm woken by an alarm of ultra-bright lights and a grinding noise.

'What?' I shout. 'What?'

If my voice before had disappeared into the silence, it's lost now to the alarm. I shut my eyes and cover my ears, cowering beneath the barrage of light and sound.

What have I done?

Light floods the room from above.

'Please,' I shout, 'please.'

And then, just as suddenly, the alarms and lights are switched off and I'm back to the silent darkness.

'No,' I say in disappointment because I'd hoped the noise might mean something, be a sign or progress of sorts. 'I'm hungry!' I shout out. 'And water – you can't leave me here without water.'

But I'm back to shouting into the void.

I whirl around in the darkness, panicking because I've lost my bearings. Only when my arm hits a wall do I calm myself. I walk around the walls, past the door and back to my corner with the bucket.

I need to pee, so I pick up the bucket and walk around the room to the diagonally opposite corner. This is the bucket's new home. I reach up to the Velcro fastening and peel it open. Too late, I remember dropping the hood in the bucket and I hear the different sound my pee makes as it hits the sacking.

Oh well, there's nothing I can do about that now. I refasten the Velcro, wipe my hands on the overalls and walk back to my corner.

The lights have left an impression behind my eyes, orange like the colour of my overalls – an orange jumpsuit. I've become a symbol.

I think about *Papillon*. I think about *The Count of Monte Cristo*. I think about *The Man in the Iron Mask*. Heroic figures – not like me. My mask – my piece of sacking – is in the bucket across the room.

I sit down in my corner. The alarms and the lights come on again and I curl up into a ball. Are they watching? Can they see me in the darkness? Is this a punishment for sitting down or for falling asleep? The noise stops but what to do? If I can't sleep, what am I to do?

I stand in my corner to let them know I'm not sleeping. So they can see I'm not sleeping. Can they hear me too? Hear me but not care what I have to say. I resolve to not speak, to not give them the satisfaction.

I have to take myself out of this room. If I tell my mind I'm no longer in this room, I will no longer be in this room. I concentrate on a mental image of the prom in Brighton – how much I love to walk along the prom. How I love the sunlight in Brighton. It's like nothing I've ever seen before. I love this town. Who would ever have thought? This is my chance to stop fucking around. It's time to make Brighton my home. I can be better than what I've become. I can't change the past, but I don't have to live with it. I have to get over my daughter; it all comes back to her. She's better off without me and what she doesn't know can't hurt her. If she's happy with her mother, surely that's something? Everything comes back to Ciara but I have to let her go.

I wake up to hear the sound of a baby crying.

'That baby's hungry,' I say out loud.

They must have allowed me to sleep because I'm slumped awkwardly on the floor. Is this still the same day? How long have I been in this room? The baby continues to cry. The crying doesn't seem to be coming from any one direction; it's in my head, like the music from a good set of headphones. I shake my head but the crying won't go away.

I must be dreaming of Ciara. It's the cry of a very young baby, the hungry cry of an infant that doesn't understand anything but its hunger. The noise increases in urgency, just like when Ciara's food wasn't coming soon enough for her.

'Just one more minute, darling,' I say, but the milk is way too hot and I have to wait for it to cool. I put her bottle in a jug of cold running water and pick her up but she's inconsolable. She thrashes around in my arms and arches her back. She wants her mother. She'd make do with her bottle but she's fast approaching the point where nothing at all will do. She'll be past caring about the milk and will make herself ill with her crying.

'Come on, come on,' I say to the bottle, testing the milk

73

on my wrist. I put the bottle to her mouth but she snatches her head away. She's impossible to hold in the crook of my arm when she's like this. She kicks out with her tiny legs at the bottle and I struggle to control my temper. I put the bottle back down in the jug of cold water and place Ciara down in her cot. I walk away across the room to calm myself but, if anything, her crying becomes louder and I can't leave her like this. I pick her up again and try to comfort her, walking around the room, putting her head across my shoulder, which is normally her favourite position but, of course, she's still hungry.

'Please, Ciara,' I say. 'Please.'

I hear my own voice above the sound of the crying in my head. This isn't a dream – they're playing the sound of a baby crying in my head. This isn't Ciara – it's just the sound of a baby crying. How can they do that? Why would they do that?

I slap my face to create a sensation other than the crying.

This is a stage set, I tell myself, a black box with added props.

I have to reorientate myself. I have to find my own corner.

I stand up.

Think.

The crying.

This is my corner. I was trying to meditate, trying to stay awake, and I wasn't very good at it. I must have fallen asleep. I was hungry and I was thinking of Ciara, so I had a dream about trying to feed her. But how would they know that?

The crying – the crying is still there in my head.

They put the sound of a baby crying in my head, so of course I dreamt of Ciara. It's okay to think of her, just as it was okay when I found it hard to care for her on my own. Everybody finds it hard with a baby at some point or other.

74

They're fucking with my head. They allowed me to fall asleep and they played the noise in my head.

How could they do that?

Never mind that – maybe it's not in my head. This is an enclosed room; they can do things with this room. They can do things to me in this room. This is not Ciara crying – it's the sound of a baby crying being played to fuck with my head.

But it doesn't stop, even though I've figured it out. That perfectly pitched cry finds me, holds me and won't let me go. I know I have to find a place to escape the crying – to take back ownership of what's inside my head – but I can't do it. Just like trying to leave Ciara alone to cry – I just can't do it.

And then the crying stops. I crumple in a heap to the floor and curl up into a ball. I'm alone again in the silence, with nothing but the sound of my own thoughts; and they make no sound at all. I count out the seconds but what are three thousand, six hundred seconds really worth? Another hour has gone by – but so what?

I count for another hour and still nothing happens.

I try exercising, a variety of stretching positions that are a combination of football training and yoga. It's not easy and, when I stand free of the wall, the falling sensation returns and I have to reach out for support. I swing my arms around – pathetic exercises but at least they're something and they act as a temporary distraction.

People are held indefinitely, I think.

Thoughts like that, I tell myself, thoughts like that aren't going to do me any good.

I'm hungry and I sit back down. The alarms and the lights come on and I shelter as best I can. It goes on for a long time. I don't know what their rules are. I can't figure out the rules.

I'm the one crying by the time the alarms are switched off – real tears this time – lying in the fetal position until the silence and the darkness are returned to my cell.

'What?' I shout. 'What do you want from me?'

But I think I know the answer – they don't want anything. They just want to do this to me.

I try to meditate again. It's not really meditation – more a case of forcing my mind not to think. I try to appropriate the darkness, focus on the nothingness. I forget about taking myself – thinking myself – out of the cell and concentrate instead on nothingness.

A voice in the dark tells me to stand up. The voice is in the cell but there's no one in the room.

'Stand up and face away from the door.'

I do so. Behind me, the seal on the door is released and the door opens. A dull light spreads across the floor and a guard comes into the room.

'Where's your hood?' he asks.

'I put it in the bucket by mistake.'

'You what?' he says and laughs.

'I'm sorry.'

'You're going to be, when you have to put it on your head.'

I turn around to look at him. He's dressed as a security guard rather than a prison guard.

'Never mind,' he says. 'Pick up your bucket and follow me.'

I do so and he leads me along a corridor, pointing out where to empty the bucket. I throw the sacking in with my own mess.

'Now take the bucket back to your cell and come back here.'

The corridor looks pretty much like any other, only with very little natural light. There's another guard at the door where I came into the building. There are other doors along the left-hand side of the corridor, similar to mine, and I wonder if they're occupied. It all seems very relaxed and quiet, like I'm heading into a job interview and not in some prison. I put the bucket inside my door and return to where the guard is waiting. The rooms on the other side of the corridor are like offices, sparsely furnished with desks and chairs. It's very strange, like they're making do with a building not fit for its purpose.

'This way,' the guard says, and he leads me into one of the offices. A window looks out on to an industrial estate of warehouses and workshops. There's a guy in a suit waiting to talk to me.

'Sit down,' he says.

The guard shuts the door and takes up a position behind me where I can't see him. I sit down on a chair in front of a desk.

'What did you intend to do in Brighton?' the guy in the suit asks, standing above me. 'What were you doing at the Grand Hotel?'

I don't say anything. The daylight is disorientating after the darkness and silence of my cell.

Suit man nods his head and the guard moves forward and hits me hard in the kidneys with his fist. I double up in pain.

'Think hard about this, son,' the suit says, even though he can't be any older than I am. 'I want to know what you intended to do in Brighton. I want to know why you were in the Grand Hotel. I want names, I want details and I want concrete information. You have a few days to think about it.'

He walks out.

'Come on,' the guard says. I pick myself up and follow him back to my cell. As soon as I'm inside the door, a second

77

guard hits me across the back of my legs with a baton or a club and I fall to the ground. They kick me and I roll up into a ball to protect my head and my balls. It's a lazy beating but it hurts anyway. They leave me be and shut and seal the door. I'm back to my darkness and my silence, presumably to think about what the suit man wants me to say.

Only, they don't leave me be. Just as I'm getting my bearings again in the dark, they switch on the alarms and the lights. I crawl around the floor to my corner, waiting for it to end, but it's the longest session yet. I try to block out the noise but it takes over my whole being.

Is that why I'm here? Because of something I was about to do in Brighton?

What was I about to do?

I have nothing to tell them.

The alarms and the lights are switched off.

'Stand up,' a voice says in the dark. It's the same guard; I recognise his voice. 'Stand up and turn your face away from the door.'

I do so and the door opens. The two of them come in and hit me again, repeating the blow to the back of the legs that has me crumpling to the ground. When they leave, it's back to the alarms and the whole thing starts again. They do this again and again, without any real joy, as though it's a tedious chore. It gets so that my legs collapse in anticipation of the blows and I fall to the floor each time in a heap. This makes the guard laugh when, instead of delivering a beating, he brings me some food.

'Supper time,' he says and leaves me alone to find the food tray in the dark.

I can hardly bring myself to make it over to the door but I

have to eat and drink. It's some sort of a stew in a bowl and a plastic beaker of water. I eat and drink what I can find in the dark and crawl back to my corner.

They stop me sleeping with the alarm a couple of times but the beatings dry up and eventually they allow me to sleep. They wake me with the baby crying noise and there's porridge for breakfast. They come up with something new, playing the song 'Kim' by Eminem on a continuous loop for what I reckon to be about twelve hours – from porridge to stew time. I listen to the song, thinking about Siobhan and what she did to me.

The porridge and the stew measure out the passing of time.

I'm taken to see the suit man again but I have nothing to say. He wants to know what I was doing in North Africa. Why did I check in my bag at Stansted but not travel on the flight to Dublin? Why do I choose to live in Ireland and not in England where I was born?

I want to please him – to give him an answer and avoid being hit in the kidneys – but, again, I've nothing to say. I think back to Stansted, to what seems like a lifetime ago – though, of course, it's really only a matter of a few weeks. I remember liking the notion that they might think my bag was a bomb. This, after all, is the world they've made for themselves.

Suit man wants to know why I gave a false address in Manchester when I checked into the Grand Hotel.

As ever, the thought of sleep takes over – whatever they do to me, all I ever want to do is to sleep. My chin drops on to my chest and I'm woken by water being thrown in my face.

He wants to know what I was doing with Laura Roberts.

What does he think I was doing?

Why did I follow her from Stansted? Was she my cover for being in Brighton?

Oh Christ, what can I say to him? How do you fight that kind of stupidity? Would he understand that I was messing with Laura to get at her sister? That I wanted to fuck up their whole family? That I hated them and everything they stood for?

But suit man just looks bored. I'm nothing to these people.

'Take him away,' he says to the guard. 'He doesn't know anything. We're wasting our time here.'

Yes, I think, take me away. Lock the door and throw away the key – you'll be doing us all a huge favour. Only please – just let me sleep.

Time passes. They move me to a more conventional cell, having got nothing from me. The beatings stop, as does the *son et lumière* show. I doubt they realise how close they were to breaking me, before I gave them something – even if that something would have been a fabrication. My new cell has a steady dull light and isn't soundproofed as before. There's a bed along one wall and a strip of floor where I do my exercises, an irritating three and a half paces long. The floor space is wide enough for me to stand with my legs apart. More like a broom cupboard than a cell. At the foot of the bed is a gap for my sink and a bucket, emptied once a day. I'm given an hour's exercise each day and this new life becomes the norm.

Time passes. I measure out my life in porridge and stew. I come to understand twenty-four hours. I know how those hours work. I understand that one of those twenty-four hours will be spent in the yard and the other twenty-three in my cell. I will be fed twice. If they were to change this, I would adapt. If they were to create a new routine, I would adapt. Whether that new routine was based on hours or days or weeks or months,

I would adapt. They need a routine as much as I do to run this place.

Time passes. I sit, I stand, I pace the length of my cell. I'm dead, but still alive.

When I manage to sleep, I sleep deeply, as though I've pressed an elevator button for a floor somewhere far underground. When I wake, I come back to the surface with a gasp. I'm like Ripley in the movie *Aliens*, sleeping through time and space. Some days when I wake I can't move my right arm. It just flops around, hanging uselessly at my side. I ask to see a doctor and they laugh. The arm goes numb for a few days and then hurts so much I'd happily have it hacked off by one of my fundamentalist prison mates. Oh yes – I'm not alone here.

There's a painting by Van Gogh of the inmates at Saint-Rémy exercising in the yard of the asylum, and I'm reminded of it every day when they let us out into the yard to trudge around, one after the other, for an hour. We're not allowed to communicate to each other but I know some of them do – messages passed along the line or hurried questions and information. There were forty-two of us at one point but we're now down to thirty-three. I hear that such and such was set free or that they moved somebody somewhere but the whispered messages come to a halt when they reach me. Not because I'm worried about breaking the rules, but because I don't care enough to pass the messages on. It's the ones who fight the routine, the ones I see losing it in the yard, trying to grab a moment of collective outrage – they're the ones who won't make it. For this reason, I'm grateful for the time they came at me with their noise and their silence, with their unannounced beatings in the dark. It's helped me embrace this new life and

81

to accept their routine. I can't fight the routine and it's not mine to change, so it's pointless to try.

I was told once, as an adult, that I had a playground mentality and I don't think it was meant as a compliment. Good or bad, it allows me to recognise the types I see in the exercise yard every day and I have to tell you: they're not a very impressive bunch. These are not dangerous people and if this is the threat to the nation then the nation is quite safe. I suppose they're the idea of a threat. They're the sad cases that have somehow spilt over into the political world, and the faces I see belong to lost souls similar to my own. Sure, some of them are committed to a cause, but they lack the resources to do anything much about it. You have to be smarter than we are to overthrow the system.

I know from what I hear in the yard that our freedom – or our lack of it – is what exercises the other inmates the most, but I believe all thoughts of freedom are relative. I'm free from the responsibilities of caring for myself, of working, of earning, of learning, of shopping and of cooking. I'm free from the worries of parenthood, of relationships and of my place in the world. In truth, I'm almost content. I'm not interested in any moral outrage – either at what I've done or at what has been done to me. Apart from my hourly exercise, I'm pretty much left to my own devices. I know that to be kept in solitary confinement for twenty-three hours of each day is supposed to be a form of punishment but it seems to suit me just fine. It's all fairly half-hearted. I think the sense of injustice I pick up from the other prisoners is their refusal to accept the situation we find ourselves in. A little perspective is required: we're being held here, that's all, and eventually they'll let us go. To tell you the truth, I suspect most of us have been forgotten or are being ignored, like a memo in an in-tray full of much more pressing matters to attend to.

And anyway, what would I do if I were free to leave? Where would I go? What would I do with my freedom?

There are bad days. Days when my breathing is so messed up that I take in short snorts of breath through my nose to calm myself. Days when I think I'm fine, when I think I'm okay but I'm not. I'm a mess, but I'm here and for now this is where I stay. The rules are different in here. I was a mess out there too, out in the world. I'm locked up for my own good. *Keep the world away from me and me away from the world tried that living thing and it didn't work out guess I am a mess but it's my own mess and mine alone.*

Stop. Breathe. Calm yourself, Robert.

I've practised talking to myself – not crazy talking but listening to the sound of my own voice. When I heard other prisoners shouting or mumbling to themselves in the yard, I thought madness lay in that direction, but then I tried singing a scale of notes, hopelessly out of tune, in an attempt to retain the use of my vocal cords. This is what my isolation has brought me to. I can't remember the last time I had a conversation with another person that didn't involve being asked inane questions about why I was in Brighton. Misremembered conversations in my head: Laura morphing into Ciara, Ciara into Siobhan, Siobhan into Laura. Maybe I have gone a little crazy, talk or no talk?

Days when there's too much weight in my body, when my limbs are so heavy I can barely move. Days when I can't do my exercises, when it's a struggle even to sit up on the side of my bed. Days when the air feels like a mattress above my head. Or do I just have the flu?

I let myself fall sideways on to my bed. I sleep and time passes and I hear the door to my cell and it's time for the yard. No choice, so I get up and for the first time I'm like one of the shufflers. *Pick up your feet* I try to tell myself. *What has happened to me what have I let in can't live like this won't make it like this won't survive.* I get through the hour and back to my cell and to the next meal and to the next morning and still the heaviness weighs down on my limbs and my head. *Got to be some kind of flu or a drug have they drugged me why start that now?* I force myself to eat and I pace my cell – six, seven paces, no, that's not right but I stick with it, and I try not to shuffle around the yard. Feels like I'm being watched. Always being watched – depend on it even – but this time by the beards *what do they want from me this is not my fight it's theirs and it will be a long one it's an old one and a long one and it will run and run but it's not my fight.* Collateral damage – that's me. *Keep your war it is a war but it's not my war and it's a war we can't win who's we?* It goes on. The heaviness goes on and the war goes on and I think the heaviness will win. I dig in and I count the days: one, two, three, a week. I can't live like this. Won't make it like this. Won't survive like this. Won't survive.

I do believe they'll let me out. The problem is, it might be today or it might be tomorrow, or next week, or in a year's time. I think if they were going to send me somewhere else or bring me to trial, they'd have done so by now. They're just waiting until it's politically acceptable to let me go. Some of the beards have been in here since before I arrived, so they can't be that important. But the prisoners that disappear – I don't know if they're released or sent elsewhere. If I was that important to the people keeping me here, I wouldn't be here. They'll let me go whenever they let me go. Hoping or waiting

84

to be released will only drive me crazy. I'm here and there's nothing I can do about it. I have to find a way to cope. I will get through this. It will end. These are the tenets of my life.

If I believe I will be released, I must also believe in some future life. But if I imagine a possible future life I won't be able to get through this one.

This is no life.

It's the only life I've got.

I'd have to be alive to call it a life and I'm not.

I'm living it the best I can.

I'm living nothing. I'm dead.

I'm living it the best I can. I'm surviving. I'll do whatever I need to do to survive.

And that's it – survival?

That's all I have.

All I shall ever have?

Who knows? I have to regroup, to tell myself over and over again that this is it, there is nothing else.

When did my past life end and this present life begin?

My past life ended when I lost custody of my daughter. Or – my life ended when I agreed not to contest the custody of my daughter. Or – my life ended when I agreed never to see my daughter again. Or – my life ended when I agreed to take a wad of cash in exchange for never seeing my daughter again.

Or – I had a life. It ended. That's all, folks.

More prisoners disappear. There are fewer and fewer of us during the exercise hour and those that remain look more pitiful than ever. When it's my turn, I'm taken to an inner courtyard rather than the exercise yard, and I know immediately that something is about to change. I'm told to take off my overalls and I'm given a pair of trousers, a T-shirt and a cheap pair of runners. Outside, in the loading bay of the warehouse, there's a van with its engine running and the memory returns of my previous trip in the back of a van. I'm rattled but they don't handcuff me and there's no hood or blindfold. One of the guards opens the back door and pulls down a kind of jump seat attached to the side of the van. I climb in and sit down.

'You must have some powerful friends,' he says.

A second guard takes my left hand and fastens me to a single manacle attached to the jump seat. They must have got tired of all the vomit and shit and urine in the back of their vans. The guard shuts the back door and joins his colleague in the front. It's dark but not pitch black and I can see for balance. I'm on the move.

While I don't feel under any physical duress, I'm not indifferent to where they might be taking me. I've had a relatively easy ticket in custody. After those initial beatings I was pretty much left alone, apart from a malicious smashing of the knuckles of both hands. I've watched others cause a fuss and pay the price. The regime I've lived under has been one of 'don't bother us and we won't bother you'. I hear the muffled voices of the two rent-a-cops up front but I can't make out what they're saying. Those prisoners I've seen move on: I hope I'm not about to find out where they all went. I still regard myself as different – unusual – and I can't believe I'd be of any real interest to anyone. The worst-case scenario is that I'm handed over to the Americans and this is the one real fear I have. There's absolutely no reason why they should do so, but that hasn't stopped it happening to other prisoners. If they're transferring me to another detention centre, I know I will adapt to whatever conditions I find there; but if I get caught up with the Americans, I know enough to fear I might never get out.

I hear the jet engines while I'm still locked in the back of the van and it worries me. The van stops and a guard opens the back door. We've driven directly on to the tarmac of an airport. It's a large commercial airport – not a military airbase – and this, at least, is something. The guard unlocks my handcuff and tells me to get out. I can hardly hear him over the noise of the nearest plane. I know better than to ask what's going on. I'll find out soon enough. The guard holds out a clipboard and a pen and shows a member of the flight crew where to sign. He takes out a passport from his inside jacket pocket and hands it to the attendant.

'Is that it?' asks the attendant.

'That's it,' says the guard with the clipboard. 'You'll be met in Dublin. He stays on the plane until you sign him back over.'

I follow the attendant across to the steps leading up to the plane. It's a Ryanair flight and this adds to the unreality of the whole situation. He hands me my passport and a boarding card. I follow him up the steps and show the boarding card to the flight attendant waiting by the door. The flight is already boarded and there's a single empty seat in the front row. As I sit down, the cabin crew close and seal the aircraft door.

I'm heading back out into the world once more. This strange, strange life is about to begin all over again.

SIOBHAN

1998 to 2001

It was Siobhan who first came looking for me. She arrived part way through the launch of my second book in Dublin and, immediately, I picked up on a completely different vibe in the room. I looked up and saw Siobhan McGovern, trying – but failing miserably – to appear anonymous. She was about the only person deliberately focussing her attention on me; everybody else had that special buzz about them when they know that a star, a genuine celebrity, has walked into the room. As my publisher rounded off the formal part of the evening, I couldn't get over the fact that Siobhan McGovern was at my launch – or worse, that she was about to leave without us having had the chance to speak. But I needn't have worried; she was first in line to get a copy signed. She told me later that she didn't want to distract attention from me any more than she had already, that it was best if she just got what she came for and left. She was well used to the effect her fame might have on a crowd.

'I enjoyed your book,' she said. 'Or books – I liked this one even more than the first.'

My best friend Danny was watching me from across the room, not making this any easier.

'Not that I didn't enjoy the first one too.' She blushed. Siobhan McGovern was flustered. Her hand was shaking as she held out the book for me to sign.

'Is this for yourself,' I asked, 'or would you like me to make it out to somebody else?'

'It's for me.'

'And what's your name?' Thankfully, everybody laughed and this eased the awkwardness of the situation.

'Siobhan,' she said, smiling. 'If you could make it out to Siobhan.'

'*To Siobhan*,' I wrote. '*Thank you for all the great songs.*' I handed the book back to her and she turned to leave without looking at the inscription.

'We're going for a few drinks,' I said, 'if you'd like to join us.'

'I . . . I don't know.'

'Just around the corner in The Duke.'

'Maybe,' she said, in a way that meant she wouldn't. 'It's not so easy, being out in Dublin.' As I say, she was more than aware of her celebrity.

'We have a private room,' I added, trying hard to keep the desperation out of my voice.

'Maybe,' she said again. 'I'll see.' She turned away and left the launch.

Danny couldn't wait to have a go at me.

'We have a private room,' he said. 'Please come, please.'

The crazy thing is: she did. And when she walked into the room upstairs at The Duke, I think I already knew what was going to happen between us – however impossible it seemed at the time.

Too many people have described Siobhan elsewhere for me to add much more here. 'Vulnerable' is the word most often used; 'tiny but tough' as I wrote in one of my books, though I wasn't writing about Siobhan at the time. And always a reference to that face. That she could be so famous and still look nervous about coming into a bar full of people she didn't know – I think that says a lot about her.

'Jesus,' Danny said, 'she came.'

I walked over. It's funny how your life can change in one moment.

'I can stay for one drink,' she said, and put her hands in the back pockets of her jeans.

'What would you like that one drink to be?'

'Oh, a glass of Guinness, I think, seeing as how I'm in my home town.'

We waited awkwardly at the bar. It seemed to take an age for the Guinness to be poured and to settle.

'Dublin is still home for you?' I asked.

'It's my home but it's not where I live, if that makes any sense.'

'So where do you live – England, or America? You're not going to go all Hollywood on us, are you?'

'No, not yet,' she said. 'England, I'd say, is where I spend most of my time – well, when I'm ever in one place that is. We have a house outside London with a recording studio that we escape to whenever we can. I seem to spend most of my time on tour these days though, travelling from one country to another. A lot of time in hotels, you know?'

'That sounds just like my life too.'

'Really?'

'No, not really.' I handed Siobhan her Guinness. 'Do you and the band ever get sick of each other's company?'

'Oh yes, of course, so I tend to run back home to Ireland.

But that's not why I'm here tonight,' she added, as though I might run off to the music press with this nugget of Siobhan McGovern gossip.

'Why are you here tonight?' I asked.

'Don't you think we artists should support one another?'

'Of course, only—'

'Only?'

Only you're Siobhan McGovern, is what I wanted to say, but she was apparently determined that her coming to the launch should seem no big deal and I was happy to go along with the act. I would have gone along with anything she wanted that evening. Later too, I guess, if truth be told.

I looked over towards Danny, who was trying to act casual, and asked Siobhan if she'd like to meet a few of my friends.

'Not that you have much choice in the matter.'

It worked quite well, with Danny being as cool as you like and thankfully knowing a whole lot more about Siobhan than I would have guessed. I wanted to speak to her alone again, to ask her all the obvious questions, such as why did she like my books and what was it about me that convinced her to come to the launch. I hoped she might stay, but her drink was finished too soon and she announced she had to get going. I felt such a sap, hoping against hope I could somehow get to see her again – but I couldn't help it.

'When do you go back to England?' I asked.

'Early tomorrow – very early.'

I was close to running out on my own party. If she'd asked me there and then, I'd have left with her.

'We have a gig this weekend,' she explained.

I stood there like a fool.

'So I have to get back.'

'To the band?'

'Yes. You could come if you like.'

'What – now?'

'To the gig – on Saturday, in London. I could send you a ticket.'

'I'd like that.'

'Would you come?'

'You came to my gig, didn't you? It's the least I can do.'

I didn't really see the point of going to the gig, to tell you the truth – where was it going to get me? But I'd have taken anything at that point just to maintain some form of contact with her. I gave her my publisher's address in Dublin.

'I'll have it sent over,' she said, 'so you should have it by Thursday. Will you really come?'

'Yes,' I said. I thought I might too. What else would I have been doing?

'You could sell the ticket on eBay and make a fortune.'

'I'll be there,' I said, 'but can I be really cheeky and ask for two tickets? For Danny, I mean,' I added, in case she thought there might be someone else.

'So you really are going to sell the tickets?' She laughed and I was lost. 'Daren't you come alone?'

'It'll be more fun with Danny.'

'I came here alone, didn't I?' she asked. 'I'll be there on Saturday night – isn't that enough for you?'

'You and about ten thousand other people.'

I knew she was toying with me, but this only made the moment better to savour.

'Okay,' she said, relenting. 'I'll send you two tickets. Your Danny can meet my Danny. Thank you for such a nice evening. And thank you again for the book.'

She put her hand on my upper arm and leant up to kiss me on the cheek. She had to stand on her tiptoes to do so.

Siobhan's Danny was Danny Callinan, the guitarist in her band and the guy who wrote all her songs. My Danny was delighted to hear about the tickets and even more delighted when they arrived with a pair of VIP Access All Areas passes and a hotel voucher for the night of the gig.

'What's going on?' Danny asked.

'I don't know. I think she likes me.'

'She doesn't even know you.'

'Maybe she wants to get to know me?'

'I could tell her a thing or two,' he said.

'All the good stuff?'

'Right – the good stuff.'

I had an apartment in Smithfield in Dublin that I once shared with Danny. It was a fine apartment but the mail often went missing; this was the reason I asked Siobhan to send the tickets on to my publisher. I rented the place from Danny and it suited him to have me as a tenant: the value of his property was rising so quickly it didn't bother him that he received so little in rent. He might well have sold it to me at a good price but no mortgage company was going near a writer in his late thirties. It would be fair to say that, of the two of us, Danny had made more of a financial success of his life since we left college. What this amounted to was the simple fact that Danny was good at making money, with the obvious correlation being that I wasn't. We met at Trinity: I majored in English, Danny in Maths, but we took joint degrees in Philosophy and struck up a friendship when we discovered we were both from Manchester. Danny was always more fascinated by the logic and probability side of his course and, once we graduated, he returned to England to head up the new operation of an Irish bookmaker looking to target the UK market. I also spent as much of my time in England as in Ireland, combining my writing with renovation work on Danny's large Victorian house in Salford. Of the various rubbish jobs that kept me afloat in the years after college, painting and renovating houses was the consistent earner. However, the satisfaction of a good gloss wears off after a while and I had what might best be described as a colourful CV of little or no consequence: car park attendant, barman, library assistant, waiter, typing theses for students who grew younger as I grew older. If I'd lived in New York it would have been halfway to glamorous but I lived in Dublin and the only person – apart from my editor – who believed in my writing was Danny.

Now Danny was returning to Ireland to study Divinity at Maynooth.

'Divinity?' I'd asked when he told me a few days before the book launch. 'As in the priesthood?'

'Not necessarily the priesthood but something to do with my faith, yes.'

'Your faith? What faith?'

Frankly, I was astonished. Danny shrugged in response, as if to say *if you didn't know me before, you do now*. I hoped my incredulity didn't appear rude, but equally disconcerting for me was the realisation that Danny was likely to move back into the Smithfield apartment and I wasn't sure where that might leave me.

'I'll probably sell the house in Salford,' he said. Then he must have noticed the look on my face. 'I'll be living in college accommodation, so nothing will change for you here.'

In some ways, I may have seen this coming: there was always more to Danny than the ease with which he made his way in the world. But Divinity – what the fuck!

He stayed on with me in Smithfield after my book launch and we travelled together over to London for Siobhan's concert. He viewed the trip as a bit of fun and didn't share the weight of hope or expectation that I had for the weekend. One of my clearest memories is of him hopping from one side of the VIP line to the other.

'I'm allowed here,' he said to the bouncer, 'and I'm allowed here. Here . . . and here.'

'Not for much longer if you keep that up,' the bouncer said. 'I'll boot you out so hard you'll go from here . . . all the way back to whatever pit you crawled out from.'

'I'm allowed here . . . and—'

'Danny,' I said. 'Stop fucking around.' I'd never been backstage at a concert and I didn't want to get thrown out before it even began.

When the band appeared from their dressing room – the three guys first and Siobhan a few steps behind – there was a huge push towards Siobhan and then a similar surge back as security protected the band. Danny and I were obviously amateurs when it came to backstage life. A few blokes with cameras were plucked from the scrum and thrown out of a side door.

'Leeches,' our bouncer said.

I caught a brief glimpse of Siobhan as she was ushered through. She looked calm, even as she was being jostled to one side. I couldn't understand why these people were allowed backstage if they were going to behave like this as soon as the band appeared.

'They always find a way to get in,' the bouncer said when he saw the look on my face, 'but never fail to blow their cover. It'll be different after the gig is over.' I must have looked so innocent.

'Can we go through here?' Danny asked. The gig was about to start and we didn't really know where we should be – if we should go out front to watch the band and come backstage again once it was over.

'My friend,' the bouncer said, 'so long as you behave, you can go wherever you please.'

'See?' Danny said to me, 'he called me his friend. What's *your* name, my friend?'

'My name is Stevie.'

'And can we really watch from through there?' Danny indicated to where Siobhan and the band had gone on stage.

'My friend—'

'Danny, please,' Danny said.

'Well, Danny, I don't know how you got hold of that badge around your neck but it allows you to go just about every place you can imagine – except on stage with the band.'

I don't know what I'd expected or hoped for. I enjoyed the concert and I could see why the world was going Siobhan McGovern crazy, but I didn't really know what I was doing there. I'd had a few days to anticipate what might, just possibly, happen between us but I could see now there was absolutely no way that I was ever going to get close to Siobhan McGovern. I felt a little stupid actually and I think that's why Danny was playing the fool – to prove that if all we got out of the trip was a bit of fun, well, fun was still fun.

It was hard to equate the Siobhan on that stage with the Siobhan I'd met in Dublin. She was a performer – a singer, yes, but so much more as well. The way she wrung every last bit of feeling out of those songs was an astonishing thing to witness, especially from only a few feet away at the side of the stage. And to project that emotion out into such a large arena so that each member of her audience felt as Siobhan felt – I knew I was watching an artist at work. I remembered her saying that we artists should support one another, but I just wasn't in this league. I was happy to reach a single reader who may have been moved by my work; Siobhan was reaching thousands of people every time she took to the stage.

Backstage was a little more controlled once the concert was over, as Stevie had said it would be, but not that much more. And Siobhan still had that distant look on her face – untouchable, on another plane, call it what you will. The band went back on for an encore and then the house lights came up.

Danny and I stood looking out at the vast auditorium from the side of the stage.

'Look at the size of this place,' I said.

'That was quite something all right.'

Stevie the bouncer came up behind us.

'Did you enjoy the show, gentlemen?'

'Oh man,' Danny said, 'that was just so good.'

'She knows how to sing a tune, that's for sure.'

'Can I fetch you something?' Danny asked Stevie. 'A drink, I mean?'

'No, I don't drink,' Stevie said, 'but thank you for asking.'

'Don't drink, or don't drink while you're working?'

'Don't drink.'

'Oh man, that sucks,' Danny said. 'A coke, then, or a juice – I bet you drink juice.'

'I'm fine, really, but you go in and enjoy yourselves.'

'What time will you be working until?'

'I'll be here until you folks decide to go home – or until the band decides it's time for everyone to leave.'

'Do you work for the band or for the concert hall?'

'I work for the band. I'm responsible for their safety.'

'Man, what a great job,' Danny said. 'It's been a pleasure to meet you, Stevie, but now I have to go and check out the VIP bar.'

'You do that, my friend, you do that.'

Danny really was the ideal person to have brought along to the gig. I don't know how he did it – that easy-going, get along with everybody thing. If I'd been there on my own, there's no way I would have met Stevie, no way I would have dared watch the gig from the side of the stage.

We hung around for a while, trying to act like we were somebody and not be rumbled as nobody. It was hard work trying to look so cool for so long. The lads from the band came out after an hour or so and that created something of a stir but there was no sign of Siobhan. We were about to leave when Stevie came to find us again.

'Gentlemen,' he said, 'would you come along with me?'

'Are you throwing us out?' asked Danny.

'No, my friend, I'm not throwing you out.'

'Should we bring our drinks?'

Stevie smiled. 'Yes, you can bring your drinks along with you.'

He took us through to a back room where Siobhan was waiting in her dressing room, alone.

'I was worried you might have left,' she said.

'Not while there's still free beer to be had,' Danny said.

'I'm sorry you had to wait such a long time,' she said. 'It

takes a while sometimes to come down after a show and I didn't want you to see me in that state.'

'We've had a great time,' I said, 'really.'

'Great show,' Danny said. 'Thanks.'

'Well, thank you for coming.'

'Look,' Danny said, 'I'm going to wait outside. I've made friends with your bodyguard.'

Danny stared hard at me as he left the dressing room. *Don't mess this up* was what he was telling me.

'I really am glad you came,' Siobhan said.

'It was generous of you to ask,' I replied. 'The plane tickets too.'

Siobhan shrugged.

'It's easy to be generous when you have so much money.'

We looked at each other across the room.

'I don't—'

'I just feel—'

We laughed.

'You go first,' I said.

'I was going to say, I just feel as though I'd really like us to get to know each other.'

'And I was about to say I don't see how we can.'

'Do you want to?'

'Yes, but I'm already way out of my depth here.'

'With all this, you mean?' She nodded at the door.

'Yes and . . .'

'And what?'

'And you. I don't know what you would want with me.'

'Isn't that my decision?'

'I've just watched you perform.'

'What's that supposed to mean?'

'I guess I'm overwhelmed by how good you were – scarily good.'

'Is that a compliment?'

'You live in a different world to me.'

'There are ways around that if you're interested in trying.' She didn't wait for a reply. 'I have to find a way to live a normal life in a mad world and part of that is the freedom to get to know the friends I choose.'

'And are you free to choose?'

'I'd like to find out. How about you?'

'I'd be crazy not to try. I guess.'

Siobhan laughed.

'Or crazy to even think about it? Can I suggest something? I have to go out there now and you can probably imagine what it's going to be like: false politeness from strangers looking to be my new best friend. You and Danny should go back to the hotel so you don't have to see all that.' My face must have dropped. 'We can meet up in the morning – how about that? Not too early though,' she added.

'My flight is at one.'

'Then it's decision time,' Siobhan said, 'because there's absolutely no way I'll be up before midday tomorrow. If you're still at the hotel by the time I drag myself out of bed, I'll see you in the foyer and we can talk. If not – no hard feelings?'

I think I already knew I'd be changing my flight back to Dublin.

I forget the name of the hotel that Danny and I stayed in for the night of Siobhan's concert but it was within walking distance of Earls Court. It was expensive in an understated way. We had one last drink in the hotel bar; Danny was all for having another, but I didn't want to abuse Siobhan's hospitality. It was easy to see that most of the people still drinking in the bar were associated with the band in some way, and I wondered about the numbers of hangers-on an event like this must attract.

'Do you think the band is staying here?' Danny asked.

'I don't know. Siobhan didn't say.'

'And you didn't ask?'

I told Danny what Siobhan had said about meeting up the next day and he asked me again what I thought was going on.

'Why didn't you wait for her?'

'She didn't want me to. And I didn't want to.'

Danny was still in the mindset of my seizing this one golden opportunity to have sex with Siobhan McGovern and here he was suggesting that I'd probably blown it.

'So you're just going to see what tomorrow brings?'

'Are you staying on with me?'

'I am not. Some of us have proper jobs to go back to.'

'Have you told them about Maynooth yet?'

'Tomorrow – wish me luck.'

The next morning, Danny went all serious on me before he left for Manchester.

'What about your writing?'

'I've just had a book published. I deserve a few days off.'

'Just don't forget who you are and what you do.'

'Jesus, Danny! I'm meeting a girl for a chat is all.'

'Not just any girl. And not just any old chat.'

I checked out of the hotel once Danny had left, and called the airline about changing my flight. They told me it was such a good ticket I could turn up at the airport and get on the next available flight. I sat down to wait in the hotel foyer. There was a lot of people watching to be done, a lot of sore heads as guests checked out, and the general vibe seemed to be that the gig had been something rather special. I thought about buying a paper or taking a quick walk for some fresh air but I was content to just sit and let my mind wander. Danny was right: I really did need to find out what was going on here.

I was facing the entrance to the hotel, watching out for Siobhan, but when she finally arrived she stepped out from a lift across the lobby. She was wearing jeans, a black top and open-toed sandals. I watched her cross the lobby: she had the same look of concentration I'd seen as she walked on stage the night before, only now it was focussed on me.

'You stayed then?' she asked.

'I stayed.'

'And Danny?'

'Gone back to the real world.'

'Dublin?'

'Manchester.'

'I'm going to see about getting something to eat. Would you like something?'

'I might have a sandwich.'

'And a drink? I'm having a pot of tea.'

'Sure – I'll share a pot of tea with you.'

'Nothing stronger?'

'Never again.'

'Should I ask them to bring it over? Is this okay for you here?'

I assured her it was. Across the lobby I noticed Stevie the bouncer reading a newspaper. Once Siobhan had ordered the tea, she sat down in the opposite armchair, curling her legs beneath her into the overly large cushion.

'Did you stay the night here?' I asked.

'I did. You must have been tucked up in bed by the time I came in.'

'We might have waited up if we'd known.'

'I'm glad you didn't; it gets to be a bit much sometimes.'

'Is it always like that after a gig?'

'More or less, which is why I suggested you leave when you did. Not that it's unpleasant at all, but there's drink and there's drugs and there's phoniness and I didn't want that to be the first impression you had of me.'

'So is this here the real you or simply a different you?'

'I hope this is closer to the real me.'

A member of staff – a girl of about seventeen – brought a tray of tea to the table. Her hands were shaking and I was reminded of Siobhan's nervousness at my book launch.

'That's okay,' Siobhan said to the girl, 'we'll pour the tea.'

The girl thanked us and came back a couple of minutes later with a plate of sandwiches.

'Thank you,' I said, and the girl sneaked a quick glance to see who this person might be, drinking tea with Siobhan McGovern.

'How old are you?' I asked Siobhan.

'I'm twenty-four – why?'

'You seem to handle it all very well.'

'Years of practice. What age are you?'

'I'm over ten years older than you. I'll be thirty-seven in a couple of months.'

'That's old,' Siobhan said and laughed. 'You can be my older man.'

'Is that what this is?'

'I'm not really sure if I know what this is yet.' Siobhan took a sip of tea and put the cup back down on the saucer. 'Danny wasn't too pleased that I took a whole day off from rehearsing just to go to a book launch.'

'Your Danny might not have been but my Danny was delighted.'

'Did I come across like a stalker?'

'Not at all; I felt honoured.'

'You needn't have done. I meant it when I said I love your books. I wanted to meet you, to see what you were like – that was all.'

'Oh dear – and?'

'And here we are.'

'I'm worried that you might think I'm the same person as I appear to be from my books.'

'Aren't you?'

'I write fiction.'

'The stories come out of your head, don't they?'

'Yes, but they're not me; that's not who I am.'

'In that case, I might ask what you just asked me: which is the real you?'

I had no answer to that. My writing was all I had, the only thing I could point to and say *this is what I have done with my life*. My writing defined me, but like Siobhan when she stepped on to a stage, I went to a different place when I sat down to type the words in my head. When I left the stage, there was nothing much else to see.

'It's the women in your books who interest me,' Siobhan said. 'I want to be one of those women: strong, independent, wilful but blessed with a good heart. I want to be the kind of woman who would appear in one of your books – does that make sense? I think that to be such a woman would be as good a version of myself as I could possibly be.'

'Hmm, they tend to be quite troubled too.'

'Yes, but they find a way through by being true to themselves.'

'They're just stories.'

'They're not just stories and you know it. They're a part of you and they become a part of the reader too. They've become a part of me.'

Like any writer, I was susceptible to flattery, and praise like this from Siobhan felt like praise indeed. The women in my stories were fantasies in the sense that I invented them, I dreamt them, I made them up, but I liked them too as creations. Siobhan needn't have worried about matching up: with the little I already knew about her, plus her undeniable and singular beauty, sitting opposite Siobhan was like coming face-to-face with a woman from one of my books.

'The person – the man – who wrote those books . . . I want to know what kind of a man can reach me in that way.'

She had a disarming way of cutting to the chase that left me feeling helpless – which is the point of being disarming, I guess – yet still, I worried that I might not be the person Siobhan took me to be from my work.

All around us, the lobby was buzzing with the effect of Siobhan's presence. There was not one person who crossed that floor without sneaking a look. If they were checking out of the hotel, they left to go and tell their friends; if they were checking in, they emanated a glow of having chosen such a cool hotel. Try as I might, I couldn't ignore this; I was finding the simple act of drinking tea and eating a sandwich difficult to master. Siobhan managed both with poise and grace, maintaining a full beam on me at all times. Mind you, I guess Siobhan knew she had Stevie watching her back, discreetly tucked away across the floor, ready to step in at a moment's notice should any unlooked-for situation arise.

'I understand the danger of projecting my thoughts on to someone I don't know,' she said. 'I've had it done to myself often enough. So I was prepared to turn up the other night and get my book signed and that would be it. But when you asked if I'd join you for a drink I knew I was in trouble and that I definitely wanted to see you again. And yes – we could have had sex last night, which I'm sure would have been nice and might also have been enough. You could have left to go back to Dublin and we never had to see each other again. But I didn't want just that, and I don't think you do either.'

'Fuck! You don't hold back, do you?'

'No, I don't see the point. Maybe I'm spoilt – I know I'm spoilt – in that I can have pretty much anything I want in this world but, with you, that doesn't seem to apply.'

'Oh, I don't know,' I said and smiled.

'You know what I'm saying: I'm not entirely sure what this might lead to but I'm certain I want to find out.'

I was gone already. I was lost, adrift, all at sea. Siobhan had entered the void – the vacuum – of my non-writing life and there was only ever going to be one outcome. I had no immunity from Siobhan McGovern – the rock star, the girl, the woman, the human being – and who would have wanted immunity anyway? If Danny reckoned I'd blown my chances with Siobhan the night before, there was no way I was going to do so a second time.

'I think I'd like to find out too,' I said eventually.

There was trouble with Danny from the very beginning – Danny Callinan that is; Siobhan's Danny. There was trouble

106

with my Danny later, or if not trouble then a falling out, but it was obvious as soon as I met Danny Callinan that he resented me. This was a shame because I really liked his music and there was plenty to like about the man, but he'd made up his mind about me without us having an opportunity to get to know each other.

From the hotel, Siobhan was travelling up to the band's hideaway house in Hertfordshire and she suggested I come along for a few days. She reckoned it was the closest thing to normality available to her, which said a lot about her life at the time. Perhaps she had a point though: she didn't particularly want to go back to her family home in Dublin during the down time after a gig because it always created problems for her parents. This was at the height of Siobhan's fame and there were very few places she could go without being mobbed, so the band's refuge-cum-bolthole seemed like our best bet for some space and time together.

I didn't dwell on the strangeness of it all at the time: that Siobhan needed to travel with a bodyguard at all times, or that Stevie would chauffeur us through the streets of London, out into the country to a huge private estate where the band and their entourage could be at peace. I was already so besotted that I would have followed Siobhan anywhere, and she was trying desperately to be normal in a very unreal situation. I didn't really care about the unlikely turn my life was about to take because I was in the back seat of a car with Siobhan McGovern and she wanted to spend some time getting to know me. Stevie was a benign presence in the car and he was so obviously fond of Siobhan that he also helped put me at my ease.

The house – or mansion, I guess – seemed deserted when we first arrived, but then I heard somebody chopping vegetables in a kitchen somewhere, a vacuum cleaner working away down the hall and a guitar being strummed in an upstairs room.

'Are the other members of the band here?' I asked.

'Yes, they'll all be in their rooms. It's always like this after a gig; everybody keeps pretty much to themselves for a day or two.'

Stevie offered to show me to my room but Siobhan said she'd take me up.

'Do you need anything?' Stevie asked me. 'Toiletries, clothes, I mean?'

'No, I'm fine.' I didn't anticipate staying long enough to need much more than I'd brought over for the night of the concert. I could have done with a change of underwear but I wasn't about to ask a grown man to get that for me.

My room was at the top and the back of the house so it was even quieter. Siobhan asked me if I wanted to take a shower.

'Are you saying I need to?'

'I was thinking more of taking a shower together.'

It was a long time since I'd taken a bath or a shower with a girl and it must have shown on my face.

'Sorry,' Siobhan said. 'Too fast?'

'No, not too fast.'

'So what is it?'

What could I say – that this was unreal, or dreamlike? Pinch me? Danny had once told me, when I was given my first book contract, that authors get laid, and here if ever I doubted him was the proof. I'd pulled Siobhan McGovern because she loved my books. I said nothing more and we took a shower together.

I have to say something here about having sex with Siobhan. I say 'have to' because I don't particularly want to.

I think it helped that I wasn't a huge Siobhan McGovern fan. I enjoyed her music, sure, and I was well aware of her fame. Having moved to Ireland for college and then stayed, it was gratifying to see the local band's early success suddenly take off and morph into international superstardom. I liked their songs; I liked that Danny Callinan kept coming up with the goods; and, as did every other straight man on the planet – and quite a few women too – I liked to look at Siobhan McGovern and wonder, what if? This was a huge part of Siobhan's appeal: that she could look into a camera and let you understand that she knew her life was outrageously unreal but one day, one day, she would leave all this behind for you – because what was important in this world were not the trappings of fame but the securities of love.

My age and experience, too; Siobhan presumed – correctly – that there were elements of the women in my books that were taken from my own life. I'm sure if I'd met Siobhan when I was younger – a version of Siobhan because she would still have been a child – I might well have been intimidated into ineptitude. And no, that doesn't mean what you've just taken it to mean. It means that I was old enough to enjoy the moment, the moments, the hours spent naked together, getting to know each other's body while discovering who we were as people, as a couple, coupling.

(An example, a quote from Siobhan that even now – after everything, when I owe her nothing – feels like a betrayal of confidence: 'When you lifted both my legs over your shoulders so you could move deeper inside me – that's when I knew that you knew what you were doing.')

So, what you want to know is: what does it feel like to fuck an icon? And my answer is: the same as it does to fuck anybody. When it's right, it's right; and when it's not right, it's very, very wrong. And it was right with Siobhan.

After two days, Siobhan said Danny Callinan had a problem with my being in the house. They were due to play in Berlin the following weekend and he wanted to rehearse.

'So I should go,' I said. I had no idea what the protocol of band life was and I didn't want to fuck things up by outstaying my welcome.

'He's just being a dick,' Siobhan said. 'We rehearse on Wednesday, travel on Thursday, soundcheck on Friday and play on Saturday.'

'But if it's causing trouble for me to be here, I'd rather go.'

'It has nothing to do with Danny whether you're here or not. Like I said, he's just being a dick.'

'But still . . .'

'Still nothing. He thinks he can tell me what to do and he can't.'

'It's okay, Siobhan, really. I don't mind.'

'It's not okay at all,' she said and left me alone in the room.

Shit, I thought. I didn't know whether to follow her or stay put. Perhaps I should ask Stevie to drive me to the airport? But I was still there an hour later when Siobhan came back up to our room. She'd obviously been crying.

Here it comes, I thought. It was nice while it lasted.

'Danny and I . . .' she began.

I was probably the only person in England not to know what Siobhan was about to tell me.

'We grew up together,' she said. 'In the same street, I mean. And we started the band together, or rather – Danny formed the band and asked me to be in it. So in a way it's his band.

110

And we were together in another way for a very long time, up until the end of last year in fact.'

'But that's over now?'

'It is, but as you might imagine, it's not been particularly easy.'

'Am I the first person you've met since you were with Danny?'

'You're the first person I've been serious about since Danny and I split up, yes.'

'And he doesn't like it?'

'He doesn't like it.'

'Does he want to get back with you?'

'Yes.'

'And?'

'And what? And nothing – it's over between us.'

'Does he still love you?'

'Yes.'

'But you don't love him?'

'Not in that way. I love him because he's been my closest friend for almost ten years but we were doing each other harm by staying together for so long.'

'And the band – the band is staying together?'

'Yes, but it's a strain.'

'It didn't show the other night.'

'Thank you.'

'But my turning up has made things difficult for you?'

'Something like that, yes. We . . . we have to figure out some new boundaries, I guess.'

'And that's what you've just been doing, is it? Figuring out your new boundaries with Danny?'

'Yes.'

'And that's why you've been crying?'

'Yes.'

'Do you think he agrees with the new boundaries?'

'It doesn't matter. They're my boundaries now, whether he likes them or not.'

'I don't want to fuck up your band.'

'You're not going to fuck up the band. Whatever happens to the band has nothing to do with you.'

'It doesn't feel that way right now.' I reached for Siobhan's hand. 'Why are you doing this?'

'Doing what?'

'This – with me. Why run the risk of losing everything for someone you met only a few days ago?'

'Maybe I think you're worth it.'

'You don't even know me.'

'What I know I like. I thought you wanted to give this a go?' she said.

'I do but I'm scared.'

'Scared of what?'

'Not matching up – to you.'

'If you're thinking of giving up so easily,' Siobhan said, 'you'd best let me know.'

'I'm not thinking of giving up; I just said I was scared.'

'And you think I'm not?'

'I don't know. I don't understand any of it – why I'm here, why you would even think of being with me. I don't know what I've done to deserve this.'

'You moved me. I read your books and you moved me. I want to be with the person who could do such a thing.'

As I have said, it was flattering that Siobhan always brought it back to my work. However I might feel about my writing now, I was proud of what I'd achieved at the time. My Danny always referred back to this brief stay in Hertfordshire when we argued later, saying it set the tone for how my relationship with Siobhan would be from then on: that Siobhan called and I came running; that everything was on her terms; and that it would always be me fitting into Siobhan's world and never the other way around. He said I stopped being a writer and became Siobhan's partner. But I couldn't see the harm in that. I'd never been an obsessive type who wrote doggedly every day; if I was working on a book, fine, but I didn't beat myself up when I had nothing much to say. It had never been a problem for Danny when I spent weeks at a time over in Manchester, renovating and decorating his house; he never showed concern that taking a pneumatic drill to the concrete of his back yard was taking me away from my writing. He seemed to be implying that, sure, a quick fling would have been okay but anything more was a betrayal of my art.

Siobhan and I stayed with Danny shortly after we'd got together, when she had a gig in Manchester. Danny, it must be said, was the perfect host and Siobhan certainly appreciated the few days in a home rather than a hotel – even if by then Danny's house was already on the market.

'I feel like I recognise your house from Robert's books,' I heard her tell Danny. 'Won't you miss it?'

'I will, but it's time to move on,' said Danny.

I was grateful to Siobhan for taking an interest in Danny moving to Maynooth. Once you scratched the surface of Danny he could be quite intimidating, but Siobhan persisted, with one question following another. If Danny had acted younger than his age at the gig in London to ease my nervousness,

Siobhan seemed wiser than her years for the duration of that stay at Danny's.

'I'm not sure he likes me so much, you know,' she whispered to me later when we were in bed.

'I don't think it's that,' I replied, but she was right to pick up on Danny's reticence.

Siobhan spent those early weeks trying to get to the heart of my friendship with Danny – a friendship I already felt was slipping away from me. Understanding Danny was one more way for Siobhan to understand me, just as without Danny Callinan I would have had an incomplete picture of Siobhan – but neither of us wanted them in our bed. Simply put, in the free time between Siobhan's band obligations, we just wanted to be together, on our own, doing the things that people do when they get to know each other. Mostly, we stayed in the apartment in Smithfield, laying low and out of sight – or so we thought – running the risk of attracting the paparazzi to our door.

'This will just end, you know,' Siobhan said one night when we were in bed in Smithfield together. She was naked and sweaty from sex, lying perpendicular to me with her head resting on my belly, small enough to fit crossways on the bed. When her words filtered through to my drowsy brain, my stomach and balls contracted into a tight knot. She lifted her head in response.

'The madness,' she said, 'the band, the touring. Oh fuck – I'm sorry; I didn't mean us.' She moved up the bed and lay on top of me. I held her and she kissed my neck and face but my secret was out: I was in deep and the thought of losing her already terrified me. How easily these things happen.

The sex being so good acted as a reassurance for both of us; sometimes it was just sex but sometimes it was a conversation too.

'What do you hope for once the madness does end?' I asked.

'I want the same as everyone else: to be loved, to have a family, to lead a normal life.'

'I'm not sure there's any such thing as a normal life.'

'As normal as possible, given the life I've already had.'

'A lot of people in the world want what you have now.'

'You mean to be in bed with you? I know, but they can't have you – you're mine!'

'Very funny; you know what I mean.'

'Yes, I do. But when the madness ends – and it will – what I'll have is who I've always been: a girl from Cabra who wants to be loved.'

I hesitated for a second and then asked:

'When you say "family", you mean you want to have kids?'

'Of course – don't you?'

'I've never been in a relationship where that has ever been remotely likely.'

'But you've thought of it, right?'

'Only in the abstract; without the right person, it's not even worth considering.'

'Okay, "in the abstract"?'

In the abstract, I'd come to accept that I was unlikely ever to find the right person, that I couldn't offer the financial security many women look for in a man – but I didn't say any of this and Siobhan let it go.

'You know the Cyndi Lauper song, "Girls Just Want To Have Fun"?' she asked. 'Well, I have news for you: they don't.'

And then . . . Argentina.

My passport had already taken a fair battering since I'd met Siobhan: mainly across to Britain and back, as well as a handful of European cities – Stockholm, Vienna, Kraków, Madrid, among others. Siobhan had stopped staying in the same hotel as the band on these trips, and we booked places in my name in the hope of stealing some time to ourselves. Obviously, we were hoping to avoid the awkwardness of my bumping into Danny Callinan, but it also meant we could enjoy the cities in a way Siobhan just wasn't accustomed to. Occasionally I'd go see her perform, but more often than not I kind of enjoyed the time alone while Siobhan was working – a little reading, some music, strolling alone through continental streets. We were certainly developing a pattern of differentiating between Siobhan's professional life and our own private life together. I became aware of the toll each performance took on her: the emotional drain, the adulation, the sheer hard work of reaching such a level of excellence. I also got used to the crazy hours she kept, the days she was away from me, even when I was in the same foreign city, because she couldn't come down. And when she did return – thirty-six, forty-eight hours later – there was still a detox period for us to go through, during which I'd catch her looking at me, thinking God knows what.

For my part, I could wait, because I considered the wait worthwhile. You didn't get to be with Siobhan McGovern for free – I understood that – and I thought the strangeness was a small price to pay because she kept coming back to me. You'd suspect drugs, it being rock and roll, but Siobhan's highs and lows were already so extreme an experience that I don't believe she touched them. My role was to be her equilibrium, her median, her mean.

I was in Bristol when Siobhan disappeared; or rather, when she never actually appeared. I was travelling alone and had checked into our hotel, waiting for her to arrive from

Hertfordshire. There were practice sessions with the band, soundchecks at the venue – it was enough for the two of us to know I would be close by for whenever it suited Siobhan for us to be together. The only unusual thing about this trip was that I was taking the opportunity to renew my British passport while I was in the UK. I expected to see her the evening I checked in but no: the day of the rehearsal came and went, the day of the soundcheck and finally the day of the concert itself, without Siobhan appearing or getting in touch. I kept checking the mobile phone Siobhan had given me for messages or missed calls. I didn't have a number I could contact her on: the only names in the phone were my Danny, Siobhan's bodyguard Stevie and Siobhan's parents. The evening of the gig, I walked into town only to see cancellation notices on the posters surrounding Colston Hall. I tried the box office but it was thronged with angry punters trying to get their money back. I walked around to the stage door but it was in darkness; there was nothing going on here tonight.

Back at the hotel, I was surprised to see a missed call from Stevie, but when I tried returning the call it went straight to message. I left my name and told him to call me, asked if he could tell me how to get in touch with Siobhan. I heard nothing back and fell asleep on top of the covers, still half-expecting her to appear in the middle of the night.

I felt like crap the next morning for not having gone to bed properly. In the hotel lobby I saw the newspapers were full of reports about the cancelled gig and also that Siobhan had gone AWOL, but I still didn't quite believe she'd gone AWOL from me. She knew I would be at the hotel until the next day and it took the following twenty-four hours for it to dawn on me that she really was gone – from Bristol, from me, to who knew where? I checked out of the hotel, grateful that the bill was covered by Siobhan's credit card, and caught a train up to Danny's in Manchester to give him a hand putting his furniture into storage. There was no 'I told you so' from Danny but it was definitely in the air.

While I was in Manchester to collect my new passport, I picked up a call on the mobile from Stevie.

'Is she with you?' he asked.

'No, I haven't seen her for over a week. Where might she—'

But he rang off abruptly.

Danny's house was changing hands in less than a week. Although he was then travelling to Ireland, I left as soon as I collected my passport, thinking – hoping – that Siobhan was either at home in Smithfield or with her parents in Cabra. Her parents' phone number was permanently engaged and I presumed they'd taken it off the hook. When I got back to Dublin, there were reporters at the gates of the Smithfield apartment block – so they knew where we lived – but thankfully they didn't yet recognise me. They were gone by the following day, as though the news story was over, and I was at least able to settle back into some sort of routine – albeit without knowing where Siobhan might be hiding.

In the end, after ten days, it was Danny who told me she was in Argentina. He had travelled to Maynooth without calling in to see me in Smithfield, which in itself was an indication of the growing distance between us; it was, after all, still Danny's apartment. The weirdness of having a soon-to-be seminarian tell me the whereabouts of my rock and roll girlfriend – because he'd read about it on the internet – wasn't lost on me, but by then I was just so sad it could have been the Dalai Lama and I wouldn't have cared. Danny

118

accused me of being too passive, but all I could do was wait and hope. She wasn't with me. She needed to be somewhere else and possibly with somebody else. South America was a step too far – financially, emotionally, physically – for me to go looking for her.

It took three months for her to call – time Siobhan spent playing a series of small solo gigs at a club in Buenos Aires that of course only had the effect of making her even more famous. She called the mobile rather than the apartment phone and, satellite technology being what it was at the time, there was a delay as her words travelled up into space and back down to earth.

'I want to come home . . . to you . . . I want to live with you . . . I want us to be together . . . I want us to have a family together . . .'

I want, I want, I want – the trouble was I wanted the same things. This was all I'd ever wanted and I'd been granted a glimpse of its possibility.

When I spoke into the phone, I didn't quite believe my words would reach her, that they could possibly cross the distance of the ocean between us.

'Should I come and get you?'

The time delay extended into silence and then into a gradual build-up of feedback in the receiver so that I thought I'd lost her again.

'I'm so ashamed,' she said. 'I'm too ashamed for you to see me here.'

I didn't know what she might be ashamed of. I didn't want to know.

'Don't worry about that. Tell me where you are and I'll come and get you.'

'No,' she said. 'No, please don't do that.'

More dead air between us.

'Then come home,' I said, 'just come home.'

The year I spent at home in Glasnevin in Dublin with Siobhan was, I think, as happy a time as anyone could reasonably ask for.

Siobhan announced to the band that once any remaining tour commitments were over she wanted to have a break for a year. If Siobhan wanted to stop, the sooner she told them the better. Her taking a year off affected their plans for a proposed tour of the States and this put a further strain on relations with the band. What Siobhan didn't tell them – or her record company – was that she wanted us to have a baby together.

I knew it was time to move on from Danny's apartment in Smithfield, but was surprised when Siobhan suggested we look for somewhere together in Dublin and surprised again when she didn't opt for the isolated grandeur that she was used to at the house in Hertfordshire. She could easily have afforded somewhere in Dalkey or Killiney, a place overlooking the sea where the residents are used to tax exiles and rock stars, but she asked me to start looking just north of the city centre, somewhere handy for visiting her parents in Cabra.

'I don't want to shut myself away,' she said. 'I want where we live to be as normal as possible.'

The fact that her life was anything but normal only made her more determined to slot back into life in Dublin.

'It'll calm down after a while,' she said.

I thought this was optimistic to say the least, but I wasn't really in a position to insist on where we set up home together; Siobhan was paying, after all. It was my job to look around for suitable places to buy and arrange times for us to go looking at houses whenever Siobhan could get away. I knew what Siobhan was doing: she was hoping for a different refuge, her own bolthole, away from the band.

'I want this to be ours,' she said. 'Just ours.'

I found a small place in a quiet cul-de-sac behind the cemetery in Glasnevin. Siobhan was pregnant before we moved in, before she'd even stopped touring. I knew it was fast, but it was what we both wanted and I couldn't believe my luck. This was, after all, everything I'd ever wanted – to love and to be loved, to take care of someone. Siobhan told me so often that I was perfect for her that I'd finally started to believe it. I was her way out of the world she'd inhabited – as a teenager and into her twenties – her golden ticket to a life less extraordinary. It never occurred to me that she might not be telling me the truth, that she wasn't even being truthful with herself. When you're with someone you want to be with, you choose to believe what they tell you – however unlikely it may seem to the rest of the world.

We bought a house, but didn't rush into buying much else. We wanted to do a few alterations – just some decorating and a couple of minor changes – so we looked for things only as we needed them. The first thing we chose together was a bed. I showed Siobhan a poem by Emily Dickinson that I'd come across in *Sophie's Choice* and she had me copy it out on to a scrap of paper which she slotted into one of the joints when we made up the bed. I couldn't stop putting my hand over her tummy when we made love, snuggling up behind her, torn between wanting to fuck her so badly and to protect her at the same time. It already felt like there were three of us in the bed together.

We didn't have a landline connected but Siobhan's mobile wouldn't stop ringing, even though only certain people were supposed to know the number. She apologised every time she took a call, but I told her it was okay; I didn't want her cut off completely from her world. When the press started calling, however, Siobhan announced she was turning off the phone for good and I did the same with mine.

We did a lot of walking, through the Botanic Gardens and the cemetery, nearly always stopping off to choose a DVD to watch in the evening, as by now we had both a sofa and a television. I was also in the process of putting a kitchen together. I wanted to cook and care for Siobhan, to make sure she was getting all the right foods and vitamins. It was still impossible for her to eat out in public without it creating a certain amount of fuss and we were soon sick of takeaways being delivered to our door. It was a pleasant experience to shop during the day for fresh produce to cook that evening and, in this way, the local shopkeepers became used to seeing Siobhan around.

Being pregnant suited Siobhan, though she didn't really show much until after almost six months. Her being so well seemed to confirm how perfect this all was, how right it was that we had chosen this life together. I keep saying it but this really was a very happy time.

Everything changed once again when Ciara was born.

'No rock and roll names,' I told Siobhan when we were trying to agree on what to call our baby. We knew she was going to be a girl and when Siobhan suggested Ciara I thought perhaps it was a little rock and roll but still – a beautiful name.

'Ciara McGovern,' I said.

'Do you mind her having my name?' Siobhan asked and I assured her it was fine. Perhaps this was a warning sign, but I didn't think twice about it. I didn't need to get married or for my daughter to carry my name. I already had everything I wanted.

Siobhan had an easy pregnancy but it wasn't an easy birth. I was there and it was hard to watch and I wasn't much use. When I read later in magazines or newspapers that Siobhan went crazy, it was hard to disagree. Something happened while she was giving birth to Ciara that affected the balance of chemicals in her body, and she was never the same Siobhan again. Sure, that was one way of rationalising the difference in her behaviour towards me; but those chemicals were already inside her, and all it took was Ciara's birth to bring them to the fore. So yes, at the time it felt like she'd gone crazy . . . but, if I'm honest with myself, I probably knew it was coming all along.

The picture I try to keep in my head is of Siobhan and Ciara together on the bed. Ciara was content and feeding at Siobhan's breast. They were both naked, on top of the sheets, and Siobhan was sitting upright with her legs crossed, almost in the lotus position. It was a beautiful thing to see; I think it is the single most beautiful thing I have ever seen or am ever likely to see. It was potent too; an image that carried an enormous amount of power, the embodiment of everything we wanted together – or that we'd told each other we wanted.

Siobhan looked up when I stepped towards the bed and I saw that she was crying. She wasn't sobbing at all but tears were streaming down her face and on to Ciara's head.

'Siobhan,' I said. 'What's wrong?'

I reached out to touch her but she pulled back and turned with Ciara to face the wall.

'Siobhan,' I said again.

'Just – stay away from me,' she said. 'Stay away from us.'

She apologised later and we hugged, but I could tell she wasn't comfortable in my arms. I decided to give her some time and space, but to be there for her all the same. I tried to talk to her about it, to tell her that it wasn't unusual to be depressed after having had a baby, but she said it wasn't that.

'So what is it then?' I asked but she wouldn't say.

She stopped breastfeeding and told me she wanted to go back to work. The band were due to record some new material and the tour of America had been set up for the summer and into the autumn.

'It's been almost a year now,' she said.

'If that's what you want, then yes.'

'That's what we agreed, wasn't it?'

Yes, this was what we had agreed.

'And we're not doing anything here, are we? It's not like you're writing at all, so you're free to look after Ciara.'

I hadn't much considered my writing since I'd met Siobhan; I was too busy living to be writing. If I thought of it at all, I presumed there'd always be time later.

'I'm happy just to be here with you and Ciara.'

'Well, we can't go on like this forever. One of us has to earn some money.'

'Do you want *me* to work or do *you* want to work? What are you saying?'

'What's the point of you working? You're never going to earn any money. No, I'll go back on tour with the band. You can stay here and mind your daughter.'

I just didn't know this Siobhan. It was the body of the person I loved in front of me but I didn't know who she had become.

'I understand if you want to go back to work,' I said. 'I never thought this break would last forever and you're good at what you do – you know you are – but I'm not interested if it's simply a question of money. I just want you to be happy and well.'

'No, you never think about the money, do you?'

'Siobhan, we have more money than we could possibly ever need.' For the whole of my adult life I had managed to get by with cash-in-hand payments for casual labour. I was given a small publisher's advance that I hadn't a hope of earning out. So yes, the ready access to cash since we'd moved in together was something I'd never experienced before and still appreciated.

'I have money,' Siobhan said. 'You have nothing.'

And so it went on. I stayed behind in Dublin with Ciara while Siobhan rejoined the band. I hoped the Siobhan I knew would come back to me once she started working again, that she'd work her way out of whatever it was she'd gotten herself into – just as she had in Argentina. We'd become so close over the past year that I couldn't imagine she would just give up on us. I thought it was worth going through anything if I could only have Siobhan be in love with me again. I still believed in the girl from Cabra who wanted to be loved.

And, of course, I had Ciara. I'm not saying it was easy or that I was a natural at looking after a baby because it certainly wasn't easy and I was anything but a natural. There were plenty of occasions when I asked myself if this was really what I wanted – was this really what I'd been waiting my whole life for? But once Ciara was about five months old, it stopped being so much about feeding and cleaning her. With the improving weather, we could get out more and it became more of a pleasure than a chore – and the answer to my question was 'yes'. Ciara and I became so close that it was impossible to think of her other than as a part of me. The times Siobhan came home on a visit, it was strange to see Ciara in the third person, from a distance, with someone else – even if that person was her mother.

I worried about the lack of variety and stimuli in Ciara's young life; she needed more than I could give her and sometimes I was too tired to even bother. I often took her around to her grandparents for that very reason, asking Siobhan's mother if such and such was normal or should I be doing things this way or was Ciara at the right stage for her age? I bought a book on a child's first year of life but I was too exhausted to read it. Siobhan's mum and dad were fine with me calling around and were always happy to make a fuss of their granddaughter. They were at a loss as to what their own daughter was playing at, though. I could see they found the whole business of Siobhan being away very strange.

But Ciara seemed to be doing okay. She was a very happy baby and I knew just how lucky I was. If she'd been a bawler, I wouldn't have known what to do. Anything could be made better by blowing on her tummy to make her laugh; it was a tonic for the two of us.

I tried at this time to get back in touch with Danny, but it didn't go well. He'd sold the apartment in Smithfield and, although he didn't come right out and say it, I suspected he'd given most of his money to the church. I knew enough about Danny to accept that he would do well at whatever he put his mind to; it's just that this had seemed such an arbitrary step.

He didn't come on too strong with the faith thing. He simply claimed that this was what he'd chosen to do with his life and that was it; all he asked of me was that I call him Daniel from now on. I felt as though I'd lost my friend, but he told me that was exactly how he'd felt when I started seeing Siobhan. The same old argument was in the air between us: what was I doing with Siobhan McGovern? Danny was great with Ciara, but I knew he thought I was being used.

'It's not unheard of for a bloke to stay at home and look after his child,' I said.

'If you can't see what's happening,' Danny said, 'I can't help you.'

'Tell me! Tell me what's happening.'

'Read the papers, can't you? Everybody seems to know apart from you.'

'Tell me what you've read that's so important.'

'That she's back with Danny Callinan, you fool.'

I either believed Danny – Daniel – or I trusted Siobhan. I chose to trust Siobhan. I was sensible enough not to challenge Siobhan about it before she left for America. If it was true, it was true; if it wasn't, I could make it true simply by asking. I just wanted her back and I was prepared to do anything to get her back.

I knew I'd lost her when Siobhan said what she said about 9/11. She went on some chat show – I forget which one, if I ever knew – and told the American people they had it coming. I knew what she meant – that they can't go on interfering in the affairs of other nation states without one day somebody interfering with theirs – but it was a stupid thing to say; an unforgivable thing to say in America.

I had watched the buildings come down with Ciara in my

arms. Siobhan and the band were in Ohio, but I couldn't help but worry. There was no way of contacting her. I knew the tour agenda but didn't know where she was staying or her dates of travel from one city to the next and her mobile was in the house in Glasnevin. I didn't know much, really.

I held Ciara and watched, dreading America's response. A part of me hoped they might finally learn, but I knew in my heart which way they'd go. It was all too predictable over the next few days . . . but I couldn't have predicted that Siobhan would say such a thing on live television.

I wanted to speak to her, to lie down next to her in bed and cup her belly in my hand and tell her it was okay, tell her to come home so we could find a way to be together. *Look at our beautiful daughter: she's all anybody could ever need.*

But when Siobhan did come home, it wasn't like that at all. The rest of the American tour had been cancelled and it looked very much like the band was about to split up for good. At first, Siobhan went back to Hertfordshire, but then she came to see us in Glasnevin.

'I want to live here,' she said. 'Without you,' she added, in case it wasn't clear what she meant.

'And where are we supposed to go?'

'I don't really care where you go, but I want Ciara to stay here with me.'

'You can't just decide things like that. I'm not about to give Ciara up just because you've decided you finally want to be her mother.'

'She's not yours to give up or to keep. She's my daughter and I get to decide what happens to her.'

'She's my daughter too.' I almost said more but even at this late stage I was still trying to placate Siobhan.

'Nevertheless, I get to decide what happens and I want you out by the end of the month. This is my house and Ciara is my daughter.'

The house was bought in Siobhan's name only.

'But I've looked after her all this time,' I said. 'She barely knows who you are. If it comes down to it, I'm the person she knows and trusts the most.'

'We'll see, shall we, what it comes down to? If you're not prepared to go willingly then I'll do whatever it takes to force you to leave.'

'What do you mean – like, through the courts? You wouldn't stand a chance, Siobhan, and you know it. I'm Ciara's parent. I'm the one left looking after her while you're off fucking your boyfriend in America.'

'You can't support Ciara,' Siobhan said. 'You have no money.'

'I can get money,' I said. 'I can find a job.'

'But then you won't be here to look after Ciara.'

'I can get another book deal.'

'I doubt that. Some people I know say you're not actually that good a writer.'

'Some people you know?'

'Forget it, Robert; the courts always side with the mother in these cases. You haven't a chance of getting custody.'

'You left us, remember?'

'Only for my own safety, and now I'm concerned for the safety of my child.'

I was so shocked by her words that I couldn't think what to say. Words on a page can be powerful, but when it came to using her voice then Siobhan had the edge on me. Siobhan raising the threat of physical violence made me want to hurt her into changing her mind – how fucked up is that? But I didn't want to be the man I knew was inside me, the one inside every man, the one who resorts to using his fists because he doesn't have the words.

That she would go to such a length to get her own way; that she would do such a thing to me – at least she had the decency to look away.

'Why?' I asked. It was all I could ask.

'I want you out of this house and out of Ciara's life.'

'You can't stop me seeing my daughter.'

'We'll see what I can and can't do,' she said. 'You have until the end of the month.'

She turned and left the house once again.

'Siobhan,' I called after her but the Siobhan I knew was already gone.

JULIETTE

2005

1

I do sleep for a while. I thought I might never be able to sleep properly again, but here I am. And when I wake up, I know where I am; it's not as though I feel lost and confused. I'm back in Ireland. I'm out of England. I'm safe, for now.

Quite where I am in Ireland, I'm not sure. I know we travelled north from the airport in Dublin but not on the Belfast road. If I had to guess, I'd say I'm somewhere in the region of Enniskillen, somewhere in that land of lakes and hills that are not quite mountains. I stopped watching for road signs or clues to my destination and gave in to my tiredness and the motion of the car. It was dark, but there were stars in the sky.

I reach out from my bed – I have a bed – and my hand touches the flex of a lamp. I trace the wire with my fingers and find the switch. A soft light comes on, easy on my eyes but not bright enough to read by. I swear to God this is what occurs to me: after the many unwelcome lights that have been shone in my eyes, or the brightness that they flooded into my cell to keep me awake, or to make me lose track of time, or whatever they thought they might achieve – and let's not pretend here, Robert, they succeeded – I'm worried that this bedside lamp might not be strong enough to read by and that if I try I might damage my eyes. Like I'm thinking of doing some reading. But as I look around me, I notice that the room is full of books; old books mainly, and I feel the familiar instinct of curiosity kick in. I know that before long I'll have to look through those shelves, just to check them out – you never know what might be there. For now, though, I keep my head on the pillow – pillows, I see, two deep pillows – and I take in the room.

It's a large room, big enough to act as both bedroom and study – about the floor space of a modern apartment. There's a door in the corner and I suspect this leads to a bathroom. It's the type of room you wouldn't see today. Everything about it suggests another age, the time of the Big House and servants and upstairs and downstairs; it's a gentleman's room.

It was so late and so dark last night and I was so tired that I barely noticed where the journey came to an end. The air smelled different – like a foreign country. I know I stepped out of the car on to a gravel driveway and someone – I don't think it was the driver – led me up some steps and in through a heavy door. I remember the flagstone floor inside; I'm in a house that's big enough and old enough to have a stone floor. Everything I noticed seemed to be down on the ground, as though I was still partially blindfolded and could peek beneath the cloth around my eyes. What type of place had they brought me to now? I wasn't sure if this was freedom; it could have been just another trick.

I'm still not sure. The room is carpeted, and I know that

132

if I were to swing my feet from the bed, the ground would be soft and comfortable to the touch. But I don't trust that carpet yet; I know that prisons come in many different shapes and sizes.

Have they handed me back to the Irish? Given up on the problem case – *here, if you want him you can have him*. It doesn't make sense for the Irish to keep me in custody, but since when did any of this make any sense?

What did that guard say – that I must have some powerful friends?

But I don't, do I? Unless Siobhan pulled some strings? No, I don't think so. She might not want me locked up, but she wouldn't lift a finger to help me get free.

Locked up where? I still don't know where they kept me or for how long. I don't know much, really; only that they took me in and chewed me up and now it seems they've spat me out. No longer a threat? Was I ever a threat? What did they think I might do – kill Blair? Who hasn't thought of doing that? Before that I wanted to kill Thatcher. They can't arrest everyone who ever had that thought cross their mind. Was I ever anything at all other than a vagrant, a traveller, an undesirable?

I hear a heating system come on and pipes rattle somewhere as the water starts its circulation to the radiators across the room. Like everything else here, the radiators are old and heavy, yet well looked after, it seems. I realise I can't see properly – no glasses, no contact lenses – and it's the first time it's bothered me since they took me in. There's a black bin bag on the floor across the room and I guess it might contain my things. I wonder if my glasses are inside.

I can hear birdsong, as though the heating system has woken

133

up the birds outside, but I can't hear movement elsewhere in the house. There are old-fashioned shutters across the windows; big, heavy, wooden shutters that fold back in on themselves when they open, but shut out any daylight when they're closed, as they are now. I want to move from the bed. I want to look in that bag. I want to pull back those blinds. I want to know where I am. I want to look through those books on the shelves. But I don't do any of these things. I go back to sleep; or, I lose consciousness again.

A knock at the door wakes me. I lie there, waiting to see if there's another knock. There is.

'Mr Lanaghan,' a voice says – a woman's voice.

Somebody knows my name.

Of course they know my name – they brought me here.

Somebody's using my name. I had begun to doubt my own name.

'Mr Lanaghan, I've a pot of tea here for you.'

I listen for a clue; it could be a trick. I feel more confused and disorientated now than when I was awake earlier. The bedside lamp is still on, but now I can see a tiny shaft of daylight shining into the room through a gap beneath the shutters. I hear the woman on the other side of the door place a tray down on the floor and walk away. If this is a prison, then it's a very strange one.

I try to lift my head off the pillows but it's like a dead weight. My whole body is pressing down into the bed; my chest is bearing down on me and I can't move my arms and legs. The room is stuffy from the central heating; those old radiators are effective. I wish I'd tried harder to get out of bed when I woke up earlier. I don't like the idea that people are up and about in this house while I'm immobile; incapacitated, it seems. I hear

134

the vaguest of sounds, possibly human voices, but they seem very far away.

Where am I? Have they put me in some attic? Am I in some sort of an institution – is that it?

The idea of a cup of tea helps me move my legs to the side of the bed. There's a duvet covering me, a good one that hugs my body, but I have to push it away; I have to get this thing off me. I manage to move my arm so that my hand is resting on my chest, then I push the duvet up and away from me. The touch of the duvet hurts my hand, which I think is ridiculous until I look at the bruising across my knuckles, and I remember and I feel sick with the memory of the pain. This was their parting gift to me. I realise that it isn't the weight of the duvet that is holding me down but the beatings they gave my ribs and back and upper arms and legs. I see that most of my body is still discoloured, yellow and grey. I remember when they did this to me and it hurt more back then, so I'm not going to let it defeat me now.

I swing my legs over the bed and, just as I expected, feel the soft depth of the carpet beneath my feet. I don't give in to it; I know they could take it away at any moment.

I'm wearing my own underwear. I don't remember undressing. It's like I've already started the necessary process of forgetting. I felt so naked for so long, even when I was wearing their orange overalls, that I still felt exposed and vulnerable.

I try standing and it hurts. I'm weak and dizzy – too dizzy, so I sit down.

This room – it's like something out of *Brideshead Revisited*. There are some clothes on an armchair: a T-shirt and trousers that I must have worn to travel across to Ireland last night. I pull on the T-shirt but I can't attempt the trousers. I think I might fall over if I try.

I walk to the door and listen, but hear nothing. I try the door and at first I think it's locked, but it's just the door handle that's old and stiff to turn. The door is also difficult to pull back; it's heavy and rubs against the depth of the pile in the carpet. Just as the woman said, there's a pot of tea outside the door. I look down the long corridor of a hallway, half-expecting someone to come rushing out now they've heard my door opening, but nothing happens. I can hear voices more clearly now, still muffled and far away. Downstairs, I think, in some back kitchen perhaps. At the end of the hallway, there's a large window with a view out on to some woodland and a lake. From what I can make out, it's very picturesque, as though the house was deliberately designed with this view in mind. It looks bright and crisp and clean out there, strong sunshine and deep shadows, some frost, a blue sky with no clouds. I'm not ready to face such a beautiful day.

I bend down to pick up the tray but almost topple over. I have to bend down on one knee and hold a dado rail running along the wall. I can't pick up the tray, so I decide to drag both it and myself back into the room. I lean against the door to close it shut and sit back in relief. They'll notice that I've taken the tray but I don't want them to see me – and I don't want to see them, whoever they are.

The tea is in a covered pot to keep it warm. There's a cup and saucer, a teaspoon, a sugar bowl and a milk jug. There's a little plate with three chocolate chip cookies on it and, like the view out on to the lake, I think the sight of this is going to break me. I close my eyes and take a deep breath and then I open my eyes and pour a drop of milk into the cup. I take the cover off the teapot and pour out the tea. I drink it where I am, sitting with my back against the door.

If this is a trick, I think, or a trap, then they've got me.

'Mr Lanaghan?'

It's a male voice this time. The light coming into the room beneath the blinds has changed again – how long have I been sitting here? I feel the vibration of his knock on the door in my back.

'Mr Lanaghan, is it okay if I come in?'

'One moment,' I say and try to push myself away from the door. I have to use the door handle to stand up and open the door a fraction. I stumble back over to the bed and I work my way round to sit on it.

The door is pushed open by a middle-aged man in an open neck shirt, sleeves rolled up, hairy arms – why am I noticing this shit? He looks at the tea tray on the floor and then at me. Whatever he sees doesn't faze him.

'Jack Reilly,' he says and reaches out a hand, but I show him my knuckles and shrug; there's no way I'm shaking anybody's hand.

He walks over to the shutters and opens one slightly, enough to let in some light but not enough to dazzle my eyes.

'How are you feeling?' he asks. 'I see you've had some tea – can I get you anything else?'

'Where am I?'

'You're in Leitrim, not far from Manorhamilton.'

'And what is this place? Am I in some sort of prison?'

'Hardly. You're on the Fitzgerald estate, in the main house. You're here as a guest of Lord Fitzgerald.'

'And he is?'

'Well, he's Lord Fitzgerald – he used to own the estate.'

'I didn't think we still had lords in Ireland.'

'Well, technically we don't. He's an English lord but he once owned everything hereabouts. He's now bequeathed it for use by the State.'

'And you are – Jack, yes?'

'I'm the director of the institute here – it's a centre for artists and writers and so on. I presume Lord Fitzgerald thought it a suitable place to send you.'

'Who the hell is he and why would he bother?'

'Well, I don't know for sure why he's helping you out, but he offered and we agreed. He doesn't ask for much, when you consider all he's done for us.'

'Am I under some sort of house arrest?'

He gives me a look of . . . pity, is it?

'No, you're free to leave here whenever you like, but I suggest you take advantage of Lord Fitzgerald's generosity to get yourself well.'

'So he's some sort of benefactor?'

'Yes, I suppose so.'

'And I'm . . . he's now my benefactor.'

'In a way, yes.'

'But you don't know why?'

'Not really, no.'

I don't like the idea of any establishment figure continuing to take an interest in me – even if it is to my benefit. I want to be rid of their world.

'So where does that leave us?' I ask.

'Well, I obviously have to look after the interests of the institute, but you're very welcome here. I suggest we regard you as a paying guest until we learn more from Lord Fitzgerald.'

He looks me in the eye and I see for the first time that there's more to him than this front of bonhomie.

'You're going to need a couple of days to get yourself together – that's okay, because everybody here is left pretty much alone. We have dinner together each evening at seven but I suspect you're not quite ready for that – am I right?'

I nod.

'Could you eat some food? Should I have something brought to your room – some soup, perhaps?'

Again, I nod. He looks at me again, taking in the bruising.

'Do you need to see a doctor? Would you like someone to come and give you the once-over?'

I shake my head. I don't think I'm damaged internally – my piss had changed back to piss from blood before they let me go.

'Maybe in a few days?' he suggests. 'I'll see what food I can find and have it sent up.'

'Thanks,' I say. I try to get up when he stands to leave but I'm going nowhere. 'Jack?' I ask as he reaches for the door.

'Yes?'

'Could you bring it in yourself? I don't really want to see anyone right now, if that's okay?' Or be seen by anyone, more to the point.

'Of course, yes.' He obviously considers this a good idea.

'Is that a bathroom over there?' I ask, indicating the door across the room.

'Yes – sorry, I should have said.'

'And was it you who helped me up here last night?'

'Yes.'

'Thank you.'

'Quite all right, quite all right. Get some rest, if you can.' He picks up the tea things and leaves.

I'm still sitting on the side of the bed when Jack returns with a fresh tray. He places it on the desk across the room. I'm going to have to move if I want anything to eat.

'I'll call in this evening,' he says. 'See how you are then, okay?'

'What . . .' I was going to ask what time it was. 'What day is it? Date, I mean?'

'It's the seventh of October. It's a Friday.'

'Thank you,' I say, and he leaves.

I push myself up to a standing position and make for the door in the corner. Halfway across, I lean on the desk for support and I can see that he's brought me a covered bowl of what I presume to be soup, along with a side plate of brown soda bread. There's also a glass jug of iced water, with slices of lemon and orange added, and a glass for drinking. I push off again and make it to the bathroom. The floor is tiled and I can feel the cold from the earth coming up through my feet. I sit down heavily on the toilet seat and pee. My head droops with weariness, as though my body is emptying itself into the toilet.

I'm shivering with the cold of the room, so I reach across for a towel from the rail to place under my feet and pull the cord on a heater fan attached to the wall. It's not a nice heat but it has an immediate effect and helps me control the shaking. I flush the toilet and turn to look in the bathroom mirror, shuffling my feet along to take the warmth of the towel with me.

It's not a pretty sight. I look like Saddam Hussein, twitching eyes included. I guess every prisoner is going to look like Saddam from now on. The growth of hair on my face is almost

140

a full beard, patchy in places and white down one side. My hair losing its colour on my face is somehow more shocking than the gradual fade to grey on my head. This doesn't look like me; the person I see doesn't look like me. Shaving off this beard will be a first step to regaining my sense of self, but for now I make do with a quick splash of cold water. I dab some water across my lips – I hadn't realised how parched I was – and try to wash away some of the collected gunk in the corner of my eyes. A lot of the discolouring on my face is dried blood that must be from weeks ago. My nose feels tender, but it doesn't look too bad and I can breathe without a problem – perhaps it wasn't broken? There's a dirty mark left on the towel from my hands and face. I turn off the heater and return to the desk in the room.

I sit down at the desk and lift the cover off the bowl of soup. My stomach lurches at the smell so I take my time. I don't know if my system is ready to digest anything. I pick up the spoon and scoop some soup from the surface. The first attempt to reach my mouth isn't a success, what with my shaking hand and the fear of scalding my mouth. The beard, too, gets in the way and I get more soup around my mouth than in it. There's a linen napkin on the tray and I use it to wipe myself. Eventually, I get the hang of it and feel the soup warm me through. I dip some of the bread into the soup. There's butter for the bread but I can't manage to use the knife; besides, it's tasty enough without.

I replace the cover on the soup bowl and try to tidy the mess I've made of the tray but then I have to get back to the bed. I lie down and pull the duvet over me. Once again, I sleep.

When next I wake, it's still daylight, but there's something different about the room. Whatever it is can wait because I have to rush to the toilet. I fear I might pass out on the floor and soil myself but I make it to the bathroom. The cold gets to me again and I reach to switch on the heater. There are so many things going on with my body – the shivering, the bruising, the aching – but funnily enough, I already feel as though I'm getting better. I'm weak but I think I could begin to get stronger – just so long as no one starts beating me again.

I don't bother with the full inventory in front of the bathroom mirror this time. I wash my hands, turn off the heater and – steadier now – walk through to the bedroom/study. The tray of soup and bread has been replaced by another tray of tea and milk and biscuits. I didn't hear anybody come back to my room and I wonder how long I've been sleeping. I take the cover off the teapot and feel for heat; it's stone cold. It must have been here for hours – is this the next day? I'm hungry again, so I pick up a biscuit. It tastes stale but I don't care. The chocolate chips rush in a wave of flavour to my forehead: my tongue, my teeth, the roof of my mouth and, finally, a spot just behind my eyes, all savour the sweet taste of the cookie. It's not that different a sensation to almost passing out a few moments ago; the same light-headedness and the danger that I might keel over at any second.

I pour some milk into the cup and drink it. I think I must have slept through another night. The shutter across the window is ajar, and outside I see a stone courtyard. I hadn't realised I was on the ground floor; they must have placed me in some out of the way wing.

Left on the desk next to the tea tray are some toiletries – a packet of disposable razors, a can of shaving foam, deodorant, scissors, nail clippers, toothbrush and paste, and a bottle of shampoo. Get the message, Robert.

142

I retreat to the bed to sit down. Cleanliness would be a start, but I'm not quite ready yet. I'm here and I'm safe – that'll do, for now.

I look in the bag on the floor. I recognise what few clothes I possess from Brighton and see my walking boots in there too. Not much else – none of my own toiletries, or my glasses or contact lenses. I take the toothbrush and paste from the desk into the bathroom. It's going to take more than a single brushing to get my teeth clean. My gums hurt and there's blood on the brush when I rinse it under the tap but I persist.

I look in the mirror again, calmer this time than when I first saw Saddam Hussein looking back at me. It's not too bad – my hair has grown longer in some places than in others. I look at the patchy mess of growth that is my beard; it's going to be a bastard to shave off. When I see the muck and grime ingrained in my face, I decide to shower before I attempt the shave.

I'm prepared for the shower to hurt but it's not too bad. Only the bruising on my knuckles is really painful; for the rest of my body, the relief from the hot water outweighs any soreness that remains. I let the water do its work as it rinses off the top layer of muck, and I enjoy the warmth it gives my body. This really is a very good shower. I'm worried in case I black out or knock my head on the soap dish but I'm okay.

I pat myself dry with the towel and step out on to the mat on the floor by the sink. I wipe the mist from the mirror and study my beard, trying to figure out the best way to approach this. The only thing to do, I guess, is to fire ahead and to see what happens – a few nicks and cuts will be a small price to pay. I fill the sink with hot water – as hot as I can bear it – and lather the shaving foam into my beard. The blade snags and catches as I run it over my face. I know it's not a perfect shave but I'm not worried – it just feels so good. When I'm done, I repeat the whole thing with a second razor. I reach behind my head and shave the hairs that are growing down my neck. I empty the water from the sink and repeatedly splash cold water across my face and neck.

When I look up in the mirror, I'm more like myself than Saddam Hussein.

Jack brings me some food again towards evening. Although the courtyard outside my window is in shade for most of the day, I can see how the daylight changes with the direction of the sun.

'I've brought you some stew,' he says.

I try to hide my response – after all, this is hardly going to be the same stew as I've lived on this past while – but it's hard. I shan't be eating porridge again in a hurry, that's for sure.

'Is that okay?' Jack asks when he sees my reaction. 'I thought it would be the type of food you could manage.'

'Thank you – really. It's hard to get used to, that's all – being looked after.'

'Well, don't get too used to it. Tomorrow, I think, I'll show you around, how the house works and all that. You can't stay in this room forever.'

I could, but I don't say this to Jack.

'And I've arranged for a doctor in town to give you the once-over, just to be sure there's nothing been done to you that we can't see.'

I like the way he's so matter of fact about what's happened to me – he doesn't skirt the issue but he asks no questions – the ideal jailor.

'You look much better,' he says.

'Cleaner, anyway.'

'Until tomorrow then,' he says and leaves me be.

By the time Jack calls for me in the morning, I'm washed and dressed and waiting for him. I don't want to put my boots on this fine carpet so I sit on the bed and wait to be collected.

'Bring the boots with you,' Jack says. 'I'll give you a brief tour of the place so you'll have an idea of the lie of the land.'

I was right – it's an example of what they call a 'Big House' in Ireland, complete with outlying buildings in various states of disrepair. The kitchen seems to be the centre of the household and I'm introduced to a Mrs Johnston, the housekeeper, who eerily reminds me of Mrs Sullivan in Brighton. There are two residents sitting at the kitchen table; Jack tells me their names but I don't catch what he says.

'You just help yourself to whatever you like during the day,' Jack says of the kitchen, 'but I have to insist that from now on you take your evening meals with the rest of the house.'

We go outside and Jack points out various views from the house, but already my head is spinning. I sit on a low stone wall and listen.

'Take your time,' Jack says. 'What I'm trying to say is: the place is here for you to use. If you want to stay in your room, by all means stay in your room, but as I say, I do need you to start joining us for the evening meal. Are you okay with that?'

I don't really feel inclined to socialise but it's not much to ask.

'And the grounds,' he says. 'It'd be a shame if you couldn't use the grounds here to help you get better. All that you see is open to you – for walking or swimming in the lake if you feel up to it, though the water's bloody cold, believe me. And there's a rowing boat you can take out, only we do ask you to wear a life jacket. There – enough for now. I'll let you get some breakfast and then we'll go into town for the doctor at eleven.'

Mrs Johnston shows me where everything is kept in the kitchen and I help myself to some cereal. I return to my room and brush my teeth. I see other residents – at least I guess they're residents – but nobody is much interested beyond saying hello.

I go in search of Jack and find him in an office under the stairs.

'Come in, come in,' he says. 'Welcome to the engine room.'

The office looks as though it's too small to keep tidy. 'Actually,' he says, 'I just have to make one phone call and I'll be with you. Do you want to wait out the front? Two minutes, I promise.'

I leave Jack and walk outside. I have a feeling this was the entrance I first came through in the dead of night – was it two, three nights ago? I look across the grounds, down to a huge lake and a hillside of tall trees beyond. It's the same view as I'd seen before, from my bedroom doorway, only now there's a greater expanse of landscape for me to see. I can't focus on the distance without my glasses so I let the whole picture wash over me. It's impossibly beautiful.

'Not a bad sight, is it?' asks Jack from behind me. 'Come on, I have the Jeep around the back.'

Jack seems equally comfortable with any silence between us as he does with the bursts of information he passes on.

'This doctor,' he says. 'I've told him what to expect and he's okay with it. He'll ask you lots of questions but don't worry

– he's not interested in anything other than making sure you get well.'

This tells me as much about Jack as it does about the doctor.

'Where are we heading?'

'The nearest town is Manorhamilton or, at least, it's the nearest for what we need today. Anything else you can think of – just let me know.'

I tell Jack I could do with being tested for my eyesight. If I'm going to be up and about, I need to be able to see.

'I'd say we could probably get that sorted today,' he says. 'It's a grand little town – a nice feel to it, I mean. Good vibes.'

'I have money to pay for this stuff,' I say. 'I just have to figure out how to get hold of it.'

Jack lifts his left hand off the steering wheel as if to dismiss the problem of money.

'We can talk about that later,' he says. I take it that he means at a later date.

Jack has arranged for me to see the doctor – a Dr Wilson – out of surgery hours. After a few minutes I'm called through and Jack goes off to see about an optician.

'Now, how's it going, young man?' asks Dr Wilson.

'Not so young any more, that's for sure.'

'No, maybe not, maybe not, but let's see what we can do for you, eh?'

I strip down to my underwear and he walks around me, prodding gently, probing my ribcage and asking me to move my arms and breathe deeply while he listens to what's going on inside me.

'Do you feel as if anything is damaged?'

'No bones,' I say. I tell him how worried I was when I was pissing blood but that this seems to have stopped.

'And what about these?' he asks, pointing to my knuckles.

'I can move them, so I think they'll be okay. They look worse because they're the most recent. They stopped hitting me properly a while ago.'

'I think you're lucky they did.'

'I don't feel so lucky.'

'No, well, now – maybe not. I'll be giving you a thorough going-over myself – only not quite in the same way, of course. I need samples of your blood and urine and the other one too, if that's okay, and I'd like to send you for some X-rays to check for broken bones. I can't do it here but I have a dentist friend down the road who can improvise with his equipment to help us out. He knows how to keep his mouth shut, if you know what I mean.' He laughs at his own joke. 'I'm also going to prescribe a few things to toughen you up a little. But I think, more than anything, you need to eat well and take a lot of exercise; not too well and not too much exercise, but enough to get back on track.'

He does what he needs to do. When he takes the samples of my blood, I have to sit down with my head between my knees for at least two minutes.

I thank him and say goodbye. Jack takes me to the optician where I'm given a full sight test and a fitting for a pair of glasses. It'll take a couple of days, but they say they can send the glasses up to the house when they're ready. Jack takes me to the dentist who (as well as X-raying my knuckles and ribs) gives my teeth a good cleaning. I've never been so thoroughly examined. We stop off at the chemist on the way back to the Jeep. While we wait for the prescription, I pick up a pair of tweezers. Jack raises his eyebrows, but after several months of neglect I have hairs growing out of my ears and my nose – everywhere but where I'd like my hair to grow.

By the time we arrive back at the house, I'm hungry and exhausted. I meet a few more residents in the kitchen, make myself a sandwich and retire to my room. I sleep for the afternoon. It's hard to motivate myself to join the rest of the house for dinner but I do, and it's not so bad.

I have a setback a few days later. I've adopted the habit of walking in the mornings – no great distances but gradually increasing my range and the strength in my legs. The grounds are expansive and the walk back up from the lake is always a trial for my legs. It's not so steep but, coming at the end of a walk, I always feel as if I may have overstretched myself. I stop by the gatepost and rest for a minute or two before moving on up to the house.

There's a small package waiting for me on the kitchen table. I panic slightly about anyone knowing I'm here, but then I remember the optician. There's a little note inside suggesting I call next time I'm in town for a proper fitting. I look for Jack to thank him, but he's nowhere to be found. I decide to eat some lunch before I try on the glasses.

Although it's October, the weather is fine enough for sitting outside. The terrace at the side of the house catches the afternoon sun and is sheltered from the wind. It's a nice spot. I take a book outside with me but it remains unopened in my lap. I take out my new glasses and try them on.

The difference is astonishing. I see the stunning view clearly for the first time. I pick out individual trees on the far shore and a heron's ungainly struggle to fly before it rises powerfully above the lake.

A car comes up the driveway and passes in front of me. I half expect it to be Jack, but it's not his Jeep. Most of the residents have their own cars that they keep around the back of the house, but this one parks on the gravel close to the terrace. I recognise the person getting out of the car – it's Juliette, the politico from Brighton! I'm about to call her over when I hesitate, because I'm not sure what her being here might mean. I stand up to slip away to my room but the changed vision from my glasses unbalances me somewhat and I have to sit back down. By now, she's seen me and is on her way across the lawn – the same strong stride and ponytail that I remember from the beach at Brighton.

'Still wearing the shades, I see,' she says and I stare back blankly. I take off the glasses and notice they have reactor lenses for the sunshine, just like my old pair.

'I only got them today,' I say, pointlessly.

'I have something else for you too,' she says. 'This must be your lucky day.'

She lays my wallet on the table before me.

'There now – what do you think of that?'

'I . . .' I don't know what to think. My being brought here was out of my control and the relative isolation of the house has helped me take Jack's advice to just go with it for now. But Juliette's sudden, seemingly arbitrary appearance brings home to me that I'm here at the whim of others. What can be given to me can just as easily be taken away.

I pick up the wallet and look inside. There's no money but my credit and debit cards are all there.

'I'm sorry,' I say. 'I don't understand what you're doing here. How did you know where to find me? Why did you find me?'

'Did Jack not explain?'

'Jack's not here. Explain about what?'

'About my father? Lord Fitzgerald,' she adds, when she sees the blank look on my face.

'Your father is Lord Fitzgerald?'

'Yes.'

This doesn't really help me much.

'You'd better sit down,' I say.

'I will. Just give me a few minutes, can you? It's a long trip from Brighton.'

She strides off like she owns the place – which, of course, in a way, she does.

I put my glasses down on the table and close my eyes. I don't know what's going on, but I've learnt to accept that everything will become clear in time.

Juliette returns with a glass of water and sits down.

'Does it feel good to be free?' she asks.

'Am I free? I don't know what I'm doing here.'

'We thought this would be the best place to send you – to give you time to rest and get over what they did to you. It's a beautiful place, don't you think?'

'Who's "we"?'

'Well, myself mainly but I couldn't have managed without the help of my father.'

'I still don't understand. Why would your father help me?'

'Because I asked him to, silly.' She's very well-spoken, but this turn of phrase grates on me – and it shows.

'Okay, why would *you* help me?'

'Who wouldn't help you, if they could?'

'But why did you? Or how could you?'

She takes a sip of her water.

'As soon as we realised you'd been taken—'

'You and your father?'

'No, the comrades in the branch – the ones you met that night of the meeting?'

I give her another blank look. Is she referring to Anna? Juliette sees my confusion and tries again.

'We knew the police had organised a series of arrests throughout Brighton,' she says, 'but we didn't really know who'd been taken. It never occurred to me to think of you until I started missing you each morning on my walk with Max.'

'Your dog?'

'My dog. So at the next branch meeting I asked that guy you knew in the bar if he'd seen you around and he said no, that with any luck you'd got what was coming to you. I thought he was your friend?'

Bob the Builder.

'I knew him. He wasn't a friend.'

'So anyway, I talked to the comrades and told them who you were and that I thought you might be—'

'You told them who I am?'

'Yes.'

'Who am I?'

'You're Robert Lanaghan, the writer.'

'How do you know that?'

'I just know. So we started—'

'Did you know all along who I was?'

'No, I didn't recognise you until I saw you without your glasses, that night in the pub. So, anyway, we started posting your picture around town and that was when we were told you'd been taken.'

'Who told you?'

'Some of your neighbours, I guess. You lived over towards Hove, didn't you?'

152

'I did – briefly.' I remember my new neighbours from the morning I was taken – they were only too glad to have helped the police (or the army, or whoever the fuck it was that came to get me). 'And what then?'

'I told my father and at first he said he couldn't do anything, but when I told him who you were and that it was obviously a mistake, he agreed to look into it for me.'

'Do you know why I was taken? I mean, mistake or no mistake?'

'It was all done in the build-up to last year's Labour Party Conference. They arrested anybody they considered in the least bit suspicious.'

'What was I supposed to have done?'

'I don't know, and I guess we'll never find out; but the good news is that we now have someone who's prepared to take your case.'

'Take my case?'

'Yes – the more people we can persuade to stand up and let the world know what's happening, the better chance we have of forcing them to stop.'

'And is that why you're here? To ask me to start a case against them for what they did to me?'

'Of course! It's impossible to get any kind of coverage in the media, so we're hoping you might have some idea of where you were held so we can—'

'I've no idea where they took me.'

'But if someone like you is prepared to go public about what was done to you—'

'I'm not interested in taking a case.'

'Maybe not now, but when you're a little stronger . . .'

'I'm not interested in taking a case.'

'I understand how you—'

'You don't understand shit! I don't want anything to do with them, or with you or your case, or with anybody – don't you get it? What did you think – that I'd be grateful for some silly little rich girl asking her daddy to set me free? When it was probably her fault that I was taken in?'

'You can't mean that.'

'Do you think they'd have given me a second thought if I hadn't decided to stay on at that ridiculous meeting you held with your revolutionary comrades?'

Even as I say this, I know it not to be true: they picked me up because I checked a bag onto a plane and walked away. I pick up my book and my glasses and my wallet.

'This isn't a game, you know,' I add.

'So what – you're just going to let them get away with it?'

'Of course I'm going to let them get away with it. They can get away with whatever they want – it's their country, after all.'

'And what – this is yours? Good old Ireland, that allows US warplanes to refuel at Shannon? Or to carry rendition prisoners as part of their unchecked cargo?'

'Oh, for fuck's sake,' I say and stand up. 'Don't you see? Britain, Ireland – it doesn't matter. This is how it is. It's their world – they can do whatever they want.'

'I'm sorry you feel that way.'

'Don't be,' I say and walk away to my room. So, I think, I'm still in prison after all.

I half expect Juliette to follow me and continue the argument but she doesn't. I sit alone on my bed and nobody bothers me until gone seven in the evening. It's not Juliette that comes knocking, but Jack.

'Time for dinner, Robert,' he calls through the door.

I know it's time for dinner because I'm hungry, but the thought of going out to the dining room and seeing Juliette is keeping me in my room.

'I'm not well, Jack,' I shout.

'May I come in?'

I open the door and sit back down on my bed.

'I'm not well.'

'I have to insist you come through for dinner.'

'Could I not have something here?' I know how feeble I sound, like a child.

'No, that's not possible.'

I look at Jack and realise I have no choice.

'Juliette's gone,' he says, 'if that helps?'

I look away and shake my head. 'Do I have to leave the house?' I ask.

'On account of what went on between you and Juliette this afternoon? No, I don't think so, but if you're not prepared to follow the rules of the house you'll be gone by the morning. And one of those rules is that you join the rest of us for dinner at seven.'

Jack leaves me alone. I wait for a while and then follow him to the dining room. Nothing else is said of the matter.

We have a few days of rain but I continue to go out on my walks. I borrow some rain gear from Jack and, once I'm out in it, I actually enjoy the bad weather, although I find it hard to cope if the wind is particularly strong. I take a long shower when I return from the walks and it never fails to revive my spirits. I keep the water pressure on high and I love the pummelling it gives my body.

If I can't sit outside after lunch, I set up camp in the drawing room. I've found a copy of *Brighton Rock* and I'm amazed at how much of the novel I don't remember. I'm not sure I like it – the language seems to be from a different time, from an England I don't recognise – but I stick with it. During the occasional bursts of sunshine, I take a quick walk around the grounds and stand with my back to the west-facing wall of the house.

I'm not unsociable. There are some artists' studios out the back of the house and I've taken to calling in. It's impossible not to strike up conversations at dinner with people about their work. Nobody bothers me about my writing but, even if they get nothing out of me about my not-so-brilliant career, it's only right that I should show an interest in theirs. I like the painters the best – their work is more immediate and accessible – and they're very welcoming when I drop into their studios. I visit just before dinner because that's when they're generally finishing up for the day. I like the ambition in their work and the variety of all the different artists. They're all so technically accomplished; what matters is what they do with that ability. It's harder for me to talk to the writers, given the disdain I now feel for my own writing. Some evenings a writer might give an impromptu reading, but the best nights are when there's a crowd of musicians because the music is the great bringer-together for all the residents of the house.

The weather changes again and for a while I return to my afternoons on the terrace. I travel to Manorhamilton with Jack one day and call into the optician to say how happy I am with my glasses. I see Dr Wilson and he tells me again how lucky I am. He writes me another prescription to help build up my resistance.

'Take care,' he says. 'You're doing well but recovering

physically is only half of it. You're going to be hit by a wave of depression, so make sure you come to see me when it happens.'

I don't think I'm depressed. Certainly, my enjoyment and awareness of my surroundings has never been greater – probably as a reaction to having lived in a darkened cell for an extended period of time. If I can't appreciate the contrast, I might as well be dead.

I sit on my terrace and listen to the wind in the trees. There's so much noise in the silence. I watch the wind catching the lake; I see where it's rippled and calm and then rippled again. I wonder if the ripples feel like waves once you're out on the lake. I can hear birds but I can't always see them. I look out across the lawn, down to the meadow and across the lake to the far shore. My glasses help me pick out the colours, the shapes and the tones of the trees. I can make out the physical depth of the landscape and I know from my walks what it's like to step into that landscape – to become a part of that perfection. I take off my glasses and let the sun work its magic on my face. I realise I'm relatively content.

I ask Jack about the possibility of going out in the boat.

'Are you able?' he asks. 'It can get pretty windy out there, you know.'

He shows me where the oars are kept and the life jackets, and where the boat is moored out of sight amongst the trees. It's just a small rowing dinghy and I have to bail out the rainwater before I can go anywhere.

'Take care,' Jack says, echoing the advice of Dr Wilson, and he gives me a push away from the shore. The water is calm close in by the trees and I let myself float free for a while. I test my grip on the oars and I'm not as strong as I might be. I dip the oars into the water, pull back and try again. Perhaps this was a mistake? The wind catches the boat and turns me around, so I'm sideways on and I try to adjust my position. The lake is about a mile long and I don't want the embarrassment of being blown to the end, or the indignity of being unable to row the boat back. I pull on the oars and row towards the shore. As soon as I feel the wind disappear, I let up the oars and float in the calmer water.

My little adventure is about the only excitement on the lake. There are a few fishermen along the far shore and I wonder if they've watched my feeble attempts at rowing. But in the silence now, I become aware of the fish leaping repeatedly out of the water to create ripples of their own. A cormorant – or is it a shag? – surfaces, looks around and then dives again. I see my friend the heron amongst the reeds and adjust the boat slightly to get the evening sun on my face. When I feel the wind turn the boat again, I row back in to the shore. Landing the boat and pulling it in is hard, and by the time I'm walking up to the house for dinner, I'm exhausted. But I think I shall give it another go tomorrow.

Jack calls me in to the office one Saturday morning. I think I know what's coming: my being at the institute is okay up to a point, but only up to a point. The routine I've adopted of walking and reading and sitting in the sun doesn't include any writing. Jack's hands-off attitude to the artists works in my favour and there's no pressure to actually produce anything of artistic worth. I'm probably not the first resident to use the place in this way, though I guess the understanding is that one day soon I might have something to show for it. I have a hunch that Jack knows damn well that I have no intention of ever writing again. It was writing that led me to Siobhan.

'You're going to receive another visitor today,' he says.

I look at him. There's nobody I want to see, and I don't like the idea of anyone even knowing I'm in Ireland. The only person that occurs to me is Danny – Daniel – but this is unlikely given how things were between us when we last met.

'Actually, it's the same visitor as last time,' Jack says.

'Juliette?'

'And I'd like you to at least be civil to her – is that possible?'

'Yes, it is.'

'You might also thank her for getting you out of whatever mess you were in.'

'Yes.'

'She's gone to a lot of trouble on your account.'

'Yes,' I say again. I'm prepared to take on board whatever Jack has to say, but it seems this is the sum of it. 'Does she often come over to Ireland – to the institute, I mean?'

'Very rarely,' he says. 'She doesn't consider it her right and privilege, if that's what you're suggesting.'

'But she'll have visited twice in as many weeks now?'

'To see you.'

'And she has no other reason for being here? She has no involvement in the running of the place?'

'None other than the courtesy we show her as the daughter of Lord Fitzgerald. You might consider extending her that same courtesy.'

'Yes,' I say again.

Jack looks back down at his work. The lesson over.

I stay close to the house all morning and lunchtime comes and goes. I'm sitting in the afternoon sunshine before I see a car that I guess is Juliette arriving. Another half-hour passes before she finds me out on the terrace.

'Do you mind if I join you?' she asks. She carries an apple and a carton of yoghurt, a teaspoon and a knife.

'I was expecting you earlier,' I say.

'It's not the easiest place to get to from Brighton. Which is part of the attraction, I guess – escaping from the world for a while. Jack said I'd find you out here.'

'This is my siesta spot, where an old man can enjoy a snooze after lunch.'

'Not so old.'

'Thank you, but unfortunately that's how I feel.' I hold up the palm of my hand to block out the sunlight in my eyes. 'Jack asked me to be civil to you.'

Juliette laughs and sits down.

'Is that going to be so hard, do you think?'

She puts down the yoghurt and spoon on the table and cuts into the apple with the knife. She offers me a slice.

'No thanks,' I say. 'I'd like to apologise. I was out of order the last time you were here and I'm sorry.'

'Understandable, I think, in the circumstances.'

'But not acceptable.'

'Oh, I don't know, I've had worse. You have to take it out on someone.'

'But I think I chose the wrong person.'

'It's okay,' she says and makes the sign of the cross in the air with the knife. 'I absolve you – there, all your sins are forgiven.'

'That's a lot of sins.'

'But that's the beauty of Catholicism, isn't it?'

'You're a Catholic?'

'No, I told you – I'm a revolutionary socialist.'

'Ah, that again.'

'Yes,' she says and smiles. 'That again.'

'And what do you do when you're not busy saving the world?'

'Isn't that enough? You mean, how do I support myself?'

'Yes, I guess.'

'Do I live off my father, is that it?'

'No,' I say, but I've been rumbled.

'I work for the Arts Council in Brighton. I'm a civil servant.'

'And what do you do?'

'A lot of boring clerical work, but at least it's to do with the arts. Grant applications, things like that – nothing too exciting.'

'And do you write at all, or paint, or anything?'

'I told you, I'm a political activist; that's who I am – it's what defines me.'

'A political activist with a huge dog.'

'That's right – a political activist with a huge dog.'

'Well, your activism saved me.'

'Hardly saved – helped, shall we say? It's not often I'm in a position to actually make a difference.'

'So you hounded your dad until he agreed to get me out?'

'More or less, yes.'

'And what about the other sad saps they still have locked up? Can he get them out too?'

'No, unfortunately not. It was only because of who you are that I was able to persuade him to do anything.'

'You mean that I'm a published writer?'

'Yes. There's nothing quite like the threat of embarrassment to get the establishment worried.'

'But won't every other prisoner have an equally embarrassing story? How does your father feel about them?'

161

'I think I've got as much out of my father as I'm likely to get. He took a lot of convincing, and he wasn't too happy about sticking his neck out for you.'

'Or for you, his daughter?'

'Or for me. I think I've used up any credit I might ever have had – which wasn't much to begin with.'

'They should be more ashamed than embarrassed,' I say.

'This is why it's so important to do whatever we can to get the others freed.'

'And that's why you came to see me the other week – to ask if I would take legal action to highlight what they're doing?'

'Yes.'

'But everybody knows what they're doing; it's just that nobody cares.'

'That's not true – we got you out, didn't we?'

'You did, yes, but it didn't take them long to figure out I wasn't much of a threat to national security.'

'Why do I get the feeling you didn't exactly help yourself in that respect?'

'It's not easy when you're dealing with morons.'

'I suppose not.'

'Did you manage to find out where they took me?'

'All we know is that you were in a holding facility in Berkshire.'

'A holding facility?' I smile at the euphemism.

'They won't call it a prison because that would make you a prisoner, with a prisoner's rights.'

'So – a holding facility it is then. And Belmarsh – what about the prisoners there?'

Juliette looks away, across the fields to the lake and beyond, in acknowledgement of the enormity of her task.

'They're rounding people up on the slightest of pretexts,' I say. 'And they don't care if a few hopeless cases get caught up in the mess . . . in fact, I'd say they're delighted. You won't beat them, Juliette. They always win.'

'We have to try,' she says. 'I have to try.'

What I don't spell out to her – again – is that, in all probability, it was the life I was leading before I arrived in Brighton that had me on their radar. I was in their sights long before I stumbled into Juliette's pub meeting.

'The Brazilian they shot dead on the Tube?' I ask her.

'Jean Charles de Menezes?'

'That's the real measure of what you're up against here.'

'Don't I know it?'

'It's how England remains England.'

'I understand that,' she says.

Juliette sticks the tip of the knife into the apple core and places it on the table. She picks up the yoghurt, peels off the top and licks it clean, making a guilty face as though caught out in some act of illicit pleasure, before her thoughts return to the seriousness of what she's taking on. It's an endearing slip, a hint of a more human Juliette.

'There are better, more deserving cases than my own,' I say. 'I'm not that important.'

'Of course you are. Why wouldn't you be?'

'Not *that* important. Not enough to justify the lengths you went to; not important enough for your father to take an interest on my behalf.'

'I'd met you in Brighton. I felt responsible.'

'But still – there must be hundreds, maybe thousands of people locked up. They don't give a shit, Juliette, so why did they give a shit about me?'

163

'You know why.'

'I want to hear you say it.'

'What does it matter? We got you out, didn't we?'

'Just say it.'

'It was because of Siobhan – because of your relationship with Siobhan McGovern. They thought that if Siobhan heard about it, she might create a God Almighty fuss and draw attention to what was going on.'

'I thought so,' I say and sit quietly for a while. Juliette finishes off the yoghurt and puts the carton back on the table. 'They needn't have bothered,' I say. 'Siobhan wouldn't give a damn about me.'

'Does it matter why they let you out? Or that we used your connection to Siobhan to get you out?'

'Not really.'

'I only recognised who you were in Brighton because you once lived with Siobhan.'

'That figures.'

'Does it matter?' she asks again.

'No, it doesn't. None of it matters – you're right.'

'What happened to you and Siobhan?'

'Plenty happened.'

'But you don't want to talk about it?'

'Don't want to think about it more like.'

'That bad, huh?'

'That bad.'

Everything with Juliette so far has been political rather than personal – what happened to me, why it happened, what I'm supposed to do about it having happened. She's a political animal; she thinks politically and acts politically. She fights a political fight and wants to use me to stop the same thing

164

happening again, whereas I'd just like to sit in the October sunshine and for this to be the autumn of my days. I'm not looking for a fresh challenge or a new lease of life; I want to sit here like Michael Corleone at the end of the *Godfather* movies.

'I'm sorry,' Juliette says, 'that's your business.'

'It's fine – I don't mind you asking.'

I owe Juliette something and it might as well be this.

'You seemed so right for each other – from afar, I mean,' she says.

'From what you read in the papers?'

'It appealed to me – the idea of you and Siobhan McGovern being together – that's all.'

'Because I was a writer?'

'Yes, but also the fact you were that bit older. Plus, I was a huge fan – of Siobhan, I mean. I liked that she'd found somebody – somebody grounded.'

'I wasn't that together at the time.'

'You knew who you were and what you were about. Plus, you were good at what you did.'

'Well, I'm not writing any more.'

'Which is a shame, particularly after what has happened to you. I remember feeling good about Siobhan finding someone from outside the music industry to look after her. As I said, I was a fan and I wanted her to be happy. She needed someone to look after her – someone like you. I feared at the time that she was headed into a tailspin.'

'But she crashed anyway, regardless of having met me.'

'You helped her for a while – for quite a while actually. I really thought you guys had a chance.'

'Why would you care?'

'Because ... you'd have to realise how much Siobhan's

music meant to me – to a lot of girls my age – and you can't separate Siobhan the person from her music.'

'But they weren't even her songs.'

'She didn't write them, but they were her songs.'

'You might ask Danny Callinan about that.'

'As soon as Siobhan McGovern sang a song it became her song and then she gave those songs to us. That's why I cared so much.'

'Well, she crashed anyway,' I repeat, 'however much we all cared for her.'

Thinking back on it now in Juliette's presence, it all seems like such a long time ago.

'It's true that Danny Callinan wrote those songs for Siobhan,' Juliette says. 'As in, he wrote them about her, for her to sing, and yet she chose you instead of him.'

'Yes, she did – for a while.'

'No wonder the band fell apart.'

'Thanks a bunch.'

'I'm not saying it was necessarily your fault, just that no band could withstand that kind of personal pressure. But I also think they'd have split up even if you hadn't appeared on the scene.'

'I think so too, only perhaps not so quickly.'

'They were childhood sweethearts.'

I smile. 'Yes, I'm aware of all that.'

'And then she took your daughter away from you.'

'Her daughter too.'

'But the way it was done – why on earth did you allow that to happen?'

I look across at her to see if she's judging me, but I can't read the expression on her face.

'I think you know why.'

'Okay – how did you come to that decision?'

'I'm not proud of it, you know.'

Juliette doesn't say anything and I make an honest attempt to recall how things fell apart so absolutely and irrevocably. How Siobhan came back from that disastrous tour of the States to drop her bombshell that it was over between us. But then – that wasn't the real bombshell, because I already knew in my heart that I'd lost her. What I wasn't equipped to cope with was the prospect of losing Ciara – how could I have been?

'I was angry, of course,' I say to Juliette, 'when Siobhan told me she wanted sole custody of Ciara. Angry and full of . . .'

'Full of what?'

'I don't know what the word is.'

'Try.'

'Hatred, I guess, though however I felt was irrelevant at the time. Once Siobhan had made it obvious she was prepared to do anything to get her own way, she left me alone in the house with Ciara, who was crying and hungry and needed changing. So I did what I had to do. I soothed Ciara as though everything was fine, even though I was nearly blind with rage.'

'But what did you do once you'd calmed Ciara down?' Juliette asks. 'Once you'd calmed down yourself?'

'I never calmed down – ever and I never will. If I appear calm to you now, then believe me, you're mistaken.'

'But did you see a solicitor?'

'I saw three separate solicitors and they all told me the same thing – that I was fucked. That if Siobhan wanted to play dirty, there was very little I could do about it.'

'Play dirty?'

'She made out there was a threat of physical violence – both to herself and to Ciara.'

'But she was lying, surely? You hadn't done anything to hurt Ciara – had you?'

'It didn't matter one way or the other; it would be her mother's word against mine and I didn't have the financial resources to challenge her in court. Or the emotional resources, come to that. My legal advice was that I should put all my effort into persuading Siobhan to at least grant me some form of access to Ciara.'

'But why did she turn against you in that way?'

'I don't know. At the time, I was ready to believe that she'd actually lost her mind, or that she was being manipulated by Danny Callinan, or a whole host of things.'

'So you just gave in?'

'No, I didn't just give in. I knew this was a fight I couldn't win, so I asked the third solicitor what would happen if I simply disappeared with Ciara. He advised me not to, that eventually I'd be found and it would stand against me when the case finally came to court. Plus, how could I hope to live in a foreign country with such a young baby? England, I suppose, was a possibility but Danny – the one friend from England who might have been in a position to help – was now in Maynooth, and it would have been too easy for Siobhan to find us. Two days later, I received a letter from Siobhan's solicitor, offering me a one-off payment of half a million if I'd commit to never seeing Ciara again. I took the letter to show my guy and asked if we couldn't use it to prove how Siobhan was prepared to buy me off. He said even this – the offer of money – could be presented in the positive light of a mother who was desperate to protect the safety of her baby. He said perhaps if I refused the money, it might go easy on my appeal for at least some form of access.'

'But you took the money?'

'Yes, I took the money.'

I shift slightly on my seat but the sun has moved around the corner of the house. All of a sudden it really feels like October.

'Siobhan's solicitor and her bodyguard Stevie called at Glasnevin on the final day of that September. I still hadn't made up my mind what to do, but Stevie's presence helped. He said that I was to leave the house and that I could either go with the cheque or without it.'

'What about Ciara?'

'She was awake but quiet. She was almost one year old, so I'd put her in the playpen when Siobhan's solicitor called to the door.'

'Didn't it break your heart to say goodbye to her?'

'I didn't say goodbye and I don't think I had a heart left to break. I just signed the papers where the solicitor indicated and took the cheque from Stevie's hand on my way out the door.'

Juliette stands up to leave.

'I think you gave in too easily,' Juliette says.

I'm tempted to tell her I don't give a flying fuck what she thinks, but I remember my promise of civility to Jack.

'Always willing to fight the good fight, aren't you?' I say.

'What she did to you was wrong.'

'But I wasn't in a position to challenge her. The most I might have hoped for was occasional access to Ciara and I couldn't live with that.'

'So you gave up on everything instead?'

'I felt like I'd already lost everything anyway.'

169

'What she did was wrong,' she repeated.

'Wrong or not, that's what happened. I was her mistake and she wanted every trace of that mistake to disappear from her life, so that's what I did.'

'Her relationship with Danny Callinan didn't last.'

'I know, but from what I can gather her relationship with Ciara has.'

'She's found religion, the last I heard.'

'She always needed something and for a while there it was me. If believing in God helps Siobhan look after our daughter, then so be it.'

'And that's it? You're never going to try to see your daughter again? You have rights, Robert.'

'I have moral rights but very few practical rights; I signed those away. And don't tell me I should fight for my rights.'

'Why wouldn't I say that? What kind of a person gives up on his own daughter?'

A person like me is what I think, but I don't reply.

Juliette bristles with indignation but it's wasted on me. She gathers up the knife and spoon and empty yoghurt carton.

'It'll soon be time for me to leave,' she says.

She walks back into the house with that strong, confident stride of hers and I wonder what it must be like to be always so certain, always so sure of yourself that you know what the right thing is to do. Fight this, fight that – take on the world no matter what the odds might be. Can't she see I'm fucked?

I watch for her hire car to leave the estate. It has turned cold and I decide I'll probably take a bath but, after five minutes or so, Juliette surprises me by coming back outside.

'I'm sorry,' she says. 'I'm in no position to tell you what you should have done.'

170

I shrug and stand up, feeling stiff and achey from the drop in temperature.

'You have an opinion,' I say. 'You may as well express it.'

'Sometimes a little more consideration might be better. Please – I'd like to apologise.'

'There's nothing you can tell me that I haven't told myself a thousand times.'

'Still, I'd rather not travel back with this still between us.'

'Then apology accepted; my turn to grant absolution. I'll walk you over to your car.'

'That would be lovely,' she says, and I hear echoes of Laura.

'A long day for you, by the time you get back home to Brighton.'

'It is, but this is a nice place to visit,' she says. 'A peaceful place – even for such a short stay.'

'The old family estate, eh?'

'Yes,' she says and smiles. 'I was talking to Jack a moment ago, about your being here. He wants to know what you intend to do.'

'And what did you say?'

'I said that his guess is as good as mine, but we both understand you can't stay here indefinitely. Jack's been very good but there'll come a point where you being here will affect his running of the institute.'

'Do you think I should offer him some money?'

Juliette looks up sharply – money raising its ugly head again.

'I don't think it's a question of money,' she says. 'It's just that artists come here to work, not to convalesce.'

'Doesn't it help that I'm a writer?'

'But you're not, are you? You said so yourself: you'd have to be writing to call yourself a writer.'

Ouch, I think, point taken.

'Talk to Jack,' she says. 'I'm sure if he knows your plans you'll find him very accommodating.'

'I'd have to make some plans first.'

'Have you nowhere you can go? And I don't mean wandering aimlessly around Europe. Somewhere you could call home? Get back on your feet again?' She must see the answer to her plaintive question on my face. 'Jack's going to suggest a target to you of the end of the month, for you to decide what it is you want to do when you leave here. A target rather than a deadline – is that realistic?'

'That's very reasonable of him.'

'Well, goodbye.' Juliette holds out her hand and I take it. She rests her other palm across my bruised knuckles. 'Look after yourself, Robert Lanaghan. If ever you're in Brighton again, I could do with somebody to walk Max during the day.'

'That's appealing but I don't think I'll be returning to England in a hurry – or if I'd even be allowed in the country.'

'I'm serious; if you're stuck for somewhere to stay, I have a spare room that you're more than welcome to in exchange for dog walking duties. Think about it, at least.'

'I will, I promise. And I do appreciate your coming all this way to see me. It might not always appear that way but I'm very grateful for everything that you've done.'

Juliette opens the car door and sits inside.

'*Pas de problème*,' she says. 'No problem. You're my *cause célèbre*.'

Her French is impeccable.

2

I make a couple of stops in Dublin before I leave Ireland to return to Brighton. I revisit Smithfield and Glasnevin in a feeble attempt to muster a proper goodbye, though neither call is what you'd describe as particularly successful. Danny's apartment in Smithfield no longer exists, having been demolished and replaced by larger apartments, shops and offices. So I walk up Constitution Hill towards Glasnevin where everything is still pretty much as I remember it. There are children playing in the street where I lived with Siobhan. I hope for a second that one of them might be Ciara, but I see clearly enough that a different family now live in our old home; Siobhan and Ciara are long gone. It's a quiet neighbourhood so I can't hang around for too long without drawing attention to myself. I walk away and take a stroll around the Botanic Gardens. I stop off in the café and ask myself why I ever considered coming back to Ireland. The rest of the world has moved on; it's time I did too.

I have an agreement with Juliette that rather than take a case against the British Government – a case I don't feel I could ever win – I write down everything that has happened to me over the past few months. In exchange, I get to stay in her spare room while I get my shit together.

Flying back into Britain is difficult but I want to reclaim the right to travel to and from my own country. I make it easier on myself by booking a flight into Bournemouth rather than Gatwick. I know all the security measures will be the same but there's less chance of getting lost in Bournemouth. By 'getting lost' I mean being taken to one side, never to be seen again.

Juliette is waiting for me on the other side of passport control and it's no small comfort to know the fuss she'll create if I'm kept for any length of time. I think I might be sick as I walk past the uniformed officers. The shaking – or the rattling – of my body breaks out at exactly the wrong time and, of course, I'm stopped. Any security officer in their right mind would stop me, but they're polite enough and ask me to wait while the other passengers walk through. I have to sit down on a chair to avoid passing out and I guess I look pretty ill but they seem to find out whatever it is they're looking for by running a check on my passport.

'Okay Mr Lanaghan,' I'm told. 'You can go now, thank you.'

I walk through to Juliette in the small arrivals hall. I'm in a bit of a state and it must be apparent from my face. I cry when I see Juliette – and I mean really cry, to the extent of making a spectacle of myself. Juliette takes me to one side and stares angrily at any passers-by who dare to look in our direction.

'I'm sorry,' I say.

Juliette doesn't reply. She doesn't say it's okay because it patently isn't okay, doesn't say I have nothing to be sorry for because I obviously do. She just sits and waits for me to calm the fuck down.

'Let's get out of here,' I say eventually and we walk to the car park. 'Nice car,' I say when I see Juliette's brand new Mini Cooper.

'This is my baby,' she says.

'I thought Max was your baby.'

'Max is my big baby; this is my little baby.'

In the morning, I hear Juliette leave for her walk with Max and that's my signal to get up. I like to wait because I don't want any awkwardness over using the bathroom; plus, I suspect, she appreciates some privacy first thing in the morning. This is her place, after all, and, however generous she's been to offer me the spare room, it must take some getting used to having me around. It suits me too to wait. Juliette is up before seven to allow plenty of time for Max's walk and, by the time she's showered and out the door, I'm about ready to get up. The bathroom is very much Juliette's bathroom and I'm trying not to leave my own clutter around – there's already more than enough of that – so I tend to take my toiletries back to my room after I shower. My toothbrush and toothpaste in the glass on the windowsill is the only evidence I leave behind.

My room is a tiny box room, with barely enough space for my single bed – not that much bigger than a cell. Should she ever choose to sell, the room means Juliette can advertise it as a two-bedroom apartment, which is how it was sold to her. Before I arrived, the room was full of unpacked clothes in bin bags and shoes and shoes and more shoes. My arrival was a prompt for Juliette to sort out what she wanted to keep and what should go to the charity shop below us. She claims to have given away most of the stuff she didn't need – perhaps she's seen something of my own limited belongings – but I know she still has a cupboard full of shoes in her bedroom.

The apartment is spacious enough otherwise. Juliette's room looks out over the street, above a row of local shops that sell just about everything we need. Every now and again we go off in Juliette's car to the supermarket in search of a cheaper, wider range of groceries but there's nothing very much that we can't buy locally.

I tended at first to shy away from being recognised as a local but after a while it just seemed silly not to say hello, and to explain that I'm living in the flat upstairs with Juliette. People are just being nice, that's all. Juliette's a great favourite in the neighbourhood and it's no surprise that there's a level of interest in the guy who shares her apartment. They all seem very happy for Juliette and delighted to meet me. Short of telling them we don't sleep together, there's not much I can do but to go along with their misconceptions. I don't help matters by buying Juliette flowers on a regular basis. One evening I walked out of the curry house with a takeaway, a bottle of wine and some flowers – all bought in the local shops – and there was a warm glow of approval from some neighbours when I met them on the street.

The main living room includes a small kitchen and eating area but the best thing about the apartment is the large window that faces towards the sea. You have to stand on your tiptoes to actually see the sea but it's great just to know that it's there. A door leads to a balcony where Max spends most of his days. A set of steps lead down to what we call a garden but is really just a piece of shared common land. There are probably deeds to all the properties that spell out who owns what – exactly which square foot of ground belongs to Juliette – but the space is barely used by anyone except Max when he needs the toilet. He pads downstairs and I wait a few minutes for him to do his business before going down to clean up after him. We cross on the steps to the garden, he on his way back up and me on my way down, and he avoids eye contact because he knows what it is I've to do down there. By the time I've finished clearing up his mess, he's settled on his balcony, chin resting on his enormous front paws, staring into the middle distance – *nothing to do with me*, his look suggests.

I put on a pot of espresso for when Juliette returns from her morning walk with Max. I was always a cup of tea person to start the day but living with Juliette has changed me – it must be the influence of her French mother. I'd noticed how much she enjoyed her coffee at the weekends when she had the time to enjoy it and I could see that it frustrated her making do with instant during the week. The smell of the coffee when she comes in with Max is enough to persuade her to sit for a couple of minutes before she sets off for work; a quick shot is enough to hit the spot. She reckons she has a good breakfast for her mid-morning break but I don't know how she lasts that long – especially after having walked Max for close on an hour.

'You,' she says to me most days, 'are a genius.' She means at making coffee, which is high praise indeed from anyone with a drop of French blood in them. She brushes her teeth for a second time because she lives in fear of having them stained by the coffee.

'Are they black at all?'

'They're perfect. You're perfect and I'm a genius – now go or you'll be late.'

It's a short ten-minute stroll down St James Street for Juliette to get to work. Not that she ever strolls; Juliette steps out with a purpose wherever she goes, even to work. She bought the apartment with the intention of getting back for Max on her lunch break and she still occasionally comes home during the day but, more often now, she's content that Max is no longer shut up alone for hours on end. They enjoy a big reunion every evening.

I have a desk set up, facing out on to the balcony. If Max is outside and I shut the door, he wants to come in; if he's in and I shut the door, he wants to go out. If I leave the door ajar, he settles down. This freezes the shit out of me, given that it's almost Christmas, and I'm sure he does it to wind me up. Every hour or so, I get up to have a fight with him to keep myself warm. I give him a knuckle butty and pretend to bite his throat; he could easily stick the whole of my head in his mouth but is happy just to growl down my ear. I can stick the length of my fingers in the fur of his coat before I touch his body. He's a truly magnificent animal. I hug him and then get back to my work. He watches for a while and then flops back down.

Max doesn't think much of my writing. Time spent writing is time spent not walking him and this is what he believes is the purpose of my existence. It's as good a purpose as any, but Juliette would rather I write. I told her the other day that she reminded me of the movie *Betty Blue* – that she was in love with the idea of my being a writer.

'Yeah, you wish,' she said and I blushed as I remembered the opening of the film.

The attempt at writing is part of my deal with Juliette – that and walking Max. What I put down on paper is a detailing of events or a statement – this happened, and then this happened – for Juliette to advocate on my behalf. Actual words mean very little to me now.

I kept Max on the chain the first few times I went out with him but, after a while I was confident enough and Max was a lot happier if he just walked by my side once we got to the beach. He's impatient with me because I'm not as agile or as fast on the pebbles as Juliette, but he tolerates me as best he can. If he sees another dog or some kids playing down by the shore – which is rare in this weather – he stops while I put on his chain. Juliette found Max at the animal sanctuary when he was about seven months old and took him in despite the warnings about his size. He'd been abandoned and badly hurt and Juliette half expected him to have some behavioural problems, but these have never materialised. He's the careful one, as though he's aware that he could quite easily do what had once been done to him and he doesn't want anyone to go through that again. If excitable dogs come up to him, he stands there while they jump all over him, until they get bored or their owners drag them away. If ever they become too much, one turn of his huge head is enough to warn any dog that enough is enough.

Juliette takes Max out again when she comes home in the evening. I could go too but I think they like to have their time alone. It's quite something to see the two of them together – a beautiful thing – and I know why I so easily picked them out on the shoreline that first morning in Brighton. I tend to get some food ready while they're out on their walk. Not for the first time, I realise that this is pretty much all I want out of my life – to look after somebody I care about.

Of course, I don't express it in this way to Juliette. If I mention anything at all, it's to check that this set-up still suits her: we have an agreement that if it doesn't work out we'll be honest and tell each other.

'What's not to suit?' she asks. 'And you – what about you?'

'I'm very happy here,' I say, and I am.

I wear glasses all the time now and don't think I'll ever return to using contact lenses. The days are cold but still bright and I like the anonymity of effectively wearing sunglasses each time I leave the house. I live in a completely different area of Brighton than the Roberts family – 'the People's Republic of Kemptown', as they like to call it around here – and I'm not

179

mentally strong enough to face running into Laura. Whatever happened between us – whatever it was we had in that brief time – was ruined when they took me away. (I still haven't come up with the right words to describe what they did to me: taken away, arrested, held without trial.) I'm sure they did a good number on me for Laura's benefit once I was gone.

I've also had my hair cut very short – shaved in fact – so I doubt I can be recognised at all from a distance. Juliette loves my shaven head and can't leave it alone.

'Can I touch it?' she asks, and comes up behind my typing chair to place both her palms on my head. I make out she's a nuisance but it feels so good it gives me a hard-on – not that I let her know that. I always give it a few minutes before stepping away from my desk.

'You've missed a bit on the back of your neck,' she says.

'I think I need a cut-throat razor, like they have at the barbers.'

'Did you ever use one?'

'I've had what they call a hot towel shave in the barbers but I've never used one myself. I guess there's a skill to it.'

'I guess there is,' she says, and takes her hands away. She's a very tactile person, Juliette, in a way I'd never have anticipated. Either she just does what she feels like doing without thinking of the effect it might have on others or she's so true to herself that she doesn't care what anyone else might think. I can't decide if it's an admirable trait or a characteristic of wealth.

She returns from work one evening with the gift of a cut-throat razor, beautifully presented in its own case.

'Jesus, Juliette – are you crazy?'

'Don't you like it?'

'I love it, but you didn't have to buy me this.'

180

'I wanted to.'

'I don't even know how to use it.'

'It'll be fun to see you try.'

'Where did you find it?'

'Well, I tried the antique shops on the way into town, looking for a fancy old-fashioned one, but then I thought you might not like a second-hand blade so I called into the barber downstairs and asked him where I could buy a new one.'

'This is a lot fancier than anything I've ever seen them use downstairs.'

'There's a price to pay for the present,' she says. 'I want to be there the first time you use it.'

'You're quite mad,' I tell her and she leaves for her evening walk with Max.

I make a start on dinner because I know Juliette is due to attend some political meeting this evening, as usual. I thought at first her politics were a reaction to her more conservative father but there's more to it than that. She's determined to live her life independently of Lord Fitzgerald. When I asked her what he thought of my living with her, she said it was none of his business and I'm not even sure she's told him. It's a safe bet that somebody somewhere is keeping an eye on the two of us and they will have let her father know. While I don't possess Juliette's privileged self-assurance, I've come to accept that her open disregard of surveillance is the only rational response.

She showers when she and Max return from their walk and suggests we open a bottle of wine with dinner.

'I thought you had a meeting to go to?'

'I've decided to give it a miss.'

I look at her.

'Well, it's not that important and they won't miss me if I'm not there for once. Besides, I want to stay in and watch you try out your new razor.'

'Then I'm not sure I should be drinking any wine,' I say but we open the bottle anyway. Max slumps into his corner, content to be inside now that he's had his walk and Juliette is home.

After dinner, Juliette won't let the shaving thing go. She follows me into the bathroom.

'Jesus,' I say. 'Give me a second to get myself together.'

'I'll fetch the razor.'

I take off my shirt and look at my face in the mirror; there's a couple of days' worth of growth there. I think back to shaving off my beard in Leitrim and look at Juliette in the reflection behind me.

'What?' she asks.

'Nothing,' I say, and run hot water into the sink. I splash my face and pour some shaving oil into the palms of my hands.

She takes the razor out of its case and hands it to me.

'It's a beautiful thing,' I say.

'Just get on with it, will you?'

I do so, hesitantly at first, but then with greater confidence once I have a feel for the weight of the razor in my hand. It's as beautiful a thing to use as it is to look at. I turn on the tap and rinse the blade in hot water.

'Why are you doing that?' asks Juliette.

'I'm washing the hairs off the razor.'

'Oh.'

'And keeping the blade warm.'

'Does it work better that way?'

'I believe so.'

182

I press on. It's tricky at the top of my moustache, close to my nostrils.

'How are you going to do the dimple in your chin?' Juliette asks.

I look at her in the mirror.

'Sorry. And your Adam's apple?'

'You're a nightmare.'

'But at least I'm your nightmare.'

'There – I'm done.'

'Let me feel,' Juliette says, and she runs her hand across my chin.

'Will it do?'

'It'll do. Now, pass me the razor and I'll do the back of your neck.'

'Oh no – no way.'

'Come on. Trust me.'

'But I don't trust you; I don't trust anyone.'

She looks up at me in the mirror.

'Sorry – go ahead,' I say and pass her the razor.

'Are you sure?'

'Of course I'm sure; I was only kidding.'

'No you weren't.'

'No, but please – go ahead.'

She reaches around me to run the blade under the hot tap.

'Do I need to use the shaving oil?'

'No, I don't think so.'

'Lean your head forward.'

I do so and Juliette scratches away with the razor where the hair grows down the back of my neck.

'There,' she says. 'Does it feel good?'

'It does. It really does.'

Juliette puts down the razor. She reaches out for a towel and wraps it around my neck. She rests her hands on my shoulders and we look at each other's reflection.

'I've got such a crush on you,' she says.

'I know.'

'You know? So why not do something about it?'

'Because I don't want to mess up what we have going here.'

'It might make what we have going here even better.'

'Or it might ruin it,' I say.

'We might lose it anyway if we don't do something about it.'

'You've thought this through?' I say.

'I've thought this through.'

'And?'

'And I want to be your lover as well as your housemate.'

'Yes.'

'What do you mean – yes? Yes you know that's what I want, or yes that's what you want too?'

'Just yes,' I say.

Juliette has a very strong body but is vulnerable all the same. I undress her in the bedroom, first taking off her top to feel her against my bare chest. I hold her shoulders in the way she did mine in the bathroom, only here we face each other. I move my hand to her face. She looks up at me, like she's about to ask a question, but she doesn't say anything. I put my thumb on her lips and bend down to kiss them. She's not so tough all of a sudden. I rest my cheek against hers and it makes me smile.

'What?' she says. 'This isn't supposed to be funny.'

'Just showing off my close shave. And what's wrong with funny? Funny's good.'

184

She kisses me full on the lips – one of those kisses when you're almost scared you might lose your balance and fall over.

'You're right,' she says. 'It's a beautiful shave.'

I run my hands along the length of her spine, down to the small of her back, and feel the power in her body. We kiss again and it feels good. I move my right hand and touch her belly with my knuckles, thinking back to when I feared I might never be able to use my hands again. This is the best form of healing I could ask for. I undo the belt around her trousers and pull them down around her bottom. Her knickers look like she planned for this to happen tonight and I shake my head as I look up at her.

'What?' she says.

'You know very well what. Sit down on the bed.'

I pull off her trousers and take off my own.

'Lie back,' I say. Her knickers are so beautiful it's almost a shame to take them off. I put my finger inside her while I look her in the eye.

It's not every woman whose cunt you want to taste but I want to taste Juliette's. I want it for her and I want it for me. I never know if I'm doing this right but tonight it feels so good that I just don't care. I want her; I want the essence of Juliette and this seems to be about the best way to get it.

I look at her again and this time it's Juliette who laughs.

'I told you funny is good,' I say.

'Funny is good and so are close shaves.'

She pulls me to her.

'Do you want to make love?' I ask.

'I thought that's what we were doing. It certainly felt like it to me.'

'Okay. Do you want me to fuck you?'

185

'Er, yes.'

'Because you might have been expecting this, but I wasn't.'

'What does that mean?'

'It means I don't have a condom.'

'Do we need one?'

'I don't know. I guess not if you think not.'

'Do you trust me?'

I look at her. I don't want to make another baby, only to lose one again.

'Yes,' I say. 'Do you trust me?' I've been given so many blood tests over the past month or so that I know I won't be doing Juliette any harm.

'Yes, I do.'

'Then it's okay if I come inside you?'

'Yes, I think I would like that very much.'

Juliette lies with her legs wrapped around one of my thighs and her head on my chest. I explore her back again, down to the top of her arse. I want her all over again but there doesn't seem to be a rush, like we have plenty of time to enjoy this together.

'What?' she asks.

'If I go to the toilet, will you still be here when I get back?'

'Can I come with you?'

'Are you scared I might run away?'

'No – I'd just like to watch you take a pee.'

'That's weird.'

'That's me; that's who you're with.'

'Then let's go on a field trip to the bathroom.'

Juliette stands by my side as I wait to pee. I start laughing.

'What is it?' she asks. 'What's wrong?'

'Little boys find it hard to go when someone's watching.'

186

'Not so little.'

'Thank you.'

'What if I hold it for you?'

'Then I definitely won't be able to go.'

'Please.'

'You crazy French woman.'

'*S'il te plâit*,' she says. '*Pour moi*.'

She stands just behind me, reaching down to hold my cock.

'Nothing's happening.'

'Something else will be happening pretty soon.'

'You mean you'll be getting hard again?'

'Yes, but that won't help me take a pee.'

'So concentrate.'

'It's kind of difficult with you holding me.'

'Mm, it is kind of hard, isn't it?'

'Jesus Christ,' I say and laugh.

I hear Max padding along the floor and he takes a look at us in the bathroom.

'Great,' I say, 'why don't we all join in?'

Max looks at us like we're crazy and walks away.

'I don't think Max was too impressed,' I say.

'Max is a dog. Now come on – you can do this. Think of waterfalls and mountain streams. Should I turn on the cold tap?'

'No, just – just give me a second, okay?'

I stand there and close my eyes. It's a bit of fun but I know why Juliette's doing this.

Trust me, she's saying. Trust me enough to take a pee while I'm holding your cock. Can you do that – for me? *Pour moi*?

I pee and Juliette directs it into the bowl.

'Good boy,' she says and bends down to catch the last few drips in her mouth.

187

'Crazy French woman,' I say again and we laugh.

'Would you rather I did it like this?' she asks and puts my cock in her mouth. I love being fucked by this woman. I love that she loves to fuck me. I love that she wants me. I love that she wants to be with me. I love that she knows what she knows about me and still she wants me. I love that she's prepared to give herself to me, that she seems to have made up her mind, no questions asked. I love that somebody somewhere loves and wants me for just being me and that I've found that person and am with that person right now. I love living in this town. I love being so close to the sea. I love walking Max. I love being there when Juliette comes home from work. I love how she listens to me and I love how she talks to me. I love that she's a political animal, that she fights the fight and is prepared to fight for what she believes to be right. I love that that's who she is. I love that I can give her the freedom to be out on the streets, telling anyone who'll listen what's being done in their name. I am the centre of her world, her safe harbour. I know I don't deserve this but it doesn't seem to matter. And now she wants my cock in her mouth and of course it feels fantastic and I want her and she wants me and we move to the bedroom and we fuck and we do the things to each other that we've wanted to do for a while now and we even think of a few more and then we sleep and then we wake up and for Juliette it's a working day so she takes Max out for a walk and I make the espresso and I can't believe that we've found each other . . .

But it's not enough.

Juliette comes home from work early and we make love. I feel so close to her, it almost breaks my heart. She walks Max while I cook the dinner. She says she's tempted not to go out to whatever meeting she has planned but I insist. There's no way I want her to lose her passion for political activism. I try to let her know that what we have together is all the sweeter for her doing what she does.

'I'll meet you later in the Hand in Hand,' I say, 'at about ten.' This is our local pub, a long way from Preston Park and the world of Laura and her family. Sitting together with Juliette in the pub, holding hands, I can't believe I've been given a second chance. She empowers me. I feel like I could do anything I choose to do. She doesn't ask me about Siobhan any more. She believes that if I'm here with her now, everything else will somehow be okay. She wants me to write again and I almost believe I could make a go of it. It's what I am, after all – a writer.

In bed later, I wake up to see her watching me sleep. This woman is in love with me but, again, it's not enough.

By the end of the week I have everything in place. I know the first step is the hardest and I sit with Max on the floor for a long, long time – almost so long that I run out of time before Juliette returns home from work. I take the razor out of the gift case and open it wide. Max raises his head to check out what it is I'm doing but I stroke him back down. I hug him around his neck and he growls like we might be about to fight, but I soothe him to be quiet. I put my fingers through the thick coat around his neck and I feel for a pulse. I stick the razor in hard and Max's eyes open wide with terror. He tries to get up but already the flow of blood is so great that I can push him down with my weight. He looks at me to ask why but I shush him to sleep.

There's an ocean of blood on the floor and I step away. I wipe the blade on his coat and fold it closed. I wash my hands.

There's some of Max's blood on my trousers, but that can't be helped. I put on a jacket and drop the razor into my pocket.

I leave. There's a danger of bumping into Juliette on her way back from work so I cut down to the sea front and walk along the prom. I circle around town and then back up to the station. I have to get moving. There's a train due in less than five minutes.

Fuck you, England – this tiny country with big ideas about its place in the world – and fuck you too, Blair. You talk so much about terror. I hope one day you experience what real terror feels like. I hope to see that terror when the bomb you fear finally goes off in your face, to see your doubt for that one brief second. I hope you lose your faith in always doing the right thing. I hope you lose your faith in your God. I hope for these things and yet nothing will ever compensate for your maleficence in this world.

But really, this is all about Ciara. Everything comes back to Ciara. I miss her; I miss her so bad.

So long, baby. I doubt I shall ever get to see you again.

MARIA

1

A cell is not a cell when you're free to come and go as you please. The monks call this a cell, but it's the best cell I've ever had because it has an unlocked door. It's siesta time and the room is as cool as it's designed to be – tiles everywhere, blinds across the windows to keep out the sun – and there's always a breeze, high up here in the hills above Rome.

I have to go back to work in a little while but it's just for show. Giovanni, my boss, has a relaxed approach to work this late in the afternoon. We make a big deal out of raking a few garden beds, perhaps we turn over a little soil with a hoe, but any real work was done this morning and we don't kill ourselves in the mornings either.

I'm in the Villa San Marco, up in the Alban Hills and overlooking Lake Albano, part of the Irish College in Rome. For the life of him, Giovanni can't figure out how it is that I'm here. I don't have the Italian words to explain that it was Daniel who took me in and found me the job – Brother Daniel, perhaps one day to become Father Daniel. So, for now, I live at the villa, in the monks' old quarters that double

191

as accommodation for some of the staff. I'm not paid any wages but I get my meals and my lodging for free. I work in the garden with Giovanni and am available for any other tasks I might be asked to do. The most demanding it gets is when a new coach party arrives and they need a hand with the luggage, which is hard, heavy work in the heat of the sun. Mostly though, the guests at the villa arrive in manageable numbers and the place is so professionally run that they rarely look for my help.

The villa does the holiday thing well but Catholicism is everywhere. The guests who come here must like that combination of relaxation with either a dash or a large dose of religion. I'm in no position to judge them, one way or the other. There are all sorts of religious here, of different ranks and grades and collars and colours of shirts. Giovanni fills me in on who might be important and who we can safely ignore; naturally enough, the higher up the order the more respectful he is to their faces and the more dismissive he is once they've passed on by.

He reserves his genuine mistrust for the yet-to-be-ordained brothers, some of whom share my living quarters. They were the source of his initial suspicion that I might be some sort of spy in his garden. Once I'd convinced him I wasn't a plain-clothed monk studying for the priesthood – and was never likely to be – he relaxed, but warned me to be on my guard. At least, that's what I believed he was trying to tell me.

I don't know who first laid out the gardens in front of the villa. Giovanni hints he was responsible in some capacity, though I'm not sure I believe him, because it must have taken some seriously hard work and genuine horticultural knowledge. By comparison, maintaining the garden beds is a doddle; we water them and mow the lawns and nature does its best to make us look good. Giovanni lives close by. I guess for him it's paid work and he hints – it's all hints with Giovanni – that his family have been involved with the upkeep of the gardens for centuries. Italian bullshit is the same as any other bullshit in that it has to contain an element of truth to carry the story. Giovanni's home is in the grounds of the villa and he works in the gardens, so who am I to say?

Giovanni didn't talk to me for most of the first week, apart from a few brief instructions on how to rake a flowerbed. I don't think he was too impressed with being assigned an assistant. It's hard to decipher his short outbursts of mumbled Italian – he's no great shakes when it comes to helping me learn the language – but his attitude towards me changed at the end of my first week, and for a whole morning he wouldn't shut up. It was like he was telling me all his worries and troubles in one go, most of which were lost on me. My useless Italian didn't slow him down any, even when he asked me a direct question and I stood there grinning like an idiot, lost for an answer. I thought I knew some Italian; I *do* know some Italian, but this encounter with Giovanni showed me the huge gap between uttering a few pleasantries and actually conversing in a foreign language.

I knew I'd made it when Giovanni offered me a cigarette during one of our many breaks. I declined his offer but he insisted, so we lit up while sitting on a stone wall out of sight of the main villa and the monks' cells. The cigarette nearly blew my head off and it took me back to when I was a boy. I felt sick and light-headed but it was worth it; now I felt as though I belonged. Giovanni and I had become a team. I'm now on his side against the dark forces of his employers – the

193

monks and the priests – even if I happen to live in one of their cells.

Giovanni's taken it upon himself to teach me the language and has started to practically illustrate what it is he wants me to do in the garden each day (such as dead-heading the flowers), repeating phrases over and over as he shows me what he means. In turn, I repeat the words he tells me, though his accent is so thick and guttural I find it hard to make the same sounds come out of my mouth.

I quickly realised that Daniel was the only person I could turn to for help once I left Brighton. I caught a train to London but got off in Gatwick, convinced I had to get out the country before they arrested me again. My outrage at the world lasted all of an hour before self-preservation kicked in. (Although, if I was thinking rationally, an airport was the first place I was likely to get caught.) Sickened by what I'd done to Max and ashamed of the pain I'd left waiting for Juliette, I possessed enough self-awareness to understand that I had lost my mind – temporarily lost my mind – because I wished already that I'd taken that razor to myself instead of to Max. The insanity plea isn't an excuse, because what I did is inexcusable, but now I had to live with what I had done. How I got through airport security, I don't know. It was a miracle I had the presence of mind to dump the razor in a bin. There was the blood too, as I hadn't yet calmed down enough to buy new clothes. Not for the first time, I was in a departures hall looking for the next available flight to escape from myself. I was already inclined towards Italy and when I saw Rome come up on the board I thought of Daniel.

By the time I arrived in Rome, I was returning to some

sort of functioning normality. I cleaned myself up, got rid of the bloody clothes and presented myself at the Irish College, asking for Daniel. The college is primarily a place of study for the priesthood, but it also takes in paying guests – Catholics visiting the Eternal City – so my arriving at their door wasn't that unusual. It was disconcerting when they told me Daniel was up in the hills at the Villa San Marco, but they insisted I wait while they tried to contact him.

While considering his vocation and studying in Rome, Daniel saw how he could best serve the Church and this turned out to be in the retreat hospitality business. For its part, the Church recognised just what a valuable asset they had in Daniel and he now divided his time between the college and the Villa San Marco. There was no available room for me to stay as a guest but Daniel sent word for me to be housed with the seminarians in the college proper. It was a suitably spartan room and I was able to give in to my exhaustion and shame. I expected to see Daniel in an hour or so but he left me to fester for two days – time I spent going over and over the horror of what I had done.

I hadn't seen Daniel since the summer I was travelling up the spine of Italy. The evidence of how I'd fared since then must have been apparent as soon as he walked into my room. I wasn't the determinedly independent traveller I had once imagined myself to be; I had tried making it out in the world on my own and failed miserably. I could see how well he looked and how in control – of himself and of his surroundings. No longer did I feel like I was meeting Daniel either as an equal or as a friend.

'Have you eaten at all?' he asked, though it was obvious he already knew I hadn't.

I couldn't bring myself to think about eating. I was barely able to lift my head off the pillow. I shut my eyes and curled up into a ball on the bed.

To his credit, Daniel let me be, but he didn't leave the room. How long I lay there, I don't know. When I finally mustered the courage to look over at Daniel, he was sitting on the floor with his back against the wall, waiting.

'I need to tell you what I've done,' I said.

And, in this way, my friend became my confessor.

When I first meet Maria, it's fair to say that she's something of a bitch; the bitch in the kitchen, as I've heard some of the staff call her. Mostly, she works out of sight in the kitchen of the refectory where the monks and the staff take their meals, only occasionally visible through the serving hatches, washing the pans and dirty dishes of the guests.

Even from this distance, it's easy to see she is one unhappy bunny. Almost a caricature of the stroppy Italian mamma, she doesn't have the weight or the build to carry it off and she comes across instead as something of a spoilt brat. She's nothing to me until we come face to face across the vegetables one time when she's on food-serving duties. She barks some Italian at me that I don't quite catch and I smile and say *mi scusi* and ask for some vegetables in my best Italian, which is still not good. She points to the beans and the potatoes and the zucchini and I guess she's asking me which vegetable out of the three I want, so I take the easy route and say *tutte*, which doesn't impress her in the slightest. She slops the food on to my plate.

As I walk away, one of her colleagues has a go at her and she gives it right back. I don't know what her problem is with the world, and I don't want to know either.

I eat alone as a rule, though the long refectory tables and benches disguise my lingering tendency towards isolation. The language thing all day with Giovanni is tiring, and by dinner I'm about ready to relax into myself. Giovanni eats at home, naturally, and most of the staff here are receptionists, porters, pool attendants or waiters, and they tend to be quite young. I'm closer in years to Giovanni and I'm sure I'm thought of by my colleagues in the same way – one of the almost invisible gardeners they know work in the grounds. Plus, everybody operates on different shifts; Giovanni and I are about the only ones with consistent hours.

I'm more likely to be joined at the refectory table by one of the monks who work in various capacities around the villa and who have a clearer idea of who I am and what I'm doing here. Daniel is often in Rome, but when he's here we eat dinner together. Despite Giovanni's opinion of the other monks, I enjoy their company. Many of them are Irish, which helps, while the Italian monks like to try out their fluency in English as we eat. Daniel's Italian, as you might expect, is perfect.

I'm allowed to use the villa's library, which has books in English and Italian – and Latin too, actually. Of the English books, most are religious texts of some sort, and many are biographies or autobiographies of cardinals and popes and mystics. I've also found a collection of novels that I'm working my way through. Many of the stories are from the early part of the twentieth century, written by authors I've never heard of. I like to think about the effort it took to produce these pieces of work that have ended their days in obscurity. They must have meant so much to the writers at the time and were deemed good enough to publish, so the least I can do is to read them. The monks are very generous and encourage me to take what I like back to my cell. They ask only that I return the books to their proper place. All the volumes are beautifully bound and as I turn the pages, this adds to the reverence and gratitude I feel at the freedom of being allowed to read again. This is how I spend my evenings: alone in my cell with the door slightly open, reading. The sunshine and the gardening throughout the day help me to sleep well at night.

The library also has newspapers and I'm in the habit of reading after lunch, before my siesta. The newspapers are all in Italian and I read them to measure how well I'm progressing, to see if I can match up the words I read with the ones I hear coming out of Giovanni's mouth. Two days after the vegetable incident, I see Maria in one of the alcoves, reaching for a book from one of the higher shelves. If it was anyone else I'd offer to help, but I figure she can keep reaching. She grunts and walks along the wall to fetch the steps. She notices she's not alone and grunts again, dragging the steps along the wooden floor. A wheezing sound comes out of her and she turns to face me, barking in Italian again.

'What – because I work in the kitchen, you think I can't read?'

'I work in the garden,' I say, in my poor Italian.

It's a brainless thing to say, but I'm still not used to interacting with other people and conversing in another language. She turns back to the shelves and I wonder if I've failed to say even this simple thing correctly.

Fuck it, anyway, I think, and I leave the library for my siesta.

A siren disturbs the sleep of my siesta and I panic. I'm not free of this yet. I'll never be free of this fear: that they will come for me again but, when they do, it won't be with a siren – they'll

198

come quickly and quietly and I'll be back again, always in the cell, alone, as it should be.

The siren now is close but not coming closer. A guest must have been taken ill. It's hardly the police come to raid the villa.

I swing my legs to the floor and the cold tiles on the soles of my feet help bring me around. I'm still amazed, when I wake from a siesta, that I should fall unconscious at this time of day and yet still manage to sleep the whole night through. I think I sleep in the afternoon because it's expected of me, because it'd be a disappointment to Giovanni if I didn't. I don't remember giving in so easily when I lived in Italy before; I'd take a rest after lunch but never fall asleep.

The siren changes tone, increases in volume and moves away. I hear it again from Giovanni when we meet down by the fountain. He makes the noise and whirls his hand about his head.

'Scotch,' he says. 'Scotch.' And he points at me.

It's unusual for him to use any English but I still don't understand what he's getting at – one of the guests drank too much whisky and was taken away in an ambulance? I try nodding and smiling, but for once he won't let it go. He points at my chest – a hard jab – and then holds his own chest as he gasps for breath.

'Scotch.'

This time I use my fake understanding tone, as though I know exactly what it is he's telling me.

'Ah, *si* – scotch.'

'*Si* – scotch.'

He hands me a wide net, points to the water in the fountain, and makes scooping gestures with his thick, hairy arms. Even I can see that he's telling me to sift through the fountain for

199

leaves, only the water is perfectly clear of debris of any kind. I'm left alone with this, my job for the next two hours. I break up the time halfway through by trying to find Giovanni for a smoke, but he's nowhere to be seen.

I get the full siren story from Daniel that evening at dinner.

'The Scottish girl, the one who works in the kitchen?'

I look at him blankly.

'The girl who's always shouting,' he says. 'She had a go at you the other night.'

'She's Scottish?'

'Well, she's from Scotland. Italian parents, I believe.'

'What happened to her?' I ask.

'She has a condition of some sort.'

Yes, an unhappy one, I think to myself, but I guess that's unfair if she's been taken to hospital.

'She has difficulty breathing,' says Daniel. 'Cystic fibrosis. We knew this before she came, but we agreed to her working here anyway.'

So, Giovanni's 'Scotch' was his way of associating Maria with me. Scotland, England – what's the difference to an Italian? And holding his chest – Giovanni had the whole story within minutes of it happening. He wasn't there in the library, though, as I had been, to hear her wheezing as she reached for a book from one of the higher shelves.

I wake early the next day to the sound of rain, the first rain since I returned to Italy. Thick drops splat down on the terrace outside my window. I imagine each one with its own character that claims to define the nature of the forthcoming downpour: it will be like this, no, it will be like this. I reach up above my head to open the wooden blind to the pre-dawn sky, and as I do so, lightning flashes and lights up my room.

The flash is like that from a digital camera – two or three little attempts before the main event. I listen for the corresponding thunder, but it doesn't arrive. The raindrops become more intermittent until they stop completely and I lie down again. But this is not the last of the rain; another round of lightning, this time accompanied by thunder, announces the scale of the approaching storm. The rain starts up again with a continuous drumming sound, but it's a gentle storm with no gusts of wind, nothing like what we experience in Ireland. Like the earth outside my window, I let the sound of the rain soak into me.

The rain doesn't stop. It seems to have no intention of ever stopping and I wonder where this leaves me and Giovanni for the day, but it's still early so I roll over and sleep for a while longer.

When I wake up later – much later – it is to daylight and the sound of continuing rain. I look at the digital alarm clock on the shelf above my head and see it's half past two in the afternoon. I haven't needed to set an alarm since my arrival as I always wake long before I need to get up – but not today. The rain has worked some magic and changed all the rules. I listen to the muffled noises of the villa and wonder what the guests will do in this rain. Pray, I guess.

I'm desperate for the bathroom so I pull on a pair of shorts and a T-shirt. The cells in the dormitory run down either side of a long corridor, with a shared bathroom at the far end. You'd almost miss having your own personal bucket. I don't know what the arrangements are like for the female members of staff who live on the other side of the villa.

There's nobody around as all the monks are at work, doing whatever it is that monks do all day. I have to find Giovanni to explain myself. It's close to his siesta time, but I reckon on having forfeited my right to a siesta today. I pad along the corridor in my bare feet and sit down on the toilet to pee, slightly dizzy and disorientated from having woken up so late.

I must have needed the sleep. It's a long time since I've experienced such a lack of control over my sleeping patterns. A huge black beetle scuttles across the bathroom floor and I lift my feet in a panic. The beetle freezes for a moment and then makes a dash for a corner of the cubicle. All the years I've spent abroad in hot countries and I still haven't lost my Englishman's nervousness about foreign insects. There's nowhere for the beetle to go, so it's down to me to make a move. I flush the toilet and we both make a run for it in opposite directions.

Standing at one of the four sinks, I splash my face with cold water and try to come round. I run my wet hands through my hair and look up in the mirror to see a long-legged spider drop from above and land on my shoulder.

'Jesus Christ!' I shout – probably not the best thing to be shouting out in the bathroom of a monastery. I swat it away and don't see where the spider lands – I just get out of the bathroom fast and scamper back to my cell where I sit on my bed and laugh in relief. Robert Lanaghan, the sophisticated traveller to foreign parts. I guess the rain has also upset the routine of the local wildlife; their homes are all flooded and their children all gone.

I make a decision. I'm not going to compound my error of not turning up for work by disturbing Giovanni's siesta. I take the time to shower and have a shave, bravely sharing the bathroom with the displaced bugs and spiders, before setting off to look for Giovanni.

I have to ask around to find out where I might find Giovanni on such a wet day. The reception area of the hotel is very busy and the staff are being pestered by guests hanging around with nothing much to do. Hit the bar or hit the chapel, I feel like saying to them. The villa runs coach tours into the city, to the Vatican mainly, but today's coach would have left early this morning, and it's too late now to arrange something extra for the evening. There are guests returning from venturing out in their own cars, shaking the water from their coats and shaking their heads at the relentless nature of the rain. New guests are arriving and you can see them questioning the wisdom of basing themselves out here in the hills for the Rome leg of their holiday.

Javier, one of the bellboys who I occasionally help out with the luggage, comes through the door pushing a trolley loaded with bags. He's wearing a waterproof cloak that drips rainwater on to the carpet. Javier is Spanish but he has good English and I ask him if he's seen Giovanni. He says no and looks pointedly at my dry clothes; we gardeners obviously have it easy on days like today.

I walk outside and stand under the cover of the portico.

'You're not thinking of going out in this, are you?'

It's Daniel, looking cheery, dressed in slacks and a short-sleeved shirt, and carrying one of the villa's large complimentary umbrellas.

'I'm looking for Giovanni,' I say. 'I haven't a clue where to start.'

'Where were you working this morning?'

'That's just it – I haven't seen him all day.' I hesitate and then decide to tell Daniel the truth about having slept in. He laughs.

'Until now? It's four in the afternoon!'

There are plenty of opportunities here to drink late into the night if you're a member of staff, but Daniel knows I'm not a part of that crowd. I smile and shrug.

'I believe Giovanni spends wet days in his workshop,' Daniel tells me.

'You mean the tool shed?'

'No, he has a workshop next door to his cottage.' He looks at me. 'You don't know where his cottage is either, do you?'

'No,' I say. I get the feeling Giovanni enjoys his privacy as much as I do.

'Come on,' says Daniel. 'I've to go along to the library so I can point you in the general direction from there.'

We share the umbrella as we walk along the gravel path that skirts around the villa.

'Will Giovanni mind me calling in to his workshop?'

'I doubt it,' he says. 'You have the right idea in going to see him before the day is over.'

He hands me the umbrella at the entrance to the library.

'Won't you need this for getting back?' I ask.

'I'll be here for at least a couple of hours and the rain will have eased off by then; if not, I can cut through to the refectory from here.'

Giovanni's cottage is a long way into the woods, below the villa and towards the lake. If I hadn't been reassured by Daniel that this was the right path, I'd have given up and turned back. It seems so far because I'm unsure of the way, but Giovanni must tread this path at least four times each day as he's back and forth for his lunch and siesta. The cover from the trees is such that I don't really need the umbrella; it feels incongruous in the woods anyway. The occasional heavy drop of rain catches me on my head but the air is warm and I don't mind. The long sleep has done me good.

I call in at the cottage rather than the workshop, and rest the umbrella against the stone wall. I've psyched myself up to talk only in Italian but it throws me when Giovanni's wife opens the door. I recognise her from the kitchen in the refectory – she's one of the locals who earn their living up at the villa – and I've noticed how all the other staff defer to her when it comes to getting the work done.

I tell her I work with Giovanni and ask to speak to him, which is a little redundant, because I can see right away that she knows who I am. She introduces herself to me as Ines and walks me around to the far side of the cottage. She pulls back the large wooden door of the workshop and I see Giovanni leaning over and working at a lathe. He's running a motor of some kind and Ines has to shout over the noise. He turns around and smiles when he sees it's me, raising a pair of goggles on to his forehead. If he'd wished not to be disturbed, he doesn't show it.

'Roberto,' he shouts, and gestures for me to come over to where he's working. Ines leaves us and returns to the cottage, closing the workshop door behind her. Giovanni is keen to show me his work; he's a woodturner and there are bowls and plates and wine goblets stacked on shelving above the lathe. There's a workbench running along the length of the workshop with chisels and blades each in their allotted space on the wall; a full set of a car mechanic's wrenches and spanners; and Giovanni's own personal set of tools for the garden surrounding his cottage. I see an old petrol lawnmower that looks like an antique, plus what I presume to be a motorbike beneath a dirty tarpaulin.

Giovanni returns his chisel to a bracket on the wall and chooses another, which he hands to me. He peels the goggles off his head and holds them out. I put the chisel down and when I pull on the goggles they're warm and sweaty from Giovanni's forehead. Giovanni uses his illustrative technique for showing me what to do while he tells me in Italian. I want to interrupt to give him my prepared speech about why I didn't turn up for work today – both as a courtesy and to impress him with some sentences of actual Italian – but he shows me the foot pedal for the motor of the lathe and guides my hand and the chisel to the piece of wood he's working on. The chisel jars on the wood as I press too hard and Giovanni pulls back my hand.

'Softly, softly,' he says, like it's a piece of music for the piano, and this time he lets me do it alone. I feel the contact and lean gently into the wood. I manage to smooth out the nick I made and stand back to Giovanni's nod of approval. He turns off the lathe at the mains and the noise of the motor winds down. I hand him back the chisel and the goggles and tell him about sleeping through the morning. He listens and says fine, it's not a problem, and that we wouldn't have been doing much in the rain today anyway. He puts his arm around me and leads me out of the workshop, turning off the lights and closing up for the day.

I ask him about the woodturning – does he sell his work, or is it a hobby? I think he says he gives most of it away to friends, or to the villa, and that this way he can justify working at his lathe on rainy days. He seems genuinely pleased to see me and I'm glad I took the trouble to come.

Inside the cottage, I have my first proper Italian conversation with Giovanni and Ines. There's no hope of any stray English words to help me out. There's no shared language other than what little Italian I manage to string together, and I have no choice but to strain hard to catch what they say back to me. I'm far from perfect, I know, and what I do to their language has a physical impact on their features – it's like I'm slapping them in the face with my mistakes. But I persist. I'm told to sit while Giovanni fetches a bottle of pastis and two glasses. Ines comes through with a jug of water and a glass of ice cubes. I ask her if she's joining us for a drink and she tells me she has to go to work in about ten minutes. There's an awful lot of pointing and gesticulating going on for us to understand each other. I smile like an idiot, especially when I'm shown a photograph of their son. He's also called Giovanni and, from what I can make out, is studying to be a doctor in Rome. Giovanni goes quiet at the mention of his son and I pick up some vibe. I ask Ines if they have other children and immediately wish I hadn't. She makes a theatrical show of regret and we get over the moment but I know instinctively that this issue goes right to the heart of who she is.

The pastis is perfect but I turn down Giovanni's offer of a second, saying I have to get back. I apologise again about this morning, though he's not in the least bit concerned and jokes that he'll work me twice as hard tomorrow. Ines says she'll walk up to the villa with me, so we leave together. I carry the rolled up umbrella like a walking stick. Unlike Giovanni, Ines makes little allowance for my lack of fluent Italian, so I only pick up the bare bones of what she has to tell me, which is mainly about her son and how well he's doing in Rome. There's sadness there too, as well as pride, and I wonder what their story might be. By the time we reach the villa, my face hurts from so much polite smiling.

When Maria returns to work in the refectory kitchen, I don't recognise her at first because her hair is dyed blonde.

Ines shouts across the kitchen from the washing-up area to where I'm standing at the serving hatch and points to where Maria's dropping off some dirty dishes. Ines seems delighted that Maria is well enough to return to work and is oblivious to any bad feeling there might be between Maria and myself. Maria looks towards the serving hatch and away again when she sees it's me. I get the feeling that if it was anyone but Ines embarrassing Maria, they'd be getting an earful of abuse.

I've got into the habit of returning with Giovanni to his cottage after work for a glass of pastis before dinner. Occasionally I walk back with Ines to the villa, but more often than not she's already started her early evening shift by the time we arrive. After enjoying a little aperitif together, I return to the villa for a shower and my dinner, while Giovanni waits for Ines to return home for their evening meal. My Italian has improved and Giovanni has stopped repeating and illustrating everything he has to tell me. I still miss a lot of what he says but it doesn't seem to matter and besides, we don't always have that much to say to each other.

Away from the villa, Giovanni is relaxed and he seems comfortable having me around. Ines is much more direct than her husband and wants to know all about me. While I struggle to find the words, Giovanni waves the questions away as being unimportant and pours us another drink.

'This is Robert's business,' he says, and I'm grateful. They're both very kind and welcoming and I don't want to have to lie to them. I suspect Giovanni already knows a fair bit about me, but they're both prepared to leave me be.

I'm eating dinner with Daniel on the evening that Maria returns to work.

'It looks as though we're about to have some company for dessert,' he says. 'Or, at least, you are. I'm out of here.'

We don't always have a dessert after dinner but you can help yourself to a bowl of ice cream from the freezer in the kitchen. Daniel and I often look after each other but tonight he clears away our plates on a tray and walks out of the refectory. I see why when Maria sits down in his place.

'A peace offering,' she says and pushes a bowl of ice cream across the table. She speaks in English. 'I think we got off on the wrong foot.'

She scoops up a spoonful of ice cream; for a scary moment I think she might be about to feed me but she eats it herself. I can see she's not as young as I thought she was – I'd guess in her early twenties – and I'm not sure the blonde hair is such a good idea, as it makes her look washed out and pasty. I wonder if she's returned to work too soon.

'I was sick,' she says, 'but that's not an excuse.'

I know from Daniel what's wrong with her, but she tells me anyway.

'I have cystic fibrosis and I don't always handle it so well, even if sometimes it's my own fault.'

She takes another mouthful of ice cream. I'm not sure I fully understand what having cystic fibrosis means and I certainly don't understand how it could ever be her fault. I have a picture of Christy Brown in my head but she doesn't look sick in the way he was sick. She pulls the bowl of ice cream towards her and smiles.

'I'll get you another bowl.'

Still, I say nothing. I feel as though I'm being held in a force field. She obviously loves the ice cream – and I mean really loves it – so I wait for her to finish the bowl.

209

'When I saw you in the library . . .' I begin, and she winces in embarrassment. 'You were sick, weren't you? I watched you struggle with those steps and did nothing to help.'

'I doubt it would have made any difference.'

'I feel bad.'

'Well now,' she says, 'we can't have that.'

'I mean—'

'Don't worry, I'm just teasing. And really, it wouldn't have made any difference.' She changes tack, the library incident consigned to the past. 'Ines says your Italian is improving?'

'Slowly,' I say, 'very slowly.'

'It was Ines who suggested I come over to introduce myself properly. I'm glad she did.' She stands up from the bench, picks up the empty bowl and holds out her hand. 'My name's Maria,' she says, switching to Italian.

I shake her hand.

'Roberto,' I say.

'Well, *Roberto*,' she says, 'a little warning: from now on I'll be speaking only in Italian, so you'd best shape up.'

I watch her walk away. I'm too intimidated to follow her into the kitchen for my own bowl of ice cream so I leave the refectory and go back to my cell.

I sit in the library, looking at but not reading *Gazetta della Sport*. *La Gazetta* will only interest me when the football season starts again in a month's time. I'm thinking of Giovanni and Ines; how they're the latest in a long line of people who are determined to treat me with kindness. How, for every bad thing that might happen to me, there's somebody prepared to help me make it through. Daniel, Jack Reilly in Ireland, Juliette; these are good people that mean well.

The thought of Juliette gets me thinking of the women who have loved me and what I do with that love; how I punish them all for what Siobhan did to me. I'm not what you'd call God's gift to women but women have been God's gift to me and I've repeatedly thrown that gift away. Can I blame it all on losing Ciara? Is this how it's going to be for ever?

My life is still unreal; everything in it is unreal. I'm here and I'm free, so why does it feel as though I'm still serving time? Am I free to leave this place or am I now as much a prisoner of Daniel's kindness as I was of Juliette's? Hasn't Daniel seen what I do to the people who try to help me? And if I left – where would I go? What would I do? I'm as aimless now as I ever was, and when I'm aimless I get into trouble. I had something good with Juliette and I deliberately set about destroying it. Yes, I went a little crazy but there's no saying I wouldn't do the same thing over again. I am sorry for what I did to Max and I wish I hadn't done it. I'm ashamed that I could do such a thing to so beautiful an animal – or to any animal, for that matter. All these good people wish me nothing but good – only goodness doesn't sit well with me. There was a time when I thought it might, but I lost my capacity for goodness when I lost my daughter – when I gave my daughter away for money.

I rest my head in my hands, my elbows leaning on the library table. I think I've finally succumbed to Daniel's concern that I might be in need of some professional help; that I might indeed be in the midst of the serious depression Dr Wilson warned me about. Physically, I'm much better. Working outdoors with Giovanni, eating and sleeping well – these have all had a beneficial effect on my weight, strength and physical health. I may look a lot older than I'd like to, I may have lost a lot of hair and what remains may be turning grey, but I'm learning to accept it. The past few years are written on my face and I can't ever erase them. No, the problems arise when I ask what happens next. I can function within the workings of the villa, but how am I ever going to reconnect to the world? I don't trust myself sufficiently to ever leave my latest refuge, my latest prison.

Lost in my thoughts, I'm none too pleased when Maria sits down on the chair beside me. She sits sideways on, facing me, and appears flushed and upset.

'You're Robert Lanaghan, the writer,' she says in Italian. 'You had a baby with Siobhan McGovern.'

I don't need Maria to remind me who I am but the fact that she knows surprises me. She puts a hand on my forearm and rests it there.

'I'm so sorry,' she says in English. 'I had no idea.'

She stays for only a minute or two – there's nothing to say, nothing for either of us to say – and then she leaves.

Maria starts joining me each day in the library before siesta. If we're alone – which is mostly the case – then we can talk. She hasn't stuck to her promise to speak only Italian, having realised pretty quickly that if it's conversation she wants then it has to be in English – especially when she's explaining about her illness. Her being around stops me dwelling too much on myself and she seems to enjoy my company. I still have my cell if I want to be alone, so it would be churlish to resent the intrusion into my space.

'Sometimes I get so angry at what is happening to me,' she tells me, 'that I don't behave as well as I might. And then I get angry at myself for behaving badly and my behaviour

212

gets worse. I know how it looks and I don't want to be that person. I don't want to spend what limited time I have being that person. I want to be fun and friendly and popular but I end up alienating everyone around me by being such a bitch.'

'So what is happening to you?'

'Slowly but surely, my lungs are being destroyed, that's what's happening to me.'

'And is there nothing they can do?'

'There are lots of things that make it easier, yes.'

'Like what?'

'My diet, mainly; I need lots of protein and fats and energy foods because I can't absorb the nutrients in what I eat. I take enzymes with every meal to help me digest my food. If I'm upset, I take it out on not eating properly and that's usually the reason I get sick – or sicker than usual.'

'Is that what happened the other week?'

'More or less; it's never just the one thing. I pick up a lot of infections, but still forget to take my antibiotics. Or I refuse to do my physiotherapy exercises. When I lose it, everything goes wrong.'

'And you end up in hospital?'

'Yes, only sometimes that can make things worse. I'm likely to catch a different infection if there's no isolation unit or, if they don't know I have CF, they'll try to give me some medication that could kill me. I can't go anywhere without making sure the local hospital knows all about me.'

'And is there no cure?'

'No.'

'So, long term, what will happen to you?'

'There is no long term, Robert. This is it.'

Maria has reverted to her natural hair colour, or what she

tells me is the closest to her natural colour she can find in a bottle.

'The blonde wasn't really you,' I tell her.

All her colours are earthy – her eyes, her hair, her lips, her skin – made all the more so by a seemingly unlimited supply of white dresses that she chooses to wear whenever she's not working in the refectory.

'I dyed my hair blonde to irritate Mama. She flew over to look after me when I was taken into hospital.'

'And you paid her back by dyeing your hair?'

'That was my way of telling her it was time to leave.'

'Nice.'

'I know; I'm not proud of myself. And I've spoken to her since and apologised.'

'Didn't you want her around?'

'When I'm alone and so sick I can't speak or lift my head off the pillow, and strange doctors are making bad decisions as though I'm not even there – as though because I'm the patient I'm somehow also an idiot – then yes, there's nothing better than Mama coming in and taking charge, telling them what they can and cannot do.'

'But there always comes a point when you want her to leave?'

'Yes, and it's hard for her to take after she's come all the way from Scotland.'

'She wants to stay to look after her baby?'

Maria looks up sharply and I half-expect a diatribe but it doesn't come.

'Yes,' she says, 'I'll always be her baby. No matter what age I live to be, I'll always be her baby.'

'Well, that's something.'

214

'It's something, yes. The problem is, I'm twenty-two and I need to live my own life.'

'And being here, working at the villa – is this you living your own life?'

'No, not really; this is a compromise with Papa. He found me work here for the summer, before I start university in Pisa.'

An article in the newspaper on the desk between us catches her eye and she turns the paper, absorbed for a paragraph or two.

'How is being here a compromise?' I ask.

'I wanted to study for the summer in Rome and support myself while I was there. Papa wasn't happy about my coming to Italy at all, so he arranged this job through the church knowing there'd be people here who could watch out for me.'

'That doesn't seem so bad.'

'There's a difference between people watching out for you and people keeping an eye on you. And there's nowhere to study here – no texts, I mean. Papa promised me this library but there's nothing here I can use.'

'It's . . . limited, that's for sure,' I say.

'It's okay if you're studying for the priesthood, but I'm not. I have to prepare a thesis on Italian foreign policy since 9/11 and there's not much source material on that in this library.'

'No,' I agree.

We sit in silence for a while.

'Isn't your papa delighted that you want to study in Italy?' I ask.

'He might have been if I'd chosen to go to Naples, but then I'd have had to stay with his family and they wouldn't allow me out the door.'

'It sounds like he's concerned, that's all.'

'He wants to control me and I won't be controlled.'

'No, I guess not.'

This is one strong-willed young woman.

'He uses my illness as a way of keeping his little girl in check,' she says, 'but I'm no longer his little girl.'

'Maybe he can't stop thinking of you in that way.'

'Well, he's going to have to. I'll stay here for the summer, but after that I'm out on my own in Pisa and there's nothing he can do about it.'

Her attention returns to the newspaper but I think it may just be cover as she opens up to me about how her illness dictates how she lives her life.

'Where do your parents live?' I ask.

'They live in the arsehole of Scotland.'

'Does the arsehole of Scotland have a name?'

'Ardrossan,' she says, spitting out the name.

'I was there one time; it's where you catch the ferry to Arran.'

'Then you already know everything about it.'

'Is it that bad?'

'Worse,' she says.

'We all have to come from somewhere, I guess.'

'Papa thought it would be a good place for business. He has a fish and chip shop on the main street.'

'But why choose Ardrossan?'

'I've no idea; you'd have to ask him yourself. He's from Naples – or from a small fishing port just outside Naples – and he viewed the map of Britain like an upside-down Italy. Glasgow was to London what Naples was to Milan, so he figured Ardrossan would be similar to what he knew.'

'And when he got there?'

'If he ever realised how wrong he was, he never admitted it. Pig-headed doesn't even begin to describe him.'

I reckon some of that pig-headedness might have rubbed off on his daughter.

'Why did he leave Naples – to find work?' I ask.

'That's the story but really – the west coast of Scotland?'

'You think he was running away from something?'

'Or someone – who knows? I haven't been told and I'm never likely to be – certainly not by him.'

'What about your mother – your mama?'

'She'd never go against Papa. The only time she takes a stand is when it comes to my being sick, like when she visited me here in hospital the other week. That was a huge thing for her to do.'

'And you dyed your hair blonde to thank her?'

'I dyed my hair blonde to thank her.'

'Didn't your papa want her to come?'

'Papa and I aren't talking since I insisted on going to university in Pisa,' she says.

'How long will that last – him not talking to you?'

'I don't know, but he took it pretty hard. He'll come around. I know he loves me; he just has to learn to let his little girl live her own life.'

'Families, eh?'

'Families is right, Robert; families is right.' She looks up at the books on the library shelves, making up her mind about how much to tell me. 'Because it's a genetically inherited disorder, Papa thinks he's to blame for making me ill. He believes it's his fault, whereas it took both my parents to make me this way; they're both carriers of the gene. They were lucky with my brother and my sister and unlucky with me.'

217

'They didn't know – obviously?'

'How would they have known? It's not something you automatically think about. So many people are carriers, yet the gene isn't always passed on. By the time my sister was born, they knew I was CF but they still had no clear idea what it might mean. I was just a very sickly baby.'

'And your sister's okay?'

'Yes, thank God; she's completely free of the gene. That would have been terrible for Papa – if Bea was sick after they'd been told about me. Although I think Mama was pregnant with Bea before I'd been diagnosed, so there wasn't much they could do.'

'But they got lucky?'

'They got lucky.'

'What about your brother?'

'Lucha's one year older than I am and is just a carrier.'

'So it's just you who's sick?'

'Bit of a bummer, yes?'

I listen to the birds while I lie in my bed. Italian sparrows are a lot louder than their English or Irish relations. There's one bird in particular making a lot of noise, flying around and asking the same questions over and over again. *What's the story? What's happening? Where's the food?*

I've seen him, my sparrow – I'm guessing he's a he – and it's hard to believe that so small a bird could make so much noise. He's a plucky little fucker, I'll give him that. There are other, larger birds just itching to take over his patch, but he's having none of it. I love him and I love that he's the start of my day.

When the dogs of the neighbourhood join the birds and start howling their morning chorus, I give up trying to sleep and open the window. I don't switch on the lamp until I have the mosquito screen in place. I like to get down to the refectory to make myself a cup of tea before the rest of the villa is awake – or, at least, before any of the monks start to stir from their cells. My guess is that Daniel knows I steal down for this pre-dawn cup of tea and he waits for me to return to my cell before he goes for his shower. He understands how I need my routine, making the morning I slept through the storm all that more surprising.

The dogs belong to a house about two kilometres away, in the opposite direction to Giovanni's cottage. They're big dogs and friendly, only I didn't know this when I first met them. I was out walking one Saturday afternoon and, as I turned a corner, they came bounding and barking along the lane. I talked to them and held out my arm, offering them the back of my hand to sniff and hoping to God they didn't bite it off. Their wagging tails were a bit of a giveaway, but that didn't stop my heart from pounding. One dog is an Alsatian and the other a Doberman so they could easily have overpowered me. It took a few minutes for the relief to kick in and the experience was a reminder of how rural and isolated we are up at the villa. Stepping outside the grounds is like stepping into a different time.

I drink my tea and listen to the dogs and the birds, to the monks leaving for Matins and to the staff starting up in the kitchen. Each of these sounds reminds me how lucky I am and I say my own prayer of thanks – not to any god, but to Daniel for having got me here once I left England.

Every day is like Sunday at the villa but Sundays even more so. There are lots of priests here who each have to celebrate

Mass, so that's a lot of services to get through. Breakfast is served for guests until eleven and the main meal on a Sunday is at two in the afternoon. Maria gets a break once breakfast is over and she knows to find me in the library. Sunday is the most oppressively Catholic day for me and the library is about the best place to hide. I could stay in my cell but I think the library is healthier – it's a progress of sorts.

Sometimes Maria is a child and at other times she's an adult. Sometimes I'm the grown-up she can talk to but often I'm the infuriating Englishman who doesn't speak Italian. Most of our conversations now begin in Italian and deteriorate into English. At home, she tells me, they speak Italian all the time. Her English is accented by Italy rather than by Scotland. She speaks both languages perfectly but finds it hard sometimes to flip from one to the other.

'I googled you,' she tells me and I guess I don't react in the way she expects. 'I looked you up on the internet?'

'I know what you mean; I just hadn't thought of myself as being on Google.' The idea of Maria – or anybody, for that matter – getting an instant biography on me through a search engine was new to me but it doesn't take a genius to guess what they'd find. My public life doesn't amount to much. I've resisted the temptation to look because I think it would depress me.

'I'm sorry,' she says, a little chastened. 'Everybody does it.'

I can see how innocent, or even prehistoric, I must appear to Maria, but I've also got into the habit of looking up cystic fibrosis online to learn more about her illness without having to ask directly. I guess this is how we learn about each other these days. The access to so much information is something of a shock, but not as shocking as what Maria lives with on a daily basis. Like her white dresses, Maria wears her illness lightly. I've seen at first hand what happens when it becomes too much for her but you'd never guess how ill she really is. She's light and chatty and breezy, though still liable to go off on one at any moment. She's a handful. She's a headache. She's a nuisance. She's a life force. She's all these things and yet I feel a weight fall from me whenever I'm with her. She makes me smile and it's a long time since I've done that on a regular basis.

'Why are you laughing?' she asks.

'I'm smiling.'

'Why?'

I can't tell her. She's a good thing in my life that I didn't see coming.

But what I am to Maria, I don't yet know.

Once I've seen Maria and she's gone back to work, I often go for a long walk out in the woods before lunch, or I might hang with Javier and the other bellboys at the front door. Today though, once their shift is over, Ines has invited me (and Maria) to the cottage for a late lunch.

The sight of Ines and Maria walking along the path that emerges from the woodland at Giovanni's cottage is a tonic. They look so happy and so close that they might well be mother and daughter. It occurs to me that, in a very short period of time, Maria has become the daughter Ines never had.

They step out from the dark of the woodland into the bright afternoon sunlight, Ines still in her work overalls and Maria in yet another white dress. Giovanni, sitting next to me in the shade of the cottage, has made an effort and is dressed in a clean white shirt. My clothes are clean too, but I wish I owned a wider selection to choose from. I stop in mid-sentence as they walk towards us. Giovanni looks over at his wife and nods in agreement with a sentiment I haven't even expressed: Ines and Maria make an almost perfect scene complete.

Giovanni stands up to greet them in the overly demonstrative manner only an Italian man can get away with. He kisses Maria on each cheek and stands back in appreciation of Ines' beauty. Ines gives him the brush off but she's obviously delighted. She gives me a little wave, blows me a kiss, and goes inside to get changed.

'So,' Maria says. 'While we women are out at work, you boys sit around drinking beer. Why am I not surprised?'

'Thank you for calling us boys,' I say.

I arrived with a bottle of red that I bought from the bar up at the villa. Giovanni offered me our usual pastis, but we both agreed a cold beer was called for on such a hot day. He fetches more beers from the kitchen and we sit down to wait for Ines. Our one job – the boys, the old men – is to light the coals for the outside grill. The meat is marinating in the fridge, along with the salad and a lasagne that Ines prepared before she left for work.

'Life is good,' Giovanni says, as a toast.

'Life is good,' we agree.

I cope well with the language all afternoon and into the evening. It's easier because there are four of us and it doesn't matter so much if I miss the occasional word or sentence. I can always pick up on the gist of what is being said. I spend a lot of the dinner grinning like an idiot; the food, drink and company are perfect. Maria and I stay late and we all move inside once the mosquitoes get to be too much.

Eventually, though, it's time to leave. There are lots of jokes about me not turning up for work tomorrow or sleeping through the day again. I try in my best Italian to tell Giovanni and Ines how grateful I am but I wouldn't have the words in English, never mind in Italian. Giovanni and Ines shrug it off as nothing and they kiss and hug us goodbye.

It's dark and Maria and I have to trust to memory and the sound of our feet on the path to find our way home. Maria takes my arm for guidance. We walk slowly and carefully through the woods.

'Ines couldn't have any more children after she gave birth to their son,' Maria tells me. 'She was devastated – she still is.'

'I can imagine.'

'And now Giovanni is fighting with the younger Giovanni all the time because his son wants to be a doctor and not the gardener at the villa.'

'I'd kind of guessed there was something like that going on.'

'It's the same old father-and-son bullshit,' Maria says.

'It might have been different, I suppose, if they'd had more children?'

'Ines says Giovanni's still hurting; that it's just his way of showing how he wishes things had been different.'

'You'd think he'd be proud of his son.'

'I think he is but he can't help being upset. His family have had a connection to the villa for generations.'

'And now that's about to change. How do you know all this?'

'Ines told me.'

I know I only have limited Italian but I can't imagine Giovanni and myself discussing these things if we worked together for the rest of our lives. A thought occurs to me.

'Is that why Giovanni was so set against having an assistant? Because he wished it was his son working with him instead?'

'You get there in the end, don't you? A little slow but you get there.'

'And now – please don't tell me he's expecting me to take the place of his son?' I say.

'No, but it's a measure of how much he likes you that he's so happy to have you around.'

'Why, I wonder?'

'Are you fishing for compliments?'

'No, I mean it – it can't have been easy for him.'

'Ines told him to grow up,' she says.

'Are you serious?'

'More or less; plus, she thinks you need looking after – just like me. We're both surrogate children to Giovanni and Ines and it gives them the opportunity to act out their role as parents all over again.'

'I'm a little old to be a surrogate child.'

'They still want to look after you. It might look like all Giovanni wants is a buddy to share a beer with at the end of the day – and he does, I agree – but he also gets to play at being Papa again.'

'And Ines gets to be your mama?'

'It's nice – don't you think? Having people care about you?'

We walk along in the darkness. I can smell the damp of the wood and the sounds are different to those during the day – softer and more muted.

'I worry for anyone who gets to care about me,' I say. 'There always comes a time when I let people down.'

'It's just a theory, Robert; it's just the wine talking. Don't worry – they're nice people, that's all.'

'They are, aren't they?'

As the trodden path of the woods turns into the gravel that surrounds the villa, Maria and I step away from each other.

'You can kiss me,' she says, 'if you like.'

'I'd like to, but I'm not going to.'

'You don't want to?' she asks.

'Of course I want to, but I don't think I should.'

'You don't like me in that way?'

'I just don't think it's a good idea. You don't know me and I'm old enough to be your father.'

'Actually, I think you might be older than my father,' she says and laughs.

'Great.'

'I'd like you to kiss me.'

'Yes, but I don't think you would if you knew everything about me.'

'Isn't that my decision? I'm not a child, you know.'

'No but you seem like one to me,' I say.

'I've wanted you to kiss me since the first time we met.'

'That's why you were shouting at me across the vegetables?'

'I didn't know what else to do.'

'I'm sorry,' I say. 'I can't.'

'It's just a kiss.'

'A kiss is never just a kiss. Things happen and I can't let them happen.'

'They've already happened – for me anyway. I have no choice.'

'You do; you do have a choice. You can turn around and go inside. We've had a beautiful day—'

'Hold me then,' she insists.

'No.'

'You won't even give me a hug?'

'Maria.' I've done my best to avoid this. 'I'm not . . .' I'm not what – not nice? I'm not what I appear to be? If you have a dog, I'll kill your dog?

'I don't care, Robert. I don't care what you've done.'

'But you should care, Maria, or I'll find a way to make you care. I'll find out the best way to hurt you and I'll go ahead and do it.'

'I don't believe you.'

'But you will, if you ever get close to me. That's why I'm not going to kiss you or hold you or hug you.'

'You're wrong, you know. You're wrong about yourself.'

'I don't think so.'

'I'll show you. Not tonight, maybe, but I will show you.'

'No, Maria – you won't.'

I don't hold out for long. How could I? A woman like Maria tells me she wants to be with me – what else am I going to do? A girl like Maria; she's less than half my age, so it's hard to think of her as anything but a child. And her answer to this?

'But Robert – I'm going to die before you do.'

What am I to do? This girl/child/woman has already come to terms with her own death, so who am I to question what she wants? I know enough about her not to underestimate her determination to get whatever that might be. Like choosing Pisa to go to college: an Italian city, away from Naples, with a world-renowned hospital situated right next to the university. Nothing her papa could do or say was going to change her mind.

But still.

'I'm not a virgin, if that's what you're afraid of,' she says.

226

'Oh, Jesus!'

We're together in the library of the villa, after lunch and before siesta.

'That's not really the issue here,' I say.

'But you wondered, right? Not that it was anything to write home about.'

'Please, Maria – stop. Can we just . . . stop a moment?'

She's almost giddy. Last night, after we'd all had dinner together at Giovanni's cottage, I finally relented and hugged her before she went off to her room. It had been such a beautiful day. The food, drink, company and sunshine were enough to make anyone feel good – even me. I put Maria's desire for a kiss down to the wine and the day that we'd had.

When I woke this morning, I was still smiling. There was none of that 'Oh my God, what have I done?' feeling that follows some huge mistake – just a warm feeling of happiness at the thought of the day we'd spent together. The feeling continued as I met up with Giovanni for work and it occurred to me just how happy I'd become with my new life here at the villa. But then at lunch I saw Maria in the refectory and I knew immediately that she was in love with me. That's not a conceit; you always know when someone is in love with you, just as you always know when someone is not.

So now, here in the library, I have to tell her. I have to put her straight about me. It's the young girl who has decided she loves me and I have to make the woman understand – only she sees it coming.

'Don't even begin to suggest that you're not good enough for me.' She stands up, fierce all of a sudden, the sweetness all gone. 'This is my choice and I know what I'm doing. Do you think I'd waste one moment of my life on you if I didn't think we were right for each other?'

She walks out of the library, none too quietly, and I'm grateful there's no one else around. I admire her spirit but still believe she's mistaken. It isn't that I'm not good enough for Maria; it's that I'm not good enough for anyone. I can only get through this life in one way and that's alone.

Daniel is the first person I ask about Maria, partly because I need to do this in English and also because I won't get anything but glowing approval from Giovanni and Ines. I tell Daniel at dinner that I believe Maria has a crush on me.

'You don't say.'

'Is it that obvious?' I ask.

'When did you finally get it?'

'She asked me to kiss her last night.'

'And did you?'

'No, but that doesn't seem to have put her off.'

'Why would you want to put her off?' he asks.

'Do you not think it a little inappropriate?'

'You mean the age thing?'

'Yes, I mean the age thing,' I say.

'She's not a child.'

'That's exactly what Maria says.'

'And she's right. If she's okay with it, what's the problem? You have to respect her choice.'

'I'm flattered, but—'

'Do yourself a favour and don't tell her you're flattered. That'd be the end of it right there. Unless that's what you want, of course.'

He waves across at a small group of visiting dignitaries

228

waiting by the entrance to the refectory and points to a spare table where they can all sit together.

'I don't know what I want,' I say. 'I'm surprised more than anything.'

'You didn't see this coming?'

'And you did?' I ask.

'I did, and so did just about everybody else at the Villa San Marco. There are a few guests who might not yet know but they only arrived today. We all think you're perfect for each other.'

'Why?'

'Er, mainly because she's crazy about you and she's gorgeous. Did you really have no idea?'

'I never even considered it a possibility.'

'Because she's so gorgeous? Or because she's so sick?'

'Because of who I am,' I say.

'What does that mean?'

'It means I'm not a suitable person for her.'

'Again – what does that mean? If she thinks you're suitable, then you are.'

'She doesn't know me.'

'She wants to get to know you and that's a start. But then this isn't really about her, is it? It's about you and your inability to forgive yourself.'

'I know I'm poison when it comes to relationships, if that's what you're getting at.'

'That's exactly what I'm getting at,' he says. 'Good things can happen to bad people, you know.'

'I'm not sure how to take that.'

'You know what the saddest thing about this is? Asking a man who's studying for the priesthood for advice on relationships.'

'I thought you were trained in that sort of thing? Besides, there aren't too many people around here to ask.'

'Well, as you're asking, here's what I recommend: go for it.'

'Go for it – that's it?'

'What more do you want? It's a no-brainer. My only reservation is that she really is quite ill. I don't see any happy endings where Maria is concerned and no one would think badly of you if you were to say it's too much to take on. But she's a beautiful woman and she likes you. You've had a tough few years and you deserve a break, so take it. You've been hurt in the past, so here's to looking to the future. How many more self-help clichés do you need?'

The next day, I don't see Maria in the refectory at breakfast and I don't see her at lunchtime either. I wait for longer than usual in the library before my siesta, long enough for it to feel as though she's now deliberately avoiding me. I can't begin to guess if this might be through embarrassment or annoyance – there's no telling with Maria – but I do know I need to talk to her. The problem is, I'm still not sure what it is I have to say. I don't want to fall out with her, but I've no control over that Italian temperament. I'm at a loss as to how to play this – clueless, in fact. A girl like Maria doesn't come along every day.

I'm about to leave the library when Ines comes in.

'Robert,' she beckons in a loud stage whisper, unused to the surroundings of the library. 'Come with me. Maria – yes?'

It had occurred to me to ask Ines if she knew where Maria might be, but I was giving it until this evening.

'She's sick,' Ines says, but I haven't heard any ambulance sirens and I'm sure Giovanni would have told me if Maria was back at the hospital. I follow Ines out of the library. She doesn't seem too distressed. She sets her mouth shut, shakes her head and shrugs but that's about it – an expression I take to mean 'here we go again'. She leads me to the opposite side of the villa, where I know the female members of staff have their sleeping quarters. It's as far away from the monks' cells as it is possible to be and I wonder if I'm allowed to be here.

'It's okay – yes?' I ask Ines. My reverting to simple Italian because I'm alone with Ines irritates me, so I ask the question again, properly. 'Is it okay for me to be here?'

'Bah!' she says, which I guess means we don't need to worry what anyone might think. 'Maria was asking to see you.'

'Is she very sick?'

'No – yes – no, not like last time. But she's weak – not strong?' she asks, making sure I understand her correctly.

The female quarters are like a purpose-built replica of the monks' cell dormitory – small rooms running along either side of a long corridor. It's not quite so spartan, however, and has quite a homely feel. There are one or two members of staff about and they're surprised to see me but my being accompanied by Ines makes my presence here acceptable.

Ines stops at one of the doorways and ushers me inside. Maria is lying in one of the two single beds and she smiles when she sees it's me.

'Hello handsome,' she says, and promptly starts coughing. Ines goes over to the bed but there's little she can do but hover and wait for Maria to stop coughing. There's a bowl for Maria to use on the bedside cabinet but she brings up nothing she can spit out. I've never heard a cough like it before – a dry rattle that runs through Maria's whole body, with something solid in her chest that you just know is never going to budge. The coughing is followed by a minute or so of heavy wheezing as Maria tries to regain her breath. Ines wipes Maria's forehead with a damp cloth and passes her first a nebulizer and then a glass of water.

I feel like I shouldn't be here. From what I know of Maria's illness she can easily pick up infections from other people just by being in the same room. Come to that, I don't think *Maria* should be here; she should be in an isolation ward at the hospital.

Ines straightens up, replaces the glass on the bedside table and asks me to rinse the cloth in the washbasin.

'I'll let them know you're here,' she says to me, 'and I'll be back to collect you at about four so you can get back to work. And you,' she says to Maria, 'softly, softly,' just as Giovanni said to me when showing me how to use his lathe down at the workshop.

There's a chair at the desk, so I wheel it over to sit beside the bed. The room is kitted out like a student residency and I wonder if it's actually used in this way at other times of the year, away from the summer holiday season.

'Have you a room-mate?' I ask and Maria shakes her head.

'No,' she says, 'just me.'

This makes sense if Maria's so prone to infection. It's another measure of how far they're prepared to accommodate oddities such as Maria and myself at the villa.

'Am I a danger to you, being here?'

Again, she shakes her head. I guess I'll be doing most of the talking here, given Maria's performance when I first came in.

'Shouldn't you be in hospital?'

She's lying on her side, facing me, and she lifts her head slightly to wipe some drool away from the side of her mouth.

'It's not so bad,' she whispers, and eases her head back into her pillow. It might not be so bad but it doesn't look too good either. This thought must be obvious on my face because Maria smiles. 'Honest,' she says.

I wonder if I did this to her when she got agitated at me in the library, but then I remember her saying it's never just the one thing. Our argument can't have helped, though.

'If I take it easy today and tomorrow,' she says, 'I should be okay.'

She looks weak and sleepy and so very different from her normal vivacious self. I suspect the Maria persona is something of a front, or perhaps it's her determination to live life to the full whenever she's able. I see her now, drifting off to sleep, but then she snaps open her eyes in alarm to make sure I'm still here.

'It's okay – go to sleep.'

'Will you stay?'

'Of course; until Ines comes back.'

'What about later – and tomorrow?'

'I'll be here as much as I'm allowed to be,' I say. There must come a point in the evening when they won't tolerate me being in this part of the villa.

Maria slips a hand out from under the bedclothes and I take it into my own. In the end, it's that simple. How could I not love her?

There are enough books and A4 folders of notes on Maria's desk for it to be obvious she's serious about her studies. I reach across and take a look, still holding on to Maria's hand. The notes are handwritten in Italian so they're hard to make out. I look around the room: the open wardrobe is full of kitchen uniforms and Maria-type white dresses; lots of toiletries around the sink; medicines and novels on the bedside cabinet. One of the novels is written by me. This should be disquieting, only it's not. I should be bored, just sitting by the side of her bed, only I'm not. I think about Maria making up her mind about me without my even knowing it. I think about her white dresses and how their simplicity contrasts with the medical mess going on inside her.

Maria is still fast asleep and doesn't stir when Ines returns soon after four. Ines suggests I go and see Giovanni to tell him what's happening – that I'm to return here so Ines can go to work in an hour's time.

'Tell him I say this is what must happen,' she says. I can't imagine Giovanni objecting and he certainly won't go against Ines. 'Maria has to eat and take her medication, so I shall bring her some food when I finish at the refectory.'

I ask Ines to bring me some food too – so I can eat here with Maria.

'Will she be okay?' I ask.

'If she eats and sleeps well tonight, she should be okay tomorrow. If not, it's the hospital again.'

Something occurs to me.

'You sleep here, don't you, when she's sick?'

'I do. Now, go; tell my husband what he needs to know.'

Giovanni's easy to find and already seems to have guessed what the arrangements for the evening are to be.

'How is she?'

I tell him Maria looks very sick to me, but that she and Ines seem to believe it's not too bad.

'This is how it is,' Giovanni says, the philosopher. He tells me to forget about work and to freshen up in my own room for a while before I go back in to Ines and Maria. The biggest deal for Giovanni seems to be that I've missed out on my siesta.

I go back to my cell but there's nothing I need to do except maybe splash my face with water. I can't stop to think about what I'm getting into here – what I'm already deep into – but it does occur to me that I'm no longer more dead than alive.

Maria is still sleeping when I get back to her room, so Ines slips out and leaves us alone together again. As she shuts the door behind her, I jump up and open the door again. I call quietly after her down the corridor.

'Ines, are you sure this is okay – me being here?' Although most of the female employees that live in at the villa are still at work, they're likely to start drifting back to their rooms at some point this evening.

Ines shrugs and smiles.

'They all know, Robert. Everybody knows.'

Maria is awake and smiling when I go back into her room.

'Will you be safe,' she asks, 'among all these women?'

I sit back down on the chair beside Maria and hold her hand again.

'I'm trying to figure out if Ines means that the people in charge of the villa know I'm here . . . or that everyone along this corridor knows why I'm here.'

'Both, I guess,' Maria says, but she pays the price of talking with another coughing fit. I copy what Ines did earlier with the cloth and I hold the glass of water for Maria to take a few sips. She looks all in.

'Lie back,' I say. I can see her mind is working overtime and under different circumstances there are a thousand things

235

she might be coming out with right now, but the effort is too exhausting. 'It's okay to sleep.'

I tell Maria what Ines plans to do this evening but she dozes off again as I speak. The sound of her breathing is disturbing but it's a relief that she's calm enough to sleep.

Ines comes in later with two plates of food wrapped in silver foil on a tray. I wheel the chair away so Ines can get to Maria. She passes me the tray of food and I leave it to one side on the desk. Ines has no qualms about waking Maria and I watch as she helps Maria sit up in bed, pours her some fresh water, and hands her some tablets. Maria doesn't object, as though she knows this is what she has to do. Ines shows me the packet of tablets and says something I don't understand.

'Enzymes,' translates Maria. 'To help digest the food.'

Ines gives Maria a stern look for talking, but I can see her heart isn't in it. She looks well used to having to deal with this particular patient.

'Now, eat,' she says to the two of us.

I take my own plate and pass the tray over to Ines, who positions it on Maria's lap. She's brought us a bowl of pasta with what looks like a sausage and bean sauce – easy food to manage away from the table. Ines tells me to make sure Maria eats it all.

'After,' she says, 'Maria takes two of these.' She holds up a second packet of tablets and two fingers of her free hand. 'And then – sleep. I'll be back between eight and nine this evening. Is this okay?' I must look nervous or something. 'If you need me, you come down to the cottage.'

'No, I'll be fine,' I say, although the cottage seems quite a distance in any kind of an emergency. Ines leans in to kiss Maria on the forehead. Maria closes her eyes in appreciation;

she doesn't say thank you but it's obvious she doesn't need to. Ines tries out her stern look on me, tells me not to forget the tablets, and leaves the two of us alone.

'Antibiotics,' Maria says. 'You're learning all my secrets.'

'Eat,' I say. 'Don't speak.' Already I've learnt this much.

It's quiet, though, with just the noise of the two of us eating, and it's not much of a first date. I try to ask Maria questions she can answer with a nod or a shake of her head. Is this really not such a bad episode? *Yes*. Does Ines often have to stay the night? *No*. Is this Maria's normal medication? *Yes*. Will she sleep through the night? *Yes*. Is she going to dye her hair blonde again? *No*. Will she let her parents know she's been sick again? *No*. Does she get scared? *Yes*.

I take the tray away once Maria's finished her plate of pasta.

'Are you ready for these now?' I ask, holding up the tablets.

'Please.'

I take out two tablets, hand them to Maria, and hold the glass of water for her as she drinks to swallow them. There's a second glass over by the sink, so I pour myself some water from the bottle at the bedside.

'Will this be enough water for the whole night?'

'Ines will bring another bottle.'

She looks at me strangely.

'I need to pee – before I go to sleep.'

Great – Ines didn't think about this one. It means a stroll down the corridor to the bathroom. I don't want to insult Maria by asking her if she can walk, but she tells me anyway.

'Don't worry – I can get there myself.'

She pushes back her bedclothes and swings her legs to the floor. She's wearing a long cotton nightdress – white, of course.

'Chaste, huh?' she says.

I stand and hold out my hand to help her out of bed, and then lead her to the door.

'Okay,' she says. 'Wait here. There's only so much I want you to see.'

This is fine by me but I can't help worrying that she's too weak to make it along the corridor on her own. I open the door and step out into the corridor with Maria. There's a girl I recognise from reception at the far end and I call to her before she goes into her room. I ask her if she'll just watch out for Maria as she goes to the bathroom. If she thinks it a strange request, it doesn't show, and I leave the two of them to it. I sit back down in Maria's bedroom.

'Thank you,' Maria says when she gets back to the room. She heads straight for the bed and lies down. I pull the bedclothes up to her shoulder, but she takes out her arm so I can hold her hand.

'I washed my hands,' she says, and smiles. Her breathing sounds easier and it doesn't seem like she'll have a coughing fit every time she tries to speak. 'I'll probably fall asleep now.'

'Well, I'll be here until Ines gets back.'

'You don't mind?'

'No,' I say.

'You'll be bored.'

'I can read one of your books. Go to sleep.'

'You're not mad at me?' she asks.

'No – go to sleep, and get well.'

'You can listen to my iPod if you like,' she says and laughs at the blank look on my face. 'My music? Here, I'll show you.'

'No, go to sleep,' I repeat.

I lean over and kiss Maria's forehead in the way I saw Ines

do earlier. There's a slight sheen of sweat on her face so I wipe it gently with the cloth. She's already asleep. I cover her again with the bedclothes and sit back in the chair. I watch her sleep and it doesn't feel wrong. She wheezes, pretty much as I heard her wheeze that first time she was reaching for a book in the library.

Watching Maria, I'm anything but bored. Whatever troubles I might have had are nothing compared to what Maria has to live with each and every day. I think about the support provided by Ines and Giovanni and how they've taken it upon themselves to look after myself and Maria – the latest in a succession of people who are determined to see me well.

I scroll through the list of albums on Maria's iPod. Most of the names mean nothing to me and I guess this is how it should be for a woman of Maria's age. A Morrissey album surprises me, whereas Blondie's *Greatest Hits* doesn't for some reason. I check and all of Siobhan's early albums are there. I don't know what to think about this except that Siobhan's songs always did mean a lot to young women in their twenties. I select *Best of Bowie* but even the gentle opening bars of 'Space Oddity' put me in mind of Eminem's 'Kim' being blasted repeatedly into my cell. It's so disturbing I take the headphones out of my ears.

I wait a few minutes before listening again, telling myself this will be okay; it's just David Bowie, singing songs from a happier time, from a different lifetime, it seems. I'm not going to let them take that away from me. I click the play button again and put the headphones back in my ears.

If only I'd known: to feel like a human being again, all I had to do was listen to music.

When I turn up for work the next morning, Giovanni tells me to forget the gardens and spend the day with Maria. Maria is sitting up in bed and looking much improved. She's had a wash and brushed her hair. I've a feeling Ines has helped Maria freshen up, though she's also left strict instructions for Maria to stay in bed for the whole day.

I try to explain to Maria how the music made me feel last night, but I don't have the words.

'I've made such a mess of my life,' I tell her.

She gives me a look that makes her seem older than her years.

'It's not too late to put that right,' she says.

'The odds are I'm likely to fuck it up all over again.'

'You can't help the things that have happened to you.'

'It's the things that I've done rather than the things that have been done to me,' I say. 'Things I regret.'

I don't know how much Maria knows about me, and I don't know how much I want her to know. I know she's googled me but how much would that tell her? That I lived with Siobhan? That I as good as sold my daughter? What I did to Max and Juliette? It feels like full disclosure time, whatever that might mean. I don't want her to underestimate what she's dealing with here, and I need her to realise that I'm someone who can do her harm.

'What I do – what I've done in the past – seems to be out of all proportion. And out of control. I think I lose my mind.'

'Everybody feels like that at some time in their lives.'

'But I can't remember what ... the thought processes ... I can't recall the thought processes I go through to make me act in that way.'

'Do you have to?' she asks.

'I think I do, if I want to stop the same from happening again.'

'If it's that important, why not write it all down?'

'What good would that do?' I say.

'Write it out in Italian and I can correct your homework each evening.'

'This isn't a joke, you know.'

'Who's joking? It'll improve your Italian and get you writing again.'

I hesitate, but only for a second.

'There was a girl in Brighton,' I say. 'I've tried to forget her name – because I'm so ashamed – but she's important because you remind me of her in some way. You're a similar age, I guess, and so trusting – she had the same misplaced trust in me. I deliberately created that trust in her, from nothing, so she'd fall in love with me. I wanted her to fall in love with me so I could get to her sister – so I could find a way of hurting her sister. The only reason I can think of for this is that her sister – whose name I try to forget as well – had what looked like a perfect family and I wanted to break up that family. By the time I realised what I really wanted – that I might have had a shot at living a normal life – it was too late because I was arrested and the police must have told her that everything she thought she knew about me was a pack of lies. When I got out of prison, the woman who'd worked so hard to get me released – I remember her name, it was Juliette – she eventually fell in love with me too. And for a reason I can't explain, I killed her dog. I slit her dog's throat with a cut-throat razor. Max – that was her dog's name. I loved Juliette and I loved Max and they loved me, so I don't understand why I did that. I wish I hadn't. I haven't found a way yet to hurt my friend Daniel for helping me out and bringing me here, but no doubt I will. And Giovanni, and Ines, and you – I'll get around to you all in the end.'

Maria's crying.

'See – that's what words can do for you,' I say.

'I'm not crying because of your words. I'm not crying because of what you've done but because of what's been done to you.'

'Anything that's been done to me, I more than had coming.'

'You miss your baby girl, that's all. You miss your baby girl.'

Maria mentioning Ciara hits me hard.

'I gave my baby girl away,' I say.

See what I can do? My words can make Maria cry. She doesn't need this, today or any other day. She needs rest and love and care. She needs to get better, even if she'll never be well again, and all I do is to make her cry. I'm tempted to leave her room – for her sake, not mine – only I suspect that might hurt her even more. I'm poison and I haven't even got started yet – these are just the words.

I sit and stare without really seeing: the things on Maria's desk, maybe, or my work shoes that I took off when I came into Maria's room this morning. I should be in my own cell. I should be in a real cell. I curse Juliette for having got me out, and Daniel for having brought me here. Things are so much simpler when there's just a regular routine of twenty-three hours in your cell and one in the yard. Is this what Daniel hoped for – that I should carry on from where I left off, fucking up everything and everybody? I doubt it somehow.

'I know all those things about you,' Maria says.

She's lying on her side, with her hands beneath her cheek on the pillow, palms together.

'Things you read on the internet – you think that's really getting to know someone?' I say.

'I'm not saying that. I know those things about you, those

242

things that you've done. You don't have to go through all that for my sake – to shock me into disliking you. I can tell you the names of those girls, if you like – would it make a difference? It might – to you, I guess. Laura and Paula – there you go. Get it down on paper and then throw it away. What use is it? Everybody knows you're sorry for what you did; everybody that counts, that is. You can talk to me about it all day long if that's what you want. Or talk about it whenever you feel the need to – I don't care – but I do care about you. I know that I want to be with you and for you to want to be with me.'

'Why, when you know what you know about me and I'm here telling you I might well do the same thing again?'

'Well, I have to believe you won't—'

'You see – that's it right there. I know I'll mess up again – mess up big time – and yet you choose to believe otherwise.'

'I'm not the only one: Giovanni and Ines know all about you and they still believe in you, and Brother Daniel.'

I drop my head in shame at the thought of Giovanni and Ines knowing what I've done, but then, what did I expect?

'None of you can know everything about me.'

'Sorry, yes – you're right. I meant we all know certain things about you – the things you've done and the things that have happened to you – and still we believe in you.'

'That doesn't make sense.'

'No, but it's our choice. It's my choice.'

'Believers,' I say, quietly – too quietly for Maria to hear. She lifts her head off the pillow and looks up for me to repeat what I said.

'Daniel,' I explain. 'Brother Daniel – he has faith. He might have certain issues with the Church but he has faith – and I don't.'

243

'You don't have to believe in God to believe in a person. Do you think I believe in some entity that has done this to me? And if that God did exist, do you think I'd want anything from him but to see him suffer in pain for making me the way I am? He can hang on his cross for all I care. But I can choose to believe in other things, other beings – human beings. I also believe it's worth my while fighting for the right to study in Pisa, even though it means falling out with Papa; even if there's every chance I won't live to finish the course. And when you turned up at the villa – when I learnt who you are and the shitload of grief that you carry along with you, all that fucking history you drag around wherever you go – how come something in me told me I wanted to be with you? I don't need any extra trouble in my life but I made a choice, and that choice was to believe in you.'

'Again – why?'

'Because life's too short; my life's too short.' She waits a second or two before adding, with a sly grin, 'Plus, I have to admit, there's something about you having lived with Siobhan McGovern. I wanted to know what it would feel like to be with one of her old boyfriends.'

I ask Maria what the arrangement is today for her medication. She tells me Ines is going to stop by again with some lunch, after which it's the usual routine of enzymes, food and antibiotics.

'And then I might well get sleepy again.'

'Explain to me again about the food.'

'My body can't break down the goodness in the food I eat, so that's what the enzymes are for.'

'And are there specific foods you should be sticking to?'

'All the foods that are good for you but, really, I just need to eat lots of everything.'

244

'And that gets tiresome?'

'Now and then, like when you can't taste the food for all the mucus. It helps if you have someone like Ines watching your diet. I'm going to miss her care and attention when I move to Pisa.'

'You'll have to shop and cook for yourself?'

'Yes, and that's Papa's big concern about my being there alone.'

'Because he's seen what happens when you don't eat properly?'

'There's been the odd occasion when I use not eating as a way of hitting back – though it's always me that ends up paying the price.'

'Hitting back at your papa?'

'At Papa, at being like this – everything and nothing at all.'

'Tell me about your chest,' I say and then blush. 'Your lungs, I mean.'

'I thought you'd never ask.'

'You know what I mean.'

'My lungs are the main event. My body creates too much mucus and it just sits there in my lungs and pancreas, affecting my digestive system. It's never good but once it becomes infected I take a turn for the worse.'

'And that's what the antibiotics are for?'

'Yes.'

'And there's no cure?'

'Not yet. They'll probably wait until I'm dead.'

'Stop – don't say that.'

'I'm serious – we don't tend to hang around.' She lets this comment hang around, though. 'Not much of a come-on for the boys, is it?'

245

'What will happen?'

'As in – what does the future hold for me? A lung transplant possibly, if I'm lucky and they find a suitable donor, followed by an early death.'

'And there's nothing they can do about it?'

'There's plenty but most of it adds up to fresh air and exercise.' Maria's flippancy is obviously her get-out clause, her safety net and self-protection. She sees this doesn't work for me and so gives me a fuller explanation. 'There are lots of exercises I can be doing, and physiotherapy – Pisa will be good for all that because the facilities at the hospital are so good. Running up and down stairs is perfect, particularly up the stairs – anything to get that mucus moving – and there's a special vest they've invented that constantly jogs your lungs, only I've yet to try it out. I believe it's only available in the States but they might have one in Pisa by the time I get there. In fact, you can make yourself useful and give me a massage.'

Maria flips her body over on to her other side, with her back facing me. She pulls the bedclothes down away from her and wraps her arms around her body so she can show me what to do. She moves her hands in a circular motion up and down her side, underneath her arms and round towards her breasts.

'You've got to be kidding me,' I say.

She turns round and smiles, the mood in the room lightened.

'I can show you the leaflet with the instructions, if you don't believe me.'

I get down on to my knees so I'm at a better angle.

'Here,' she says and she guides my hand to her right side. Just to touch her through her cotton nightdress is enough to know exactly what she's up to, and enough to know she's got me good. She moves my hand along her side and of course

246

I can feel her breasts with my fingertips with each motion of my hand.

'You have to press firmly with your fingers – not too hard, but firmly enough to get that mucus moving inside me. And here.' She shows me her other hand underneath her body. 'On this side too, at the same time, so you're really manipulating my lungs.'

I know which of us is doing the manipulating here, but I'm not complaining. I get into a steady rhythm and feel the give in Maria's body. I do this for about ten minutes, until my hands and fingers begin to cramp.

She looks back at me over her shoulder.

'It's a dirty job, isn't it?' I pull away and she turns to face me. 'What do you think – are you interested, on a trial basis, maybe? There are perks.' She reaches for my right hand and holds it between her own and to her breasts. Nothing I have can hold out against her.

I know Ines senses the change in the room when she arrives after her lunchtime shift. One look from Maria to me and back to Maria is enough for her to know. She's brought food for me too, but asks if I'd prefer her to stay with Maria while I get some rest. I tell her I'm fine.

'You're fine too?' she asks Maria.

'Much better, thanks.'

'Yes, I see. Work tomorrow, I think – yes?'

Maria does a mock pout and Ines puts on her stern face. The mood in the room is so much lighter than the day before – relief, I guess, that Maria's not heading back to the hospital. Ines reminds me about Maria's tablets, as though it's still my responsibility, and says she'll be back again this evening. Maria and I eat our lunch – soup in mugs and salami and

247

cheese on ciabatta – and Maria takes her tablets. I clear the tray away and leave it to the side on the desk.

'Will you sleep now?' I ask her.

'Maybe – you don't mind?'

'No.'

Hours, days, weeks and months alone in a cell much smaller than this room have left me perfectly equipped to handle stillness and quiet. Compared to solitary confinement, there's a riot going on here.

'Lock the door,' Maria says.

I do so and when I turn round she's pushed back against the wall to make space for me on the bed.

'Lie down,' she says.

I can see where her nightdress has climbed up her thigh.

'You won't get much sleep with me in there.'

'We can rest – please?'

I lie on my side, fully clothed, with Maria curled up behind me. It's a narrow bed, probably designed to deter this very thing from happening, but I do rest and I hear Maria's breathing steady into a deep sleep. Of course, I feel her breasts pressed into my back and they give me plenty to think about. Her bare knees are curled into the backs of my thighs and her left arm is wrapped around my chest.

So this is it, I think. *This is how it happens, once again.*

I must doze for a while, because I wake up with the knowledge that Maria is awake behind me. Her breathing is different and she moves her hand from my chest to my shoulder and through my hair.

'I feel like an old man,' I say.

'You're an older man,' she says, 'but you're not old.'

248

When she says this, I hear the echo of Siobhan saying just about the same thing to me and it's disturbing. Years gone, and I'm all those years older. Maria shares Siobhan's vulnerability, and I wonder what that says about me.

I don't want to repeat any part of my life, particularly the part with Siobhan, and I don't want my whole life to have been given over to the fact that I once lived with her; but of course it's not – it's given over to the fact of Ciara.

'I feel old, a lot of the time,' I say.

'You seem to be getting better, living here and working outside with Giovanni.'

'That's true.'

'What you need is a younger woman,' she says.

'Have you anyone in mind?'

'Perhaps – only you'll have to buck up your ideas. Raise your game a little.'

I sit up at the side of the bed and look down at Maria. She flops onto her back. I pour some water for each of us and she leans up on one elbow to drink it. Her nightdress isn't revealing at all, but I'm hyper-aware of her body beneath it. I've a feeling she's hit by a sudden wave of shyness, so I look away.

'All those things,' I tell her. 'All my issues – I don't want you to think we can ignore them or hide them away. I think I've got real problems, and I don't want them to become your problems.'

'My issues too,' she says. 'It's pointless us being together if you can't accept that I won't live forever. And that's not something I want to dump on just anybody.'

'I read about the life expectancy of people with cystic fibrosis. It doesn't look good.'

249

'So,' she says, and laughs, 'you've been checking up on the internet too? It varies from country to country but yes, I'll be lucky to see thirty.'

'Shit.'

'Shit is right. On the other hand, it does kind of give you a little focus. If you see someone you like, you tend to act on it.'

'I've noticed.'

'How much have you noticed?'

'I've noticed you have nothing else on apart from that nightdress.'

'Thank Christ for that! I was beginning to wonder.'

I look at Maria again and, for all the bold talk, I can see the shyness is still there. I'd like to reassure her and tell her there's no rush, only I'm not sure how good I'm going to be at taking this slow.

'We have a lot of finding out to do,' I say.

'Yes.'

'And not the things we'd find on the internet.'

'I think you might be wrong about that, but yes – I'd rather we went about this together and not in cyberspace.'

'You want us to be lovers?'

'I think so.' The shyness again. 'Maybe you could start by kissing me?'

'A kiss is never just a kiss, remember?' I say.

'I don't want it to be.'

A kiss is never just a kiss. It lets you know immediately how things are going to be. A kiss can tell you this is going to be about sex and sex only, or it can tell you this is the real deal. It's an odd thing to do – to put your mouth on someone else's mouth – but no stranger than sex. I wonder who first figured it out; how would they have known? Like babies sticking everything in their mouths? Do you have to taste something to really know if you like it? I remember Ciara grabbing whatever she could, and every time it went straight to her mouth to help her understand what it might be – if this was a good thing or not. A lot of that was probably her teething, but so many of her early discoveries were through her mouth.

I stop and realise this is the first time in years that I've thought of Ciara without feeling the bitterness of having lost her. I look down at Maria. I look in her eyes and see she's smiling. I look at her mouth and I know just how much I want her. I know how this kiss is going to feel. I close my eyes and lean down to place my lips on her lips. I rest them there – it's not really a kiss, more just a touching of lips. The closeness is like a shock through my body. I feel exposed, but I know Maria's feeling this way too. I pull away and see she's still smiling.

'You closed your eyes,' she says.

There'll be time for other kisses, I know – proper kisses, open-mouthed and open-eyed kisses – but for now I rest my lips on Maria's once more and I let the feeling flow through my whole body. Maybe we can take it slow after all, because I don't want to miss any of this; this perfection.

Maria surprises me by focussing on my body so much, running her hands along my legs, my back and my arms. I'm not complaining. She tells me it was the first thing she noticed when she saw me working in the gardens with Giovanni. We've just had sex and we're both feeling lazy and a little bit sleepy. We're in my room at siesta time. This has become our one opportunity to get together – to be naked together, that is. It was tolerated that I might be in the girls' corridor while Maria was sick but not once Maria had improved and returned to work. The monks and brothers don't do siesta, so Maria and I switched from meeting after lunch in the library to meeting here in my cell. Neither of us wants to step out of line but, also, we don't want to miss out on our time alone, so we're as discreet as we can be in the circumstances. Things happen between other members of staff – we're not unique – and the monks turn a blind eye so long as it's not rubbed in their faces. They have to make allowances for the villa being run as a tourist destination despite most of the guests using the villa to get closer to God rather than to each other. Maria and I are kind of guests ourselves – in that we've both been given our employment as a favour – and we don't want to behave badly or to appear ungrateful. I'm sure Daniel knows what's going on because he's no fool, yet I'm also sure that Ines would let us know if we ever stepped out of line.

'This here,' Maria says, holding one of my calves, 'this here is prime beef.'

'That there is the result of pacing up and down a cell for twenty-three hours each day.'

She moves her hand and rests it on my cock.

'What was it like?' she asks.

'Being shut up in a cell all day? I focussed on my exercise routine to stop me from going out of my mind.' Maria looks up at me from where her head is resting on my chest. 'Not that it always worked,' I add.

Maria gives me the look. There are often moments like this, when one of us will touch on matters that the other can only imagine, matters that you wouldn't want the other to experience. Maria's acceptance of her life expectancy is one such matter for me; what happened to my head while I was in solitary is one for her. I can't make light of having been inside, but I always try to convince Maria that it wasn't as bad as she imagines it to have been – that in a way it suited me. I think back to the fragile state of my body – and my mind, too, I guess – during the repeated beatings, when they still thought of me as being worth their effort. I try to describe to Maria the relief when they finally left me alone, but she doesn't share my appreciation.

'The exercises helped pass the time,' I explain, 'and pushing myself more each day helped tire me out and get some sleep. I was trying to stop my muscles from wasting away through inactivity.'

'Well, you succeeded,' she says.

She doesn't need to know everything. I'm happy that she likes my body the way it is. It's not such a fine specimen, but I'm relieved to have regained my physical health.

'What about sex?' she asks.

'What about it?'

'I mean, when you were locked up. What did you do about sex?'

'Tried not to think about it? Maybe they gave us something to lower our sex drive, I don't know. There were times when I just couldn't help myself, but I knew it could send me crazy if I gave in to it, so it was back to the exercise routine to wear me out.'

What I don't tell Maria is that most of my energy was spent on trying to stay sane, so much so that I think I must have failed.

'Let's sleep for a while,' I say to Maria but she drags her leg across my body and I slip inside her. Sometimes we're like the

253

dead fucking the soon-to-be dead, but this is what we have together. At other times it's different.

I keep catching Giovanni as he watches me work. If I'm setting the sprinklers and he's away in some other part of the garden, I can sense his stillness, his inactivity, as he stares across at me. When I look up, he doesn't look away. It has nothing to do with my gardening skills. More and more, he's leaving me alone to get on with my chores without explaining how exactly he wants something to be done. No, this is about Maria.

I think he might be having second thoughts about Maria and I getting together. Giovanni and Ines care for the two of us, I know that, but they're bound to care more for Maria. She's the vulnerable one here, the one most likely to be hurt, and I think Giovanni's worried that he may have been wrong about me. There's nothing I can say or do to reassure him, and only time will tell. I don't want to hurt Maria, but who knows how this will pan out?

It's easy being Maria's lover. I don't mean she's a pushover or an easy lay – not easy in that way. I mean I follow my instincts and do the things that feel right, at the times they feel right – things that are good and if they're good and right for me then they must be good and right for Maria too. These are the advantages of age. I talk to her and I ask her: *This feels good to me, does it to you? I want to kiss you here. I want to kiss you there but only if it feels like the right thing for you. I want to see you naked.* We enjoy her nervousness – well, we don't deny it or let it get in the way, but I'm selfish too. She's told me she wants us to be lovers so I'm not about to let this go. I want it all. I want everything. Sure, I care about her but I also want this for me. My self-interest drives me on. I want to be her lover; I want to be the one. I'm as considerate and as gentle as can be, but only so she'll get to the point where she forgets herself, to the point where it has to be me she has inside her. She says I have 'fatherly hands'. Every woman is some man's daughter, every woman has been some man's little girl. If I can't be a father to Ciara, at least I can be the best person possible for Maria. There's a part of me knows this is fucked up but there's Maria's need and there's my need, there's what she wants and there's what I want, and we seem to meet somewhere in the middle.

Don't ask too many questions, I tell myself. She's young and she looks at me in a certain way, in a way I understand without her having to say. She's putting her trust in me, she's trusting me to be inside her, she's trusting me not to hurt her, with my sex, with my words, with my mind, or with my fists. Let's make this nice, she's saying. And I do.

It's not all straightforward. One evening at dinner it's like the day we met, with Maria stropping around the kitchen, shouting and banging dishes and being shouted at in turn by Ines. I realise I can't just walk away, that I'm a part of this now, and if she's making a scene it's because she's sick and because she needs our love, the love of Ines, Giovanni and myself. She needs the understanding of those around her, only she's going the wrong way about getting it. I see the raised eyebrows of some of the staff and the puzzled looks of the few guests in the main dining room and I don't know what to do. I see Ines rest her hand on Maria's arm and speak to her gently. Maria shrugs off the hand and shouts out to the whole room that she's not sick, she knows when she's sick and she knows when she's not sick and she's not sick so please just back off and for once give her some space. Ines steps away and I try to read her expression, but it's hard from where I am in the refectory. If I were to guess, I'd say it's an expression of sadness.

'Did you get all that?' Daniel asks, across from me at the dinner table. 'As in, did you understand everything she said?'

'Loud and clear,' I say.

'I thought she'd been feeling a lot better recently?'

'I thought so too.'

What was I thinking – that because we were lovers Maria would no longer be sick? A few of the staff glance over in my direction, waiting to see what I do. I don't want to inflame the situation, but it looks pretty heartless to just sit at the table and finish my dinner.

'You're going to have to go over there,' Daniel says but, as soon as I start across the refectory floor, Maria sees me coming and turns to bury her head in Ines' shoulder. I can see she's sobbing. Ines wraps her arms around Maria and motions for me to sit back down. This feels a little harsh in front of all the staff, only Ines makes a face as if to say, trust me, this will be okay. It seems a long way from okay to me.

'Oh dear,' Daniel says when I sit back down.

'Oh dear is right.' I push my plate away.

'Ines knows what she's doing.'

'Yes, but do I?'

'Meaning?'

'Meaning, what the fuck am I doing here?'

Daniel looks at me with a hard expression.

'Sorry,' I say but he shrugs off the bad language.

'What are you doing here at the villa, or what are you doing at the villa with Maria?'

'Both, I guess. No, I know what I'm doing at the villa.'

256

'And what's that?'

'Getting well and staying out of trouble – somewhere safe until you figure out what to do with me.'

'And that's it?'

'I'm not ungrateful,' I say.

'I didn't think for one moment that you were, but you just waiting for me to tell you what to do next: don't you think that's something you should be deciding for yourself?'

How can I tell him I don't know how?

'And Giovanni?' he asks.

'What about Giovanni?'

'In your terms: what the fuck are you doing with Giovanni?'

'I work with him. He's my friend. What do you want me to say?'

'Just interested, that's all. So you and Maria are lovers, is that right?'

'Yes.'

'And that just happened?'

Again – I don't understand what Daniel is getting at.

'You just let that happen, without thinking about it, without thinking about the consequences?'

'No, it wasn't like that. You know it wasn't like that. You encouraged me, remember?'

'So, if you thought it through, then you must have known there'd be times like this. You know she's sick and that she gets irrational and irritable and quite irritating, actually. We all know she won't be here for very much longer, but what about you? What will you do when she leaves to go to Pisa? Carry on tending the gardens with Giovanni? Or go live in Pisa with Maria?'

'I don't know.'

'No, so I'm thinking Maria doesn't know either.'

'Don't make out that tonight's outburst was my fault.'

'I'm not; I'm just trying to figure out what it is you think you're at – what both of you are at, for that matter. I encouraged you because I thought you were so well suited and I think I was right – you're perfect for each other. I'd just rather you were perfect for each other elsewhere.'

The evening gets worse. I leave the refectory and consider calling in on Maria, but decide against it. My guess is that Ines is with her, trying to calm her down, and I believe she's doing a better job at it than I ever could. I don't trust my patience. I'm completely out of my depth when it comes to looking after Maria. I think about Ines' reassuring look to tell me I should leave this to her. It makes me feel shut out, and yet I'm not so sure I want to be let in. What on earth was I thinking, getting involved in this way?

I go back to my room, to my cell, and lie down on the bed. I could do with a cigarette, and I curse Giovanni. I smoke two or three a day now, always with Giovanni on a break from work, and here I am – thinking about having a smoke after my dinner. Or a drink; I could do with a drink. I think about walking to Giovanni's. Might Ines have taken Maria down to the cottage? And what was Daniel getting at when he mentioned Giovanni? That I was using him? Giovanni knows what I'm doing at the villa and he understands it won't be forever. I'm not a replacement for his son. I'm living in a place I'll have to leave one day, just as I was in Leitrim with Jack Reilly. I understand this and I'm sure Giovanni does too.

When I left Leitrim I was okay for a while, but then I wasn't okay at all. Christ, I need a cigarette. I try to concentrate on my breathing and to black out the thoughts in my head, of cigarettes and beer, of Maria and Giovanni and Ines and Daniel, of Leitrim and Brighton, of Siobhan and Juliette, of Laura and Paula, of Max, of Ciara – it's no use, but I try.

I listen to Morrissey, having borrowed Maria's iPod. It sounds like he's living in Rome, and I wonder if he's feeling as displaced as I am right now.

There's a knock at my door and Maria comes into my cell. She's still in her work clothes and her face is blotchy from crying. She looks like shit.

'Hey,' she says.

I turn off the music, bring my feet round to the floor and sit on the edge of the bed.

'Sit down,' I say, and Maria sits next to me on the bed.

'I've come to apologise,' she says

'You can't help being sick.'

'That's not what I've come to apologise for.'

I can appreciate why Maria might throw a hissy fit every once in a while, but I don't know how to say this without insulting her. This is the life she's been dealt, so who am I to say what her reaction should be? My problem with what happened in the refectory is all about me.

'I don't know what to do in a situation like that,' I say. 'Whether I should offer to help or leave Ines to it, or what?'

'You don't have to do anything. You're not under any obligation.'

'It doesn't feel like an obligation, more like unknown territory. I don't feel like I'm any use to you, compared to Ines.'

'Ines has had a lot more practice at coping with my tantrums.'

'It isn't the tantrums; it's more about not knowing how to cope with you being so sick.'

'But I'm not sick. I mean, I'm not particularly sick tonight.'

'So what was going on earlier?'

'That's what I've come to apologise for.'

I'm still in foreign territory. Maria might be half my age, but she has baggage I can only imagine. I feel like the junior partner here, but when I turn to look at her she seems so young and scared – too young to be carrying the weight of her sickness around – and I tell her it's okay, whatever she needs to do, however she needs to act to get through the day, is okay with me.

'You won't think so once I say what I came to say,' she says.

'You're about to finish with me?'

This sounds so juvenile. Finish with me? She doesn't need to finish with me; she's leaving for Pisa in a couple of weeks so she can rid herself of me quite easily without a scene. Our relationship has barely started, and I'd understand if this was her choice.

'I think you might be about to finish with me,' she says.

Again, this is relationship talk, and it's been a long time.

'Tell me what you came to say.'

If this is just about the two of us being together, I feel on safer ground. What unnerves me is the whole 'Maria's likely to die' thing.

'When I told you I was on the Pill, I wasn't being entirely honest.'

This is a surprise. We talked a lot about contraception before we started having sex – in great detail, actually – and, as in all things medical, Maria knew exactly what she was at. She told me she was on the Pill, primarily to help regulate her periods.

260

Her menstrual cycle, like so many different parts of her body, is shot to fuck – in this instance by her poor nutrition. So, this is one form of medication her papa doesn't know about. I listened as Maria gave me the low-down on having sex with someone who has cystic fibrosis. I think she was trying to see if it grossed me out, if it would turn me off wanting to be her lover. The antibiotics increase the yeast content in her body, which results in Maria repeatedly suffering from thrush. She often has bad breath, either from a chest infection or from her medication. She might have a coughing fit at any time, particularly during vigorous exercise like sex. And the mucus she produces isn't just in her lungs.

The biggest deal, though, is how prone she is to picking up infection – any infection – so she can't have unprotected sex without a condom. This was fine by me, only I had to tell her I didn't have any condoms on me and that I couldn't imagine being able to buy any at the villa. Maria had an unopened packet of five that we checked the date on. She wanted me to know she had to keep some with her at all times, just in case, and I said this was fine too, that I thought she was right to do so. The only problem was that when we actually got to the condom stage, Maria told me she really didn't want to use a condom; that this was part of the problem of sex for her and anyway, she didn't want to use one with me. What about the risk of infection? I asked, and she said she didn't care and I said she should care but she said no, she really didn't want to, so I said okay, but let's not have sex until we've talked this through.

I told her about the blood and medical tests I'd had in Leitrim. I told her that since then I'd had sex with Juliette – unprotected sex – and that so far as I knew I had no infections or diseases, but who knows what we carry without our knowing? She told me it was as much about cleanliness as about STDs and I said come on, let's just use a condom, but she said no it's my choice, and I said it's my choice too, and so we left it for another day. I read up on it and it seemed to me that not wearing a condom was just not an option; most sites said 'must' rather than 'should'. When I pointed this out to Maria, she told me she wanted to have sex with me but she didn't want to use a condom, and I said I understood, but she was asking me to put her in danger, and she said she was already in danger, so why worry about picking up one more infection?

'Because this might be the one that kills you,' I said.

'I'm going to die anyway,' she replied, which was kind of final. When she saw the effect this had on me, she told me it was a matter of trust and that she trusted me and finally I thought . . . who am I kidding?

But this is different now.

'Why did you tell me you were on the Pill?'

'I was on the Pill. I am on the Pill. Only, when I don't take my medication, I stop taking *all* my medication – including the Pill – so for the past month I can't honestly say I've been on the Pill.'

'So you could get pregnant?'

'It's unlikely but yes, I might.'

'Unlikely?'

'With a menstrual cycle like mine, I don't stand much chance of ever getting pregnant.'

'But you knew what you were doing? When we were having sex, you knew you might get pregnant?'

'I told you – it's unlikely.'

'I lost my daughter. I don't want to lose another.'

'I know – I'm sorry. Ines told me how stupid I've been – and selfish.'

'Is that what all the shouting was about earlier?'

'Yes. She asked me if I had any idea what you'd been through.'

'Forget about me – what if you were to become pregnant?' I ask.

'Then I'd have the baby.'

'What about college?'

Maria shrugs.

'Jesus, Maria!'

'Jesus yourself!' she shouts, and stands up. 'I might not get another chance.'

'What?'

'I might not get another chance,' she repeats.

'Are you saying you were deliberately trying to get pregnant?'

'No, it wasn't like that.'

'How was it then?'

'I don't know. I wouldn't mind, that's all; I wouldn't mind if I did.'

I look at her. If she was anyone else I'd think she was simple and that would be an end to it, and an end to us. But she's not simple; she's a mess, but she's no fool. I'm angry, but not as angry as I'd have thought I might be.

'I can't go through that again. I wish you'd told me.'

'You wouldn't have had sex with me.'

'I'm not your last chance,' I say. 'This isn't even our last chance. We can wait a month before having sex again.'

Even as I say this, I'm conscious of the fact that Maria will have gone to Pisa before that month is through.

'It sometimes feels like my last chance.'

This is one of the saddest things I've ever heard. It's hard to equate what I hear with the beautiful young woman in front of me.

'Do you forgive me?' she asks eventually.

'For not telling me you might get pregnant?'

'Yes.'

'Of course,' I say.

As if I have a choice.

I call on Giovanni at the cottage after work one day and again, it's obvious that something is on his mind. I hear the sound of his lathe in the workshop and, when I open the door, he looks up briefly and acknowledges me with the slightest of salutes from his chisel. He turns back to the piece of wood he's working on, and I hesitate. Even a fool like me can see we've lost the early ease we once had together. Thinking about it, most of that ease was down to Giovanni's geniality and his willingness to take me under his wing. Time at work is fine because we have clear roles and jobs to get done, but it's like he's reconsidering the whole friendship thing and it's a shame.

I decide to leave him at his lathe and I walk around the cottage to the seats on the terrace where we usually drink our aperitifs. I sit and wait for Giovanni to finish with his woodturning and he takes his sweet time – so long that it begins to feel like he's sending a message for me to leave, but I stay.

Giovanni goes directly from the workshop into the cottage and I hear him washing his hands in the bathroom. He knows I'm still here, and I know he knows we need to talk. We either sort this out or my days spent working in the villa gardens are over. He walks out on to the terrace, a bottle of pastis in one hand and two glasses with ice in the other. He pours the drinks, raises his glass and says *salute* but that's all; he puts the glass back down on the table. It's not unusual for us to sit in silence – through necessity when we first met – but this is different. I must have offended him in some way, and I feel sure it's something to do with Maria. I'm a little pissed off about this because Giovanni was all for Maria and I getting together, just as Daniel was, and it's a bit late now for him to be having second thoughts.

'I care about Maria,' I say.

I know this sounds stupid but I can't stand the avoidance any longer. Giovanni looks up, distracted.

'What? Oh – that's good,' he says and takes a sip of his pastis.

'In case you were worried.' I'm determined not to let this go, but Giovanni doesn't react. I watch his attention drift away again. We've shared drinks at this table so many times now and there have been other awkward moments – lots of them – but it's never been like this before.

'What's wrong, Giovanni? Have I done something to offend you?'

He shakes his head.

'No,' he says, but he's not convincing.

'I know there's something wrong – something not right.'

He still doesn't respond.

'You're going to have to tell me,' I say, not knowing what the equivalent of 'spell it out for me' might be in Italian.

Giovanni pours more pastis into both glasses.

'You have a daughter,' he says.

Christ – what has that got to do with anything? I *had* a daughter, I feel like correcting him.

'You have a daughter,' Giovanni says again, 'so I believe you care for Maria.' He takes a sip of pastis and then drains the glass. It's unlike him to knock it back so fast. 'She's very beautiful, yes?'

I presume he means Maria.

'Yes, she's very beautiful.'

'But very sick too; lots of work, I think.'

'Yes – lots of work.' High maintenance, I say to myself in English.

'But worth it.'

'Yes, she's worth it.'

'So you see – I know you care for Maria.'

'What is it then? I need to know if I've done something wrong.'

Just as with the monks and the brothers up at the villa, Maria and I could easily have crossed some behavioural line with Giovanni and Ines without even knowing it. There's a world of difference between them encouraging us to get together and them approving of us fucking like rabbits.

'I think I might offend you,' Giovanni says. I can tell he's deliberately speaking in simple sentences. 'But I have to ask you something.'

'So ask.'

'Do you still miss your daughter?'

This is what he's been building up his courage to ask? This is the reason for the long looks and the silences? I'm not offended; invaded maybe, but not offended.

'I'm sorry,' Giovanni says, 'of course you still miss her. What I mean is does it get any easier? Does it still hurt the same?' He looks down at the ground and then away across the garden. 'Sorry, these are stupid questions.'

266

I see through Giovanni's embarrassment and understand that he's talking about his son and not about my daughter. All this time I thought he was being off with me when really he was just looking for someone to talk to about being a father. Daniel would be proud of me. There was a time when I couldn't get past my anger over losing Ciara, but now all I feel is an overwhelming sadness for Giovanni and his son.

'No, it doesn't get any easier,' I say. 'It changes but it still hurts the same.'

'Is there nothing you can do?'

I don't need to answer this. I don't need to tell Giovanni I know what he's talking about. I don't need to add to his embarrassment. I don't need to tell him I wish I'd fought to keep Ciara. I don't need to tell him I still believe I'd have lost that fight, but that I might have held on to something, some self-respect perhaps, or maybe even some form of access that allowed Ciara to learn who I was as she grew up. I don't need to say I wish I'd done things differently. I don't need to tell Giovanni that for me it's too late, that the best thing I can do for Ciara is to let her go, to let her live her life and hope it's a happy one.

Now, I really need that drink and I too knock back the full glass of pastis. Giovanni's a proud man and I'm not about to ask him to spill his guts. I don't want to know why he and Ines couldn't have any more children, but I'd love to find a way for him to be happier with the son that he has. What is it in Giovanni's head that won't accept his son has to find his own way, especially when the younger Giovanni is doing so well? I want to warn him that if he's not careful the years will get away from him, that one day he'll realise it's too late, but I can't tell Giovanni how to live his life. I think about Maria's

267

father – how he must know he doesn't have the luxury of time and yet still he remains pig-headed about his daughter. I'd like to be able to tell them both: do whatever you can, whenever you can, not to lose your child. I'd like to be the example for them not to follow.

'I was a good father,' I say, and Giovanni smiles.

'Well, that's something at least.'

'Only, it came to an end.'

'Yes.'

We sit for a while in silence – companionable silence now, until it's time for me return to the villa for my dinner.

'Do you mind if I ask you a question before I leave?'

'Yes, of course,' Giovanni says, though I can hear the unease in his reply.

'Is that your son's motorbike in the workshop?'

'It is, yes.'

'And is it in working condition?'

'It hasn't been used for a long time, but there's no reason why it shouldn't still work.'

'Do you think he'd mind if I cleaned it up?'

'I think he'd be happy if you did – me too. Ines keeps on at me to get rid of it, but it's my son's bike so it's his decision.' Giovanni laughs. 'Ines never liked him riding it. I was in trouble with her for months for encouraging him, but what can you do? Boys like bikes. She seemed to forget that we did most of our early courting on that motorbike.'

'Will I be in trouble with her if I get it going again?'

'That's a risk you're going to have to take. What do you know about bikes?'

'Nothing, but I'd like to give it a try.'

'It's a good bike,' says Giovanni, 'very manageable for a

268

beginner. In fact, that was why I chose that particular bike, so you'll soon master the gears.'

'Be nice to get out,' I say. 'Maybe I could take Maria out on her day off?'

'I suggest you check with Ines first,' he says. 'Good luck with that.'

When I see Daniel in the refectory, he apologises for being so forthright at dinner the other day. He needn't have worried. I tell him it's refreshing to hear some home truths every now and again – that I kind of miss his attempts to goad me into taking better care of myself. We'll never again be as close as we once were, but I'm grateful for all he's done for me.

'I have a suggestion to make,' he says. 'A way for you to perhaps move on from being Giovanni's assistant in the gardens.'

'What do you have in mind?' I ask.

'That you get in touch with your old publisher.'

'Why would I want to do that?'

'To see if they're interested in the book you're going to write.'

'Which book is that?' I ask.

'It's what you do, isn't it?'

'It's what I did – a long time ago.'

'I think it would be good for you to do so again.'

'Even if I were to write such a book, I can't imagine it would ever get published.'

'I believe otherwise,' he says. 'Actually, I know otherwise. I contacted your publisher and they expressed an interest in seeing what you have written.'

'You've already been in touch with them?'

'With your editor – she's with a different publisher now but she said she'd certainly take a look.'

'You shouldn't have done that,' I say.

'I'll do whatever I think is right for me, as you well know,' Daniel says. 'The issue here is what you intend to do. I'm telling you now that your credit with the villa has run out and that the only reason you're still here is Giovanni.'

'Giovanni?'

'Yes, he insists he's getting old and that he needs an assistant, but the villa won't pay for two gardeners.'

'I don't get paid – you know that.'

'No, but you're staying at the villa for free. You're an anomaly, and the longer you're here the more questions are asked. Plus, you might become politically awkward – particularly if you decide to write a book.'

'I won't be writing any books.'

'Whatever you decide to do,' Daniel says, 'the current set-up is unsustainable. You either take over from Giovanni as the villa gardener – which is unlikely and also has implications for Giovanni and Ines living down at their cottage – or you move on at the end of the summer.'

'Move on to where?'

'That's your decision, but the first thing you have to do is find a way of supporting yourself – hence my suggestion. I'm thinking ahead, even if you aren't.'

What is it with my having once been a writer? Daniel was always fixated on my writing, and now he's at it again. I remember how important it was to Juliette that I write everything down and look how that worked out. And before that – a lifetime ago it seems, Ciara's lifetime at least – there was Siobhan.

270

'Writing doesn't pay that well,' I say.

'It must pay better than what you're on here.'

'Don't bet on it.' I think for a moment about what Daniel is really telling me. 'I need to find somewhere else to live, don't I?'

'Now you're getting it.'

'Have you any suggestions?'

'You're sleeping with her.'

'Maria? You mean for me to live in Pisa with Maria?'

'Of course that's what I mean,' he says. 'Are you really that slow?'

I leave Daniel in the refectory and go looking for Maria, but I can't find her anywhere. I knock at her door and get no reply. A girl I haven't seen before passes by and I ask if she's seen Maria. She shrugs and suggests I try the bar. This is unlikely – staff members aren't supposed to use the guests' bar until after closing – but I try anyway.

I see Javier, the Spanish bellboy, who's doing an extra shift behind the bar. He tells me he hasn't seen Maria. I think about walking down to the cottage, but Ines and Giovanni will be sitting down to dinner. There's a chance Maria might be with them, but I need to see her alone. I walk around the grounds for a while. I see plenty of guests but no Maria, so I take a rest on one of the garden benches. The evening is still warm and it's pleasant just to sit on my own for a while.

It's obvious I haven't thought this through properly, however many hours I spend alone in my room. I should have been looking beyond the chances of getting laid. Something so nice is never for free, but it's kind of hard not to take first and ask questions later. I haven't made any promises Maria

271

can hold me to and, if I'm honest, I was expecting her leaving for Pisa to be an end to what we have together – an end to us. The sex is good but the costings are high and in so many ways Maria is the last thing I need. I can't look after myself, never mind start to care for somebody else.

And, like Juliette, Maria's always pushing me back into my past as if that's where the key to any future might lie. She's clever enough not to mention Ciara directly, but she asks about Daniel and the life I had before I met Siobhan, the life I was making for myself as a writer – like I could go back there somehow and everything would be okay. I know she's only trying to help, but she doesn't. There's no going back anywhere for me. And now it looks as though I have to be moving on again – leaving yet another institution, just as I did Leitrim – and, despite Daniel's best efforts, I'm not equipped to do so. One thing I do know: things will be safer for Maria if I try to make it on my own.

It would be better for everybody if they just let me be. Part of me wants to get myself arrested again. This is what people don't understand: that I prefer a strict routine, the safe knowledge that every day will be the same, with no decisions to make, no personal contact to distract me from the one true path of getting to the end of this life without having suffered or inflicted more pain, of simply waiting to die. It's not that I want to die; it's just that I don't want anything else either.

I need to find another place to be.

I try Maria's room again, but she's not there. I go back to my cell and lie on the bed. I'm half expecting Maria to come and find me here, only I suspect she might also be starting to realise there's no future in whatever we have together

– however brief and enjoyable it has been. I'm not the man for her. I'm not the man for anyone in their right mind.

It's still quite early – about nine – but I close my door and tell myself it's lockdown for the night. I lie on top of the bed covers, still in my clothes, too full of food to exercise, wanting a smoke but not having any cigarettes, thinking of drinking, thinking of the music I'd like to be listening to, thinking of Maria and last hopes, last chances, thinking of Maria instead of Ciara, and then thinking of Ciara and how she's no longer the baby I left behind. Thinking how I wouldn't recognise Ciara even if I were to see her, and how maybe that's a good thing. Thinking how I hope she never learns about me, how this is for the best, the only way it can be, and how I'm no longer sad and angry, only sad and sorry, or just sad, really.

A few hours later there's a knock at my door and when I answer I'm surprised to see Ines rather than Maria. She looks agitated.

'You need to come,' she says, and I guess we have another Maria situation on our hands. There's a pattern here. I follow Ines along the corridor and out into the night air. It's late and the villa grounds are deserted. I hear Ines say something like 'Maria's fuming', but she doesn't hang around to make sure I've understood. I sense for the first time that Ines' patience has a limit.

Instead of heading to the female quarters, she turns into the main guest entrance of the villa and we have to wait for the night porter to let us in. From there we make our way to the bar where many of the younger staff tend to stay on after-hours for a few late drinks. I rarely join them – mainly because of the age difference – though I recognise a few faces and see Maria sitting at the bar with her back to the doorway, still in her overalls from her shift in the kitchen. The room is thick with smoke and as soon as I see this I understand what Ines was trying to tell me: that Maria has been smoking. Her friends should know better, even if they don't fully understand what's wrong with Maria, but I can imagine the mouthful of abuse she'd give to anyone who tried stopping her – the same abuse heading my way, if the sudden silence in the bar is anything to go by.

'Maria,' I say.

She doesn't turn around, but looks at me in the mirror above the bar. She takes a drag on her cigarette and blows the smoke into the air to obscure the reflection.

'Maria,' Ines repeats.

Maria turns on the stool to face Ines.

'Can you not leave me alone for one night?' She's had a lot to drink and she waves the cigarette about in the air, pointing it at Ines and almost catching the hair of the girl sitting on the bar stool next to her.

'Please, Maria,' Ines says.

Maria closes her eyes and then opens them to look up at the ceiling.

'Please, Maria,' she mimics.

This is too much for Ines and she leaves the bar. Maria watches her go and then turns to stare at me.

'What?' she shouts.

I can see that Ines leaving the bar has at least made an impression on Maria, but she's still in a rage. A couple of the staff start up a conversation in an attempt to defuse the tension, while a few others finish off their drinks and call it a night.

'Come on, Maria,' I say. 'Let's go.'

274

Thankfully, Javier helps out by closing the bar. Everybody gets the hint and Maria's treatment of Ines has killed the atmosphere anyway. Everybody loves Ines, and Maria lost the room by turning on her. Nothing I say is going to help, so I stand and wait for Maria. I see her watching me in the mirror, her thoughts all over the place. Eventually, her head drops down and she covers her face in her hands. Javier is still cleaning up and keeping busy, but it's time I got Maria out of here and back to her room. I don't want to provoke her, but if she's about to cry then it'll be better if she doesn't do so here. I step up behind her and put a hand on her shoulder.

'Come on,' I say, 'I'll walk you back to your room.'

I'm expecting a mouthful of abuse but it doesn't materialise. She slips off the bar stool and stands unsteadily against me.

'My bag,' she says.

I pick up her purse from the bar and leave the almost full packet of cigarettes for Javier.

'Is this what you meant by finding a way to hurt me?' asks Maria. She pushes against my chest in an effort to stand on her own.

'No,' I reply, 'this is you hurting yourself.'

Actually, this is the closest thing to a suicide attempt I've ever seen, and I came across quite a few desperate people in that exercise yard. I hold out my hand but Maria pushes it away.

'I'm not some fucking French chick you can just turn on and off, you know.'

She says this in English and there's something about her phrasing that's funny, only it's not really a laughing matter. She switches back to Italian, mumbling something I can't quite hear. I hold out my hand again and this time she takes

275

it. She links my arm and leans in against me and we make our way to the door. I nod my thanks to Javier and he tips the empty glass he's polishing in acknowledgement.

I have to ring the bell for the night porter to come and let us out. We could go through the villa, but I'm hoping the night air might have some beneficial and sobering effect on Maria. She's over the tearful stage and heading towards morose. I want to get her to her room before she collapses.

'Ines must hate me,' she says.

'Ines loves you.'

'But she must hate me.'

This is going nowhere so I concentrate on keeping up a steady pace across the grounds. Even as a drunk there's very little weight in Maria for me to support. When we get to the female quarters it takes an age for her to find her key and I dread having to wake someone up to let us in. Maria then insists on using the key and I have to stand to one side, waiting until she manages to unlock the door.

'Sorry,' she says, as if she's only now aware that she might be trying my patience.

'Will you be okay now?' I ask.

'Aren't you coming in?'

'I'm not allowed. You know I'm not allowed.'

'Please.'

I walk her to her room, half expecting Ines to be inside, only she's not and this isn't lost on Maria. I recognise the oh-so-familiar sensation of alienating those closest to you and I feel for her. Of course Ines is at home with Giovanni; there's only so much a person can be expected to take.

'Do you need the bathroom before you go to sleep?'

The sooner Maria gets to bed the better.

'No.'

She sits down on the edge of her bed.

'Are you going to be sick?'

'No – at least, I don't think so.'

I look around for a bowl, just in case, but there's nothing of much use in the room and I'm not about to go along the corridor to look in the bathroom.

'Have you some tablets you should be taking?'

'No – I took them after dinner.'

I almost ask if she's sure but I let it go.

'Is there anything else you need?' I'm trying to think like Ines and to do what Ines might do in this situation.

'My nebulizer – I'm going to need my nebulizer.' Maria looks up at me when she says this, acknowledging how stupid she was to have been smoking. I can't find the nebulizer but then Maria remembers that this too is in her bag. I reach down to where she dropped her bag on the floor and pass the nebulizer to Maria.

'Will you stay with me?' she asks.

'I can't.'

'Please – for a while.'

'We'll get into trouble.' This sounds feeble, even to me.

'You're going to leave me, aren't you?' We both know she's not talking about leaving her alone in this room tonight. 'At least help me get undressed,' she says when I don't reply.

I know what she's doing but I fall for it anyway. I take off her overalls but not her underwear. I tell her to lie back on the bed, and that she needs to get some sleep.

'Take off my bra,' she says and flips on to her belly. I unclip the bra and take it off around her shoulders. 'Thank you.'

I pull the duvet out from beneath her and tuck her in.

277

'Please stay,' she says.

I kiss her forehead and she smiles, but her smile turns within seconds to tears and then to sobs. Maybe it's the drink, but all of a sudden this is just a baby girl who doesn't want to be left alone. I try to shush her and she calms a little. I pass her a tissue and another tissue and I know I'm going to stay the night, one way or another.

'You can make love to me if you like.'

I tell her it's not about making love or having sex and repeat that she needs to get some sleep.

'I like it when you make love to me.'

'I like it too.'

'I like it when you fuck me.'

'Yes, I like that too.'

'I don't want you to stop.'

'I don't want to stop,' I say.

'But you're going to.'

'I don't know what I'm going to do.'

'No,' Maria says and leaves it at that. She closes her eyes and I think she might be giving in to sleep but after a couple of minutes she looks up at me again. 'You're still here.'

'Yes.'

'You're staying, aren't you?'

'Yes.' I've decided I can sleep in the spare bed – the bed that Ines uses when she sleeps over – and worry about the consequences tomorrow.

'You took pity on me.'

'No.' There's a world of difference between pity and compassion.

'Will you make love to me?'

'No, go to sleep.'

'Not even out of pity? A sympathy fuck?' she asks.

'No. I'm going to wait here until you fall asleep.'

'Will you do something for me – one last thing, and then I promise to go to sleep?'

'What is it?'

'Just put your finger inside me?'

'Maria—'

'I promise – it will help me sleep.'

I don't believe her for one second, but she's true to her word. She lies on her tummy with my hand over her bum and my finger inside her and she goes to sleep.

I see Daniel at breakfast, which is unusual, and I get the feeling he's been waiting to speak to me.

'You made up with Maria then?'

I look at him and it's obvious he knows I spent the night in Maria's room – whether I was in Maria's bed or the spare bed matters little to Daniel. It took me an age to fall asleep, listening to Maria struggling for breath, angry at her for smoking but realising my occasional cigarette with Giovanni probably doesn't help much either.

'Am I in trouble?' I ask Daniel.

'With me, no, but you must realise you can't do a thing in this place without everybody knowing about it.'

'She was sick. And Ines . . . Ines had gone back to the cottage.'

'So you had to stay the night to make sure she was okay?'

'She asked me to so yes, I did.'

'And how is she now?'

'Hung-over; feeling bad about the way she treated Ines.'

Maria looked like shit as I left her room, but how much

279

this was due to drink and how much to the state of her lungs I don't know.

'Does she have work this morning?' Daniel asks.

'It's her day off, which might explain why she had so much to drink.'

'She had so much to drink because she was angry at you.'

'So, again – am I in trouble?'

'You have to find a different place to live, yes.'

'Right away?'

'Soon enough. What did you say to Giovanni?' he asks.

'About?'

'You're fixing up his son's motorbike?'

'Yes, only it doesn't really need any fixing – just a good clean and two new tyres.'

'Giovanni came and asked if I'd arrange for him to make a phone call to his son.'

'Really – he came to you?'

'Exactly – he's not the biggest fan of his employers. He didn't want Ines to know, so he asked to use the phone in the office. I get the feeling this was a first for him.'

'So how did it go?'

'Excruciatingly – at least, that's what the girls on reception told me afterwards. I left him to it and apparently he was shouting so loudly into the receiver that everybody now knows you're fixing up his son's bike – Ines too, probably.'

'Is Ines working today?'

'She left the kitchen when she saw you arrive, so I'd say right now she's letting Maria know exactly what she thinks of her behaviour last night. Plus, Ines has some bad news to pass on: Maria has to leave for Pisa much sooner than she was expecting. An ambulance has been arranged for tomorrow to take her to hospital in Pisa.'

'An ambulance – she's not that sick, is she? I mean, she's more hung-over than anything right now.'

'It'll probably be a car rather than an ambulance, but with a paramedic from the hospital in Rome to drive her up there.'

'Jesus – you guys are ruthless once you make up your minds, aren't you?'

Daniel smiles and shakes his head.

'You give us too much credit, Robert, though in a way you're right: it's Maria's father who has arranged this.'

'She's not going to be happy,' I say.

'Is she ever?'

I look up sharply at this. 'Sorry,' Daniel says, 'that's unfair. She has a lot on her plate for somebody so young. But let's say she's not exactly suited to the service industry.'

'So, what – she leaves tomorrow whether she likes it or not?'

'I don't see that she has much of a choice, do you?'

'She's going to freak.'

'Probably,' Daniel says, 'if her past record is anything to go by.'

'And she'll get so agitated she'll have to be admitted to hospital anyway.'

'Hence the paramedic. I'd say you got more than you bargained for.'

Daniel is too polite to say what we're both thinking – that this is also the ideal opportunity to rid myself of Maria, if that is what I'm hoping to do. If not now, then when?

I take my leave of Daniel and go in search of Giovanni. He's not at the tool shed and there's no sign of him in the gardens.

Recently, it's not unusual for Giovanni to take his sweet time turning up in the morning. I set the sprinklers to run for an hour or so and get to work on the rose bed. I shout *ciao* to Alessandro, the pool guy (who I got to know when an ivy plant grew too close to the water and caused a spread of algae that shut down the pool for two whole days. He wasn't best pleased but how was I to know?). Alessandro's polite enough though, and he raises the vacuum poles he's carrying by way of a greeting.

'Where's the old man?' he shouts, but he doesn't wait for a reply.

In fact, I don't see Giovanni until late in the morning and when I do it's obvious he's not interested in doing any gardening.

'We have the new tyres,' he says, referring to his son's motorbike. 'So – come, come.'

He's impatient for me to leave the roses and follow him down to the cottage. I drop my tools on the ground so, if anyone checks up on me, it'll look as though I've just popped away for a minute or two. Although, if I'm to leave the villa, then what does it really matter?

'I took the bike to the garage in the village to have it looked over,' Giovanni says. 'They fitted new tyres and the mechanic there took it out for a run. I bought the bike from his father so he was happy to see it again.'

'And is everything okay? No problems?'

'Everything is good. He changed the oil and we have a full tank of petrol. We're good to go.'

He says this last sentence in English and he's delighted with himself for having done so. When we get to the cottage, the bike is standing at the end of Giovanni's driveway. It looks like something of a period piece but that's because it is.

'It's a Moto Guzzi Galletto 160,' Giovanni says and looks to see if I understand the full import of what he's telling me – which of course I don't.

'It's a beautiful bike,' I say to appease him, though it has more character than actual beauty. 'Are you the original owner?'

Giovanni misunderstands me and tells me his son owns the bike.

'But did you buy it new?' I ask.

'Yes,' he says. 'This is the bike I was riding when I met Ines.'

'And then you gave it to your son?'

'Yes.' Giovanni shrugs. 'I'm not sure he really wanted it. He wanted a bike, but maybe not this one. He thought it was an old man's bike. I guess he was right, but it's perfect for a beginner.'

Giovanni shows me how the bike has a simple gear system, even though it's actually a moped.

'Italian postmen always used a Galletto,' he says and I realise this is where the bike gets its classic retro look. The leather saddlebags at the side are stiff and scuffed-looking but I can see why Giovanni's left them on, as they add to the bike's authenticity.

'So, jump on,' he says.

Giovanni goes through the starter mechanism and gets me to rev the engine while the bike is still on its stand. The noise and the vibration resound in my stomach. He shows me the brakes, the clutch and the indicators – pretty much in the way he first showed me a rake for clearing the garden beds and also, I guess, in the way he must have shown the younger Giovanni. While he's explaining, Ines walks by without speaking, on her way home from seeing Maria. She's not happy, and I get the feeling she's had just about enough of the three of us – Giovanni, Maria and myself – over the past twenty-four hours.

The look Ines gives Giovanni isn't wasted on him; he must know he's been a fool about his son. He pushes the bike forward off its stand and gestures for me to drive a short distance up and down the road.

'Try,' he says in English.

I do so and I feel the weight of the bike beneath me. I accelerate to keep my balance but stay in the low gear. Giovanni waves me on, shouting for me to change gear. I drive on past him, up the narrow road that leads to the villa, developing a feel for the clutch and the gears before braking and returning to Giovanni.

'Okay?' he asks. Despite Ines, I can see he's delighted to have the bike running again. 'Wait one moment,' he adds, and walks down the driveway to his cottage.

I practise setting off and holding my balance at a slower, walking pace. Giovanni returns with a couple of helmets.

'This is my son's,' he says of the newer helmet of the two. 'This one,' he says, holding up something that looks more like a horse-riding helmet, 'belongs to Ines.'

He straps this second helmet to the leather panniers and points down the hill.

'This road goes down to the village so if you have any problems you can call into the garage and they'll recognise the bike. This way, up the hill, leads to the villa but it's a long way – much further than when we walk through the woods. And when you're finished, you can leave the bike by the workshop.'

In other words, Giovanni is going in to talk to his wife and he doesn't want to be disturbed.

The young Giovanni's helmet is a good fit, even if it's awkward to put on over my glasses. Giovanni helps with the strap beneath my chin. He slaps me on the shoulder and I have to turn my head to see him through the clear plastic visor. I nod to Giovanni in acknowledgement of all he's done for me – specifically with the bike – and set off down the hill.

I take it easy, but when the road levels out I pick up speed and lean into a couple of bends. I'm nervous and it's strange to be so mobile; strange to be so free, too, I guess. I get to the village in less than five minutes without passing another vehicle on the road. I slow down and see the garage, a bar and a goods store. It makes me realise how insular I've been up at the villa, Giovanni and Ines being my only connection to this real world on my doorstep. I see a couple of villagers going about their business, a few cars parked at the side of the road and, before I know it, I've passed through and on down the hillside.

I pick up speed for a while, but have to slow right down as the road becomes steep and twisting, hugging the contours of the woodland. I'm quite alone, though I anticipate other vehicles heading towards me at each turn in the road. The cover of the trees makes it quite dark in places, with occasional flashes of bright sunshine making it hard to adapt to the lack of light. I can hear nothing over the noise of the engine.

As I ride out from under the cover of the trees, I come to a junction and I turn right on to a main road, because it's the easiest choice. The route is still very picturesque but now there's traffic to contend with; I pick up speed to go with the flow. I have a clear view of the lake to my left and I see how the road makes its way down to a lakeside town. When I see cars parked up ahead at a viewing location, I pull over and almost skid on the gravel as I brake to a standstill.

I turn off the engine and park the bike on its stand, take off the helmet and enjoy the view. It reminds me of looking across the lake in Leitrim, though this is on a much grander scale and the lake is a turquoise blue. I think back to the revelation – the gift, it felt like at the time – of being able to pick out the distant individual trees with the new glasses arranged for me by Jack Reilly. It feels strange and I'm almost giddy to be out amongst normal people again – no religious brothers, no jailers – like the freedom of the bike has gone straight to my head.

I decide I've gone far enough for one day. I'm not too keen on negotiating roads that are busy with traffic and besides, I know where I really need to be. I get back on the bike and take care as I cross over to the other side of the road. I make the left turn to get back up to Giovanni's cottage, growing in confidence, and I enjoy the ride back up through the trees. The engine has a strong guttural sound and heads turn to watch as I ride through the village. The bike is very distinctive, so perhaps they're mistaking me for Giovanni's son? I ride on by when I come to Giovanni's cottage and it takes so long to reach the villa that I suspect I may have taken a wrong turn.

Finally, I arrive at a back entrance to the villa grounds, behind the chapel and next to what were once the stables. I kill the noise of the engine and wheel the bike across to what I hope is an inconspicuous spot in the shadow of the chapel walls. The bike feels out of place here at the villa, as though I've brought a piece of the outside world on to hallowed ground.

I take off the helmet and ruffle my hair to cool the sweat on my head.

'Hey,' says Maria, from over by the door to the chapel.

Preoccupied as I was with the bike and building up the nerve to speak to Maria, it's disconcerting for her to appear in this way.

'I heard the bike,' she says by way of an explanation. 'Everybody heard the bike.'

She steps forward and the sun shows the outline of her body beneath her dress. As ever, she knows I'm looking.

'You were in the chapel?' I ask.

'Making my peace with God,' she says. 'Well, with Papa actually.'

'Daniel told me.'

She stands across from me, with the bike between us.

'I guess I only have myself to blame,' she says.

'For last night?'

'For last night; for getting drunk and smoking; for going to pieces all over again.'

'Nobody blames you for losing it every once in a while.'

'No, but I imagine it gets to be quite annoying. Besides, at least this way I get to be in Pisa sooner rather than later – set up with the hospital and such like.'

'I thought you'd be raging.'

Maria shakes her head.

'Just embarrassed,' she says.

'Don't be.'

I reach my hand across the bike but she doesn't take it.

'I wish Ines had shouted at me,' she says. 'Instead of . . .'

I can see Maria's about to cry so I hang the helmet from the handlebar and walk around the bike to hold her.

'Don't,' she says, stepping away. 'Just say what you need to say and let's have done with it.'

Even at this late stage I don't know what it is that I've come here to say. I know what Maria's expecting, but that's not it. I don't want out. The phrase 'for better or for worse' goes through my head and that's a part of it. I scare myself – that's another part of it. I'm scared of my capacity to hurt and Maria is the last person in the world who deserves to be hurt – though, God knows, Laura, Juliette and Max did nothing to deserve it either. I'm scared of not being responsible for my actions. I'm scared of ruining yet another life.

I get back on the bike, unable to articulate these things to Maria – not wanting to articulate them, because she has troubles enough of her own without taking on mine.

'I have to leave the villa too,' I say. 'Not right away but soon, in a week or so.'

'They're throwing you out because you slept in my room last night?'

'I reckon I've outstayed my welcome. My time's up.'

'What will you do?'

'Well, that's what I'm trying to decide. Make a go of it on my own, perhaps, without Daniel to look out for me; without the friendship of Giovanni and Ines.'

'You won't lose their friendship just because you're leaving the villa. I don't feel like I'm losing them and I'm moving all the way to Pisa. Despite my best efforts with Ines,' she adds.

'I've no idea where I should live,' I say. This is what it always comes down to: where on this earth am I meant to be? I've tried wandering aimlessly around Europe and North Africa. I've tried returning to Ireland. I've tried making a new start in Brighton – twice, after a fashion – so what now?

'Italy's still a foreign country to me,' I say to Maria. 'I'm not sure I belong here.'

288

'The world is a foreign country to you,' she says, 'but it doesn't have to be.'

'I want to make a life with you.'

The words are out before I stop them – for better or for worse.

Maria rests a hand on the handlebar of the bike.

'In Pisa?'

'I don't really care where I am, so long as I'm with you.'

'Are you serious? You'd really consider doing that – knowing what you know about me?'

Am I serious? Do I mean it? Or am I just saying this for the want of something to say?

'It's what I know about myself that concerns me,' I say.

'I'll be sick a lot of the time,' she says.

'Then I'd look after you.'

'I'll be too sick for you to look after me.'

'I'll do whatever I can.'

'Why? Why would you choose to do that?'

'Because you're the best chance I've got,' I say.

'I'm not some fucking charity case, you know. There are professional people who can look after me better than you can – and you know that. I'm going to be living next to one of the best hospitals in the world.'

'Yes, I do know – that's not what I meant.' This is coming out all wrong. I feel like I'm the charity case, like I'm the one to be pitied, the one who should be embarrassed and ashamed – the one who is ashamed.

'So tell me what you really mean,' Maria says.

This isn't about Maria being sick. When I look at her, that's not what I see. I want to care for her like I'd care for my own daughter, but I know that isn't the right thing to say either.

I see Maria and I want her – it's that simple and yet it's that complicated because it means engaging with the world, living out in the world, and bad things happen when I'm out in the world.

'Robert.'

Good things too, I tell myself. I think of Laura in Brighton and how close I was to happiness the night before I was arrested. No – how happy I actually was, how happy we were going to be together.

'Robert,' says Maria again.

I look up, but I can't meet her eye.

'Help me up on the bike,' she says.

I show her where to rest her foot so she can swing up on to the seat behind me. She puts her arms around my body and presses her hands to my chest. She inches forward on her bum so her groin is up against the bottom of my back. The inside of her legs are pressed flat along my own and her dress rides high up her bare thighs. She lays her head between my shoulder blades and I feel her breasts push in against me. I hear the harsh rasping breath in her chest and know beyond doubt that this is what I want, that Maria is who I want, and that this is the right thing to do.

Who needs words?

2

The train from Rome to Pisa is disappointingly modern. I have memories of trains with corridors and sliding doors, of whole Sicilian families taking up a single compartment, radiating out with diminishing age from the matriarch in the corner – an ancient woman dressed in layers of black, who overlooked the distribution of a seemingly limitless supply of food and drink for the journey. I remember the lists of destinations on the sides of trains and the knowledge that I could board any one of them and travel to a city on the other side of Europe.

I could take a train and change my life, is what I thought.

It made me feel a part of the continent of Europe. It made me believe this actually is a continent and not just some landmass separated from Asia by the Urals. It was enough just to stand on the platform in some station south of Naples, next to a train that would eventually arrive in Copenhagen, or Berlin, or Gdansk, and be filled with awe and a huge sense of the possibilities of travel.

I'm sure such trains still exist, but not this train and not today. The seats are clearly numbered and it's easy to find my reservation. I leave my bag on the seat to stake my claim and return to Daniel on the platform.

'Everything okay?' he asks.

'Yeah – my name is on a reservation ticket attached to the seat.'

'It looks busy. We were right to book.'

Daniel made the reservation for me. I wish he'd agreed to accompany me to Pisa, but he brushed off the request and asked what age was I to be thinking such a thing. I know it sounds silly but I wish I was heading anywhere but Pisa. There are too many memories. No, not memories – too many reminders of the last time I travelled up to Pisa. Back then, of course, I took mainly local trains to smaller destinations, often to the end of some branch line that meant walking or hitching a ride when it came to moving on again. I did everything to kid myself I wasn't making my way home to Dublin. I may be taking a more direct route today, and there's more than just a cheap Ryanair flight waiting for me at the other end, but the fact that it's Pisa I'm travelling to is unnerving.

I know I have to go. I want to go. I can't remain in hiding at the villa forever. It's time. I want to be with Maria; she's my one hope. She's waiting for me and she'll meet me off the train, like I'm some child. I feel like a child. I feel at the mercy of things I can't control.

'It'll be fine,' Daniel says.

'Yes,' I say, but I lack conviction.

These people that think well of me – Daniel, Giovanni and Ines, and Maria – it's a faith they have. They believe in me. They believe in some inherent goodness, but what if they're wrong? This journey isn't just a repeat trip to Pisa; it's travelling from Leitrim to Juliette in England. I was this close to happiness then too and look what happened. Ask Juliette if she believes in me now.

'She loves you,' Daniel says. 'You do know that, don't you?'

Yes, I know Maria loves me, but Juliette loved me too.

'And you love her, don't you?'

Yes, I love Maria, but I loved Juliette too.

'And she wants to be with you. That's all that's happening here. It's that simple, surely even a retard like you can understand?'

He punches me hard on my arm.

'Priests can't call people retards.'

'I'm not a priest.'

'Almost-priest, then.'

'It'll be okay,' Daniel says.

'She's going to die.'

'We all die.'

'She's going to die *soon*.'

'You don't know that. Besides – all the more reason to be with her now.'

'I'm scared.'

'Of course you are. Not everyone could do what you're doing.'

'That's not what I'm scared of.'

'Well, you should be. But again, Robert – she loves you. As in, she loves *you*. Maybe it's time you learnt to love yourself a little too?'

He takes my hand and we shake goodbye. I hug him.

'Christ,' he says, 'people will think we're gay. Will you please just get on the train?'

Daniel holds up his hand in farewell as the train pulls out of the station. I don't know when I'll see him again. I've promised to come back to see Giovanni and Ines but there's no guarantee Daniel will still be based at the villa. No doubt the Church has plans for him. Whatever – I'm cast free of my almost-priest and I'm out on my own.

There's a family taking over the best part of eight seats just along the carriage from me, two sets of seats on either side of the aisle. I can see and hear that they're American. The parents keep asking their kids to please keep it down – conscious of their American loudness – and they look down the carriage to see if anyone's taking offence but really, they have six kids, so what can they expect? And the kids aren't really that loud; there are just a lot of them, ranging in age from about sixteen down to a toddler. Two teenage girls, three boys between say seven and eleven, and the youngest – the one making all the noise. The mother is like some earth goddess who has managed to have all these kids and not be completely exhausted or ground down with the tedium of parenthood. Apart from her concern about the other passengers, she looks happy. Dad is relaxed and is the focus for most of the toddler's non-stop questions. But the other boys too, they seem to relate easily to their father – showing him a magazine across the aisle and laughing at some puzzle they're trying to figure out between them. The girls are quieter but not sulkily so, and you can see they love their little baby brother. Travelling is never easy, but these guys seem to have it sussed. It can't be cheap, either, to drag such a large group across Italy, so Dad must be on a pretty good wage, but he doesn't look like he's going to be checking in on the office any time soon and he's completely at ease amongst his family. Not every man can say that.

The guy sitting opposite from me has two seats all to himself. His long legs are stretched out below the table between us and he's stubbornly refused to move them. He has a broken arm and struggles to do the smallest thing, like take off his jacket or open a packet of sandwiches. He gives off a strong vibe of determined independence. Some time into the journey, he gets slowly to his feet and I see why he has to take up so much room; he can't bend his legs as they're both in metal callipers. I offer to give him a hand, but he thanks me and tells me he has to try to do it himself. He speaks Italian but I'm guessing he's either German or Dutch. I can see he's in a lot of pain and his movements are so slow it must hurt everyone in the carriage to watch. He reaches up to the luggage rack with his one good arm to hold on for balance as he makes his way towards the bathroom. Each step is a major triumph and I wonder what the hell has happened to him. He looks like he's broken many, many bones in his body. He's a big guy – well over six foot

– and strongly built, but his body has been smashed to pieces. I think about the enormous willpower that it must be taking for him to walk again.

The American family are quiet as he makes his way past. The whole carriage seems in awe of his struggle and I guess – like me – they're thinking we sometimes forget just how lucky we really are. The American toddler asks his dad what's wrong with that man and the earth mother groans in embarrassment. The boys laugh out loud and the teenage girls shush them but the tension has been broken. All the passengers smile; they don't need to speak English to understand. The earth mother catches my eye and shakes her head. We still have to get through the ordeal of the man with the broken body returning to his seat.

The thing is, seeing that family on the train, seeing their happiness and their togetherness, their completeness, and even knowing there'll be days when it's not like this, when there'll be fallings out and nastiness between the kids, but seeing all that love and the successful workings of a nuclear family – it makes me want to find a way to destroy it. I want to do to that family what has been done to that man's body and I don't know why. I still have this in me. And this is the person about to join Maria in Pisa.

She has no idea what it is to be a pariah amongst people I once counted as friends; to be viewed with suspicion by those who at one time trusted me; to be written off as no good, a nothing, a person you wouldn't want in your life. And because Maria is so far from even beginning to accept that this might be true, she cannot comprehend that inevitably this will one day be the way she sees me too. She talks about family, even though she's fallen out with her own father. She cites Daniel as a friend, not understanding how I have strained our friendship at times almost to breaking point. Yes, he forgives me but that's his job; he forgives me my trespasses but they have been many and he knows it. Our friendship is the one relationship in my life that I haven't fucked up in such a way as to be permanently damaged beyond repair, but it's not for lack of trying. So when Maria talks about friendship and family I can't help but think this will all end badly.

There's no denying how much Maria's faith in me helps me through each day. I feel blessed by her love. I feel blessed but unworthy of such a blessing, and this isn't just talk or false modesty. I know that not only am I unworthy of her love and her hopes and her dreams of our future together – however short that future might be – but I also know I will take her faith and her love and her hopes and her dreams and find a way to ruin them. Believe in this, Maria: if you live long enough you will live to regret that you brought me into your life. If I truly cared about you I would get off this train at the next station, before it reaches Pisa, but I won't, and that should tell you all you need to know about me.

There is something in me and it will out.

I try to sleep because my daydreams are more damning than my nightmares but it's no good so I listen to Maria's iPod, switching the play mode to shuffle. I listen to the Dixie Chicks for the first time and their aggressive vulnerability reminds me first of Maria and eventually of Siobhan.

When we reach the outskirts of Pisa, I ask the man with the broken bones if he wants a hand getting off the train or if he'd prefer to look after himself. He says he's okay, as I knew he would. I make my way along the train and wait by the door a couple of carriages down to avoid listening to the American family as they get ready for our arrival in Pisa.

Maria is waiting for me on the platform. She's wearing a white dress, naturally, and this helps me to spot her before she sees me. She looks nervous – or perhaps she's just scanning the crowd and hoping not to miss me – and I take the opportunity to watch her without being seen. The short stay in the hospital appears to have done her some good, though I know enough not to be fooled into thinking everything's okay. Maria doesn't do the miracle cure kind of getting better, only the temporary reprieve.

For what I know won't be the last time, I wonder what I've let myself in for. Only, the answer is there in front of me: even if we'd never met, I'd still pick Maria out of this crowd in Pisa station. I watch other men notice her, other women too, and know they'd never guess at the messy riot going on in her lungs. People look back after passing her by – the men to look at her body and the women to see who she's waiting for. It's me, I want to tell them; she's waiting for me. Unlike the last time I arrived at this station, there's a purpose to my destination and that purpose is Maria.

I called her last night from the villa to confirm the arrival time of my train, though we both understood it was to confirm that I really was coming.

'Is your mama still there?' I asked.

When Maria was admitted to the hospital in Pisa, her mother came over to visit again and part of my apprehension is being seen as too old by her parents.

'No, you're safe – she's gone.'

'You didn't have to dye your hair to get rid of her?'

'No, she was good.'

'Did you tell her about me?'

'I did, and of course she wanted to wait around to meet you. I told her next time.'

'And she was okay with that?'

'I told her I thought you were special, but that I wanted us to get to know each other better before I inflicted my family on you.'

'Did you tell her we'd be living together in one room?'

'No – she doesn't need to know that yet.'

'And do you think she'll tell your papa about me?'

'Probably, yes; he'll find out soon enough, anyway.'

'Does that worry you?' I asked.

'Not especially, not if we're together – does it you?'

'It's all part of the package,' I said.

Maria said nothing to this.

'I like the package,' I added.

Now, Maria sees me and waves, like it's the most natural thing in the world that I should be here. She smiles and looks puzzled when I don't wave back, but when I walk towards her she dodges past the other passengers to meet me and we hug and I feel again how slight she is in my arms but also how strong and how she makes me feel alive and in the present tense, here, now, this is it, this is all there is. We kiss like when we first kissed, lips barely touching and yet close enough together for a current of love to pass between us. Yes, this is it; I have chosen to become a believer, and what I hold here in my arms is what I believe in.

So I live in Pisa with Maria. She's the reason that I'm here.

I shop for dinner each evening and I'm happy to do so. We

use the shared kitchen in our students' residence and food tends to go missing if it's left hanging around. I don't make a fuss, as it's against the house rules for me to be living here and Maria could be reported if anyone felt that way inclined. Other students have lovers stay over but I'm the only non-student who lives in the building on a permanent basis – even when Maria's in the isolation ward at the hospital. Part of our unspoken agreement is that if residents look the other way then I'll be generous with the meals I make for myself and Maria. I tend to buy more pasta and cook more sauce than we need and any leftovers are available for whoever gets to them first. They can forget about the meat course: nothing gets past Maria.

Sharing the kitchen is no big deal; there are eight rooms on our floor but no one else actually cooks any meals. Just about everybody eats at the university canteen. The kitchen is more like a common room, so I often have company while I cook. The only thing that grates is when someone smokes without asking, though this happens less and less: either they're becoming more considerate or – more likely – Maria has had words with them. If they think it's strange that I'm with Maria, then they're polite enough not to say so – they're cool about it. They help me with my Italian and they enjoy trying out their English. They also like correcting some of my cooking techniques, like how best to chop the garlic or to tenderise the meat. This always makes me laugh and they also see the funny side of telling probably the only cook in the building just how to do it properly, but I do listen and I'm learning all the time. I also own a few recipe books that help both to increase my vocabulary and to give me fresh ideas for dinner each evening.

I do all this out of love for Maria, I know, but it's more than that. She'll get sick if she doesn't eat a full and varied diet, and my job is to make sure she eats well. There are perks and I get paid in kind.

If I'm feeling confident I'll shop in the market for vegetables but, more often than not, there's a shop I like to use in the Via San Frediano. Here, I can help myself and not have to ask for what I want. I'm getting better but I still find it hard to grasp what the stallholders are saying; it's never as simple as: *half a kilo of this please ... sure here you are, that's two euro fifty ... here's the money ... thanks very much.* There's always a question I hadn't reckoned on and it throws me and I start to sweat. I know it's nothing and this is how language works and I'll never learn if I don't put myself in these situations, but I can't go through that every day. I feel happier when Maria is with me because she steps in to explain what's being said and we can go over the words together afterwards – but I'm still exhausted after a single transaction. If I'm serving myself, I can take my time and occasionally buy something I don't recognise and ask Maria what it is when I get back to the room. Plus, the shop on San Frediano has all the extras like pasta, or stock, or oil, or rice. I have a butcher I use a few doors down and here I do have to ask specifically for what I want, though there's still a lot of pointing and gesticulating and nodding of the head that goes on. I'm pleased with myself each time I come out with whatever I went in for but it takes it out of me.

There's a note from Maria when I get back to the room this evening – she's gone to the hospital to use the trampoline in the physiotherapy department. She doesn't use it every day, but when she does it's usually at about this time, after she's finished her studies and while I'm cooking dinner. On the days when her chest is particularly bad, it helps clear some of the mucus and eases her breathing. It's tough exercise but she gets into a rhythm and it calms her down. I've tried it with her a few times and it's good fun. Once I forget how much of a twit I must look and give in to the rhythm, I feel how soothing it must be for Maria. As I get going, Maria joins me in the middle and we hold hands and bounce together. This is harder because of our differing height and weight but Maria knows how to adjust herself to keep us in sync. I don't know how she does it but she seems to keep her face level with mine. It's amazing how close it makes us feel.

Our room is small for two people to live in together and we keep it tidy through necessity. We took out the single bed and mattress supplied by the university and replaced it with a futon that we can roll up into a seat during the day. Apart from that, there's the study desk and chair, a wardrobe and a chest of drawers. I don't possess too many belongings, so most of the space is taken up by Maria's clothes. We share a laptop that Maria has borrowed from the university.

I take the ingredients for tonight's dinner along to the kitchen. The two Toni's are sitting at the table – boy and girl – and not for the first time I wonder if they're not an item for the simple reason that they share the same name. They're the best of friends and male Toni is a regular visitor to our kitchen; female Toni lives in the room facing ours. If either of them is currently seeing someone else, it gets discussed at length over coffee in this kitchen.

'Ah, Robert,' male Toni says.

'Ah, dinner, you mean,' female Toni says.

Male Toni is one of my best customers.

'What is it tonight?' he asks.

I know everybody in the building is fascinated and amused by my culinary habits. It's the most visible evidence of my living here so I'm sure they think of me as the Englishman who cooks for Maria. They have some vague understanding of Maria being sick but I can't imagine they've fully grasped the connection between Maria's lungs and her dietary needs. When I sit down and read it through in one of the many information pamphlets Maria's accumulated over the years, it makes a kind of sense – she can't break down the goodness in her food so she needs to eat as well as she can – but I get lost if ever I try to explain it to any of our friends.

I can help by making sure Maria eats a good dinner each evening, but that doesn't stop whatever damage is being done to her lungs. It's not as though she just does this one thing and everything will be okay. Eating well is like the trampoline: it helps her through the day, is all.

There are some bad days – bad in ways I didn't think possible. Days when she's hospitalised and I can't even get to see her. Days when I've no one to cook for and I wonder what the hell I'm doing living in a student residence in Pisa and what will I do when she dies? Days when I think this might be the time, though Maria's told me it won't happen in that way, that when it comes it will be a long, strong steady decline with no reverse gear. She calls these bad days 'going in for a service' but for me they're a breakdown, a write-off, a crash and it's Maria who has to give me the jump-start afterwards.

Didn't she warn me how it would be? Aren't we in this together? Don't we have each other? So I can't let her down now, because she's come to depend on me. Yes, I think, but

302

no amount of culinary expertise is going to save you. No amount of love and sex will stop what's happening to your body. No amount of living life to the full will mean you won't die. And then I feel weak and useless and ashamed that she's so much stronger than I could ever be and she says listen, do me a favour – cover my shift at El Greco's tonight, and tomorrow I'll be fine. I'll come home and you'll cook for me and we'll make love and this will be over for another little while, and so I do as she asks because she's all I have. She's my love, my life, my wife without us ever being married – though Daniel did give us his blessing and more than once Maria has offered to marry me if it would make me feel more secure.

Maria comes in to the kitchen and we kiss.

'How was it?' I ask.

'Great.'

She lifts the lid off the risotto to see what's in the pan.

'What else are we having?' she asks. She points at the spinach dish. 'What's that?'

'You're a cheeky bitch.' I say this in English because I don't know the Italian. 'And you're sweaty – go take a shower.'

I turn on the oven and take the chicken breasts out the fridge. I realise I could have had these marinating, but it's too late for that now. I score each breast a few times and put them in a bowl. I pour in some olive oil, grate in some black pepper, and rub the oil into the chicken with my hands.

'No veal tonight?' asks male Toni. He knows I have a problem with buying and cooking veal but I'm getting over it. I don't like it – the idea, I mean, not the taste – but twice now I've overcome my reservations and gone for it.

I cut a lemon in half, squeeze the juice on to the chicken,

303

and use my hands again to mix it all together. The oven's at the right temperature so I put in the spinach dish. Once I've sealed the chicken on both sides, I reduce the heat under the frying pan and relax. I turn to the two Toni's.

'Some wine now, I think, do you agree?' My Italian sentences still feel like a collection of simple phrases, but I'm getting there.

I go back to the room to fetch the bottle of wine. This too I tend to buy on a daily basis because otherwise it'd go missing. Maria's in the room, naked apart from her underwear.

'It's funny how you always come in when I have no clothes on.'

'Can you blame me?' I say.

'You have to kiss me now.'

'The chicken will burn.'

'I said – you have to kiss me now.'

'It's never just a kiss with you though, is it?'

'One kiss; I promise,' she says.

I kiss her.

'I can smell lemons.'

'They'll be burnt lemons if I don't get back to them.'

'Let me smell your hands.'

She takes my right hand and lifts it to her nose. She puts my thumb in her mouth and then places my other hand on her breast. She seems completely at her ease, completely different to her worrying distraction of the past few days. Either she has come to a decision about the baby or I'm completely off the mark about her being pregnant.

'I'm going back to my chicken now,' I say, 'and my spinach.'

'Spinach – what are you trying to do to me?'

'Feed you.'

304

'Don't you want to fuck me?' she asks, deliberately stressing the vulgarity – *scopare*.

'I do, but first we eat.'

'You don't want me any more.'

'I want you plenty, only not right now – later.'

'I might not be in the mood later.'

'Is that right? You'd best get dressed – your dinner's ready.'

The chicken's fine and I take the spinach out of the oven. I open the wine and pour out four glasses.

'Cheers, Robert,' says male Toni in English.

Maria comes through and we sit down to eat. Toni helps himself to some risotto. Maria has to take her enzymes before she eats, so she knocks back the tablets with her wine and shrugs and smiles at me. Apart from this mouthful she barely touches the wine, particularly on nights like this when she's working, but she eats all the food I put in front of her. Everything is good and already I'm thinking about what I might cook for her tomorrow.

'I have to get going,' she says.

'Your antibiotics,' I remind her.

I tend to spend my evenings going over the writing I've done during the day. That way I can make any small changes while thinking about what to write tomorrow. Daniel was right about my editor: she secured me a small advance that gives me a semblance of financial security for at least the next year. It wouldn't have impressed Siobhan, but I don't need her kind of money to survive. The balance of the settlement from Siobhan is still there to fall back on; if all else fails, I can always go back to painting and decorating – Italian style.

For a while there I had some pictures of Ciara as the background on the laptop. Maria found them on the internet and saved them for me and we had a row about it until I came to my senses. All the pictures were of Ciara with her mother, growing up in public, from when she was still a baby to when she was about five years old. I could see they were all taken to capture the various stages of Siobhan's career and not Ciara's life. It was upsetting, of course, which was why I was angry at Maria, but the more I considered the photographs the more Ciara looked like any girl might appear with her mother – sometimes happy, sometimes sad and very often bored. To the world, Ciara is Siobhan McGovern's daughter and, if anybody thinks about it at all, they probably presume Danny Callinan is her father. Does that matter? I don't know. If it makes life easier for Ciara then it's better that way. Who knows if Siobhan will ever tell Ciara about me? I believe I gave up the right to insist that she does. I learnt to appreciate the photographs of Ciara for what they are and eventually deleted them from the laptop. She's there on the internet if I ever need to see her, and knowing this somehow allows me the peace of mind to finally write about how her life is so integral to my own.

El Greco's is the only non-smoking café bar in Pisa – or at least it was until others started following suit – and Maria works there four nights a week. She waits on tables and serves at the bar and keeps everyone in good order. I've watched her and she's efficient without being charming. She wins over her customers by being good at her job. They find out just how good she is when I have to cover for her, though I tend to be given jobs like clearing tables and washing dishes rather than taking orders and serving the food. The owner, Younes (who isn't Greek at all, but Moroccan) rates Maria so highly that he's understanding and accommodating when she's too sick to work. I'm a poor substitute, but he tolerates me and we get along well. I often sit and have a drink with him at the end of the evening when I come in to collect Maria and he likes to talk about writing and books and England and the River Thames for some reason – he really loves that river.

The bar gets progressively noisier as the late evening wears on – morphing from a café bar to a drinks bar – and there's often dancing. As I arrive, the music is turned down low and the place is starting to empty out. I give Maria a hand clearing away some glasses and then sit with Younes to enjoy my drink at the bar. I watch Maria dodge between the chairs and tables, protecting her stomach but trying not to make it look so obvious. If she's pregnant, she's going to have to cut back on the trampoline.

Maria catches me looking at her and she smiles. As the bar's last few customers say thank you and goodbye, we both know it's time: we always have a dance together at the end of her shift, before I walk her home. I slip off my bar stool and hold her in my arms. We move slowly to the music. We have our favourites and tonight it's 'Across the Universe' – but there aren't enough songs in the world for this moment to last as long as we'd like it to.

'I think something is about to change our world,' I say at the song's refrain.

Maria stops moving to the music.

'You know, then?' she asks, looking up at me.

'I know, yes.'

How could I not know when we live together?

John Lennon sings on, oblivious. Younes lifts chairs onto tables. I put a hand on Maria's shoulder to pull her close, wanting her to continue dancing – for the music to help us through the things I know need to be said – but she pushes against my chest and stands obstinately still.

'I'm going to keep it,' she says, which isn't what I was thinking of at all.

'Yes,' I say, 'I presumed you would.'

'I might not be here to see it grow up, but . . .'

'Maria – it's fine, really.'

'What's fine? How can it be fine? Nothing's fine. What about you – will you be here for the baby, even if I'm not?'

'Of course I will.'

'There's no "of course" about it,' she says, defiant and on the offensive, as is her way. 'You told me you didn't want another baby, so don't go staying with me out of some sort of obligation.'

Her Italian gets faster and her voice gets louder. I should have waited until we got home.

'That was before,' I say. 'Now . . .'

'Now what?' she asks.

Younes busies himself behind the bar. I know he's waiting to mop the floor, but he doesn't want to be doing it around our feet. He knows Maria well enough to recognise the signs. The music dies away as the song tails off to an ending.

'I'm here because I choose to be,' I say.

'But you didn't reckon on this.'

'Maria – we've been having unprotected sex; it's hardly surprising that you're pregnant.'

'I told you it was unlikely to happen.'

'But it happened anyway.'

'I'm sorry,' she says, and I see she's closer to tears than anger.

'Don't be,' I say, 'there's nothing to be sorry about.'

I was well aware of the risk we were taking – a lower risk than for other couples, granted, but the chance of Maria getting pregnant was there from the day I agreed not to use a condom.

'I'm not sorry,' I say.

'But I think you'll leave me all the same.'

'I'm not going to leave you,' I say. 'You're all I have.'

I've had time to think about this, watching and waiting for this conversation to arrive. Maria's fear – and it is a fear, I do see that – is well founded. Fear of the future, or her lack of a future; fear of the person I have been since I lost Ciara – since I gave Ciara away.

I know the madness inside me, I know what I'm capable of, but now I want Maria to see the person I might become – the person I once was, actually, while I was with Ciara, while I was caring for Ciara. That was the best of me. There's only one way I can allay Maria's concerns, and it will take time – these nine months and beyond. All being well, this baby will be born and grow into a person, oblivious to the fact that he or she has been the saving of her old man. I hope that's the way it's going to be, because nobody can save her mother.

'It might even be a boy,' I say out loud.

Once again, words are not enough. Or rather, I don't have the words to make everything okay because everything isn't okay. Things are as they are and that will have to do.

Unprompted, Younes puts on 'Across the Universe' one last time and takes a crate of bottles out the back door. Maria relents and folds into my arms, surrendering to the music and to me.

'We can do this,' I say to her. 'I can do this.'

I suspect Maria will opt for us to get married, all things

considered – for my sake and for the sake of our baby. She'll be as practical about the future care of this baby as she is about her own mortality. I can only picture that future being in Italy. For all the medical tests I've had, I'm going to have to take one more for the cystic fibrosis gene to see what chance in life our baby is to be given. Like Maria, I'm grateful to be living next to one of the best hospitals in the world.

I think maybe we should also take a trip to Rome to break the news to Giovanni and Ines. I reckon we'll be looking for their help in the very near future. Giovanni recently retired from working in the villa's gardens but Ines still helps out in the kitchen; I can't imagine there are better people anywhere for us to turn to. Daniel too, and Maria's parents – they will all have to be told. It's what normal people do. Her papa is likely to go ballistic but that's his problem, not ours.

Is it my imagination or can I already feel the roundness of Maria's tummy press against me as we dance?

'Let's go home,' I say.

ACKNOWLEDGEMENTS

I'd like to thank the following people who have worked hard on behalf of this book: Jonathan Williams, Paul and Susan Feldstein, Svetlana Pironko, Michael O'Brien, David Adamson, Simon Hess and everybody at Black & White Publishing.